AMANAT

WOMEN'S
WRITING
FROM
KAZAKHSTAN

AMANAT

WOMEN'S WRITING FROM KAZAKHSTAN

selected and translated by
ZAURE BATAYEVA *and*
SHELLEY FAIRWEATHER-VEGA

with contributions by
SAM BREAZEALE AND GABRIEL MCGUIRE

stories by
ORAL ARUKENOVA, RAUSHAN BAIGUZHAYEVA, ZAURE BATAYEVA,
NADEZHDA CHERNOVA, LILYA KALAUS, AIGUL KEMELBAYEVA,
AYAGUL MANTAY, OLGA MARK, ZIRA NAURZBAYEVA, ASEL OMAR,
MADINA OMAROVA, AYA ÖMIRTAI, AND ZHUMAGUL SOLTY

Gaudy Boy Translates,
published by Gaudy Boy LLC,
an imprint of Singapore Unbound
www.singaporeunbound.org/gaudyboy
New York

For more information on ordering books, contact jkoh@singaporeunbound.org.

ISBN 978-0-9994514-8-9

Cover design by Flora Chan

Interior design by Jennifer Houle

CONTENTS

AMANAT

Contents

V

FOREWORD

I remember how when I first became interested in Central Asia I went to a university library, eagerly searching for novels or short stories from the region and returning home with a great pile of books by Chingiz Aitmatov. At the time, there was little else to be found in Western libraries for those of us unlucky enough to be limited to English translations. Things are better now. There are fine new translations of novels by Abdulhamid Cho'lpon and Hamid Ismailov from Uzbekistan, of oral literary texts from Kyrgyzstan, and of poetry from across the region. And yet I cannot think of anything quite like Zaure Batayeva and Shelley Fairweather-Vega's new book of translations, *Amanat: Women's Writing from Kazakhstan*.

Forming the background of many of these stories are the great tragedies of Kazakhstan in the 20th century, the famine and purges of the 1930s, the astonishing casualties of the Second World War, and the violence of the Jeltoqsan protests. The plots of the stories often reverberate with one another in strange and unexpected ways. In Asel Omar's "The French Beret," we see a young man arrested for the seemingly trivial offence of a single typo in an article about Stalin published in the newspaper he manages, in her "Black Snow of December," we see a young boy struggling to understand what his grandparents—survivors of purges, exiles, and wars—might think about the Jeltoqsan protests of 1986. In Lilya Kalaus's extraordinary "Operatic Drama," this becomes the stuff of black comedy, as two young men sit at a table drunkenly trying to prove whose grandparents suffered more under Stalin, only to realize that their host, the aged daughter of an NKVD agent, is looking at them in bewildered horror. In Nadezhda Chernova's strange and unsettling "Aslan's Bride," there is even a peculiar kind of comfort in the trauma of war, as the 'Bride' seemingly happily trades the uncertainties of life as an unmarried middle-aged woman for the identity of widow of a man lost to the Second World War.

In many of these stories, the dislocations that trouble the protagonists the most are not the self-evident traumas of wars and purges, but rather the pain that followed moves from the villages into the new cities of Soviet Kazakhstan. This is not to say that the stories here romanticize life in the village—Zhumagul Solty's "An Awkward Conversation" and Ayagul Mantay's "Orphan" show the claustrophobia and loneliness of the village as much as the comforts. Other stories, however, show the social and economic uncertainties of life in the city. In Raushan Baiguzhayeva's "Propiska," a young woman leads a precarious life in Almaty in the 1980s, as her lack of official documents forces her into trading household work for a marginal life in the apartments of relatives. In Aigul Kemelbayeva's "Hunger," another young woman finds herself in a similar situation in Moscow in the 1990s, remembering her village as a space of fantastic plenty, with "milk flowing in rivers." Aya Ömirtai's "18+" examines the precarious life of a young woman searching for work and forced to fend off the increasingly explicit sexual demands of a potential employer. The eclectic and moving portraits of old women in Zira Naurzbayeva's "The Beskempir" begin with the unsettling image of a woman on an apartment balcony wailing for her lost life in the village, but also

gives us the tragicomedy of her "Nyanya-apa" setting out to visit her
by taking buses at random, then asking people for directions, apparently unwilling to concede that, in a city like Almaty, not everyone
will know everyone else.

In other stories, we see the frustrations that followed the crumbling of the Soviet system. Zaure Batayeva's "School" offers a disqui-
eting look at the life of a teacher in a private school as she struggles
to act with honor while her employers flatter her, expect her to nego-
tiate bribes for them, and rarely remember to pay her. Zhumagul
Solty's "Romeo and Juliet" offers a more lighthearted and optimistic
vision, as a hastily arranged performance of Shakespeare's play for
the benefit of foreign visitors becomes an unexpected triumph
despite (or perhaps because of) its hurried staging. The 1990s were
also a time when foreigners—guest workers, journalists, and aca-
demics—suddenly began to arrive in Kazakhstan in great numbers.
Oral Arukenova's "Precedent" shows the bleak side of this, as a
woman gradually realizes what it is exactly her Italian boss has been
shouting at her. This history reappears in her "Procedures Within" as
part of the gossiping conversation of two old friends who meet unexpectedly in an airport café, a story that also shows the dizzying pace
of change in contemporary Kazakhstan. As the two women trade
stories about friends and former co-workers, the conversation
bounces from Atyrau to New York, from the kitchen of the Italian
restaurant to the board rooms of Big Five accounting firms.

Amidst all the sharp edges of these stories, there are also moving
accounts of Kazakh music and literature. In many of the stories,
characters play the dombyra, the traditional lute-like stringed instrument of the Kazakhs. Zira Naurzbayeva's "The Rival" offers in its few
pages an entire doctoral dissertation on the instrument, telling us

how it is made, its place in mythology, what life in a music conservatory is like for students, but above all, telling us about the bond between a musician and an instrument and the artistry of traditional Kazakh songs. In one moment, a character who has been awakened to the beauty of this music describes the pain of walking down a city street, forced to hear "foul, filthy words and voices, timbres and tunes" spilling out of the cafes around her. Again, this is a moment when reading one story suddenly illuminates another, allowing one to understand the significance of the final scene in Oral Arukenova's "Amanat," with its young man glimpsed through a kitchen door playing the dombyra to his girlfriend as she peels potatoes, or the moment in Zaure Batayeva's "The Anthropologists" when a school director grabs another musician's dombyra in order to show off his own skill.

In talking about these stories, I have committed the sin of treating them as though they matter because of what they tell us of Kazakh history and culture, of talking about them as though they were encyclopedias or guidebooks rather than works of fiction—and remarkably beautiful ones at that. This is a disservice to the craft of these writers, and it has also had the unfortunate side effect of making me neglect the stories that don't lend themselves easily to that kind of analysis. Stories like Lilya Kalaus's "A Woman Over Fifty" and "How Men Think" are at once remarkably granular in their sense of how people inhabit their homes and lives and yet also seem to float free of any particular time or place. In her "The Stairwell," we hear an entire lifetime of trips up and down the stairs of an old apartment block, of "percussive rappings, two steps at a time, elegant glides, a flickering cha-cha-cha, now much more even, slower, calmer, now careful." We could be anywhere, and yet somehow we also know exactly where we are, in the poured concrete stairwell of an old Soviet block of apartments, with their steps worn smooth and their blue and white paint. And we know, too, that it might be almost any one of the women we have met in these stories whose footsteps we overhear on their endless trips up and down the stairwells leading to their homes.

Gabriel McGuire

Professor of Literature, Astana, Kazakhstan

TRANSLATORS' INTRODUCTION TO AMANAT

This collection features the stories of women writers from Kazakhstan over the past thirty years, and it is the first anthology of its kind to make the attempt. Their country is the world's ninth largest by landmass, but it is also a relatively young nation, independently existing as the Republic of Kazakhstan only since December 1991. That is just thirty years ago, a single generation, in a land where tradition dictates that people must know and honor the names of seven generations of their ancestors. One goal of this anthology is to collect what women have written during and about this relatively short period of time, now that the dust has largely settled from the latest cataclysmic change in Kazakh history.

As a title for this diverse collection, we chose *Amanat*, a Kazakh word with many meanings. An amanat is a promise entwined with hope for the future. It is frequently a task that comes with moral obligation, and often it is a legacy, an item of value, handed down for us to cherish and protect. This collection is our promise, to these writers and the ones who have come before and who will come after them, that their legacy will be honored and continued. Our task as translators is to share their work as well as we can with the wider world. The title is borrowed from Oral Arukenova's story, of course, but its meaning is fully embodied in the themes of Zira Naurzbayeva's essay that concludes this collection: a realization that, even in a newly independent country, the present moment never exists independently from the past and the future and that women have a sacred role to play in escorting our families and our nations through times of both joy and sorrow.

We know that women writers are underrepresented in translation from all languages into English, and this is certainly true for Kazakhstan. Of the three major translations from Kazakhstan published in the United States in the past several years, two are novels by men of the Soviet generation (Talasbek Asemkulov's *A Life at Noon* and Rollan Seisenbayev's *The Dead Wander in the Desert*) and one is a poetry collection by a woman (Aigerim Tazhi's *Paper-Thin Skin*). The last attempt we know of to collect Central Asian women's writing, as a matter of fact, was the 2008 Russian-language anthology *Solovei v kletke*, edited by Lilya Kalaus, an author who contributed several pieces of her own to this volume. The Kazakhstani government has been funding huge volumes of translation into and out of the languages of Kazakhstan lately, but those grants and contracts go overwhelmingly to male authors and to those of older generations who were well entrenched in the official Soviet writing bureaucracy and who remain in those positions today. Those projects also tend to funnel all the writing through Russian translation, even if it was not written in Russian or intended to be read that way. *Amanat* pays both its Kazakh- and Russian-language stories the respect of translation directly into English. And it spotlights a different kind of writer, the ones passed over for government support and making their own way in a decentralized—but still hierarchical, patriarchal, and occasionally authoritarian—political and cultural system. We want to make sure that writing by women since the end of the Soviet era, from any language and any region, has a chance to be read and considered as part of the ancient and still-evolving culture of Kazakhstan.

One more point on the duality of languages represented in *Amanat*: we strove to include an equal number of Russian-language and Kazakh-language authors. With the exception of Aya Ömirtai, our youngest author and an immigrant to Kazakhstan, both sets of women were mostly educated in the Soviet system, where Russian language and literature held pride of place; with that system officially discarded, they are more free to creatively build on—or disregard entirely—the Russian literary traditions they learned. Kazakhstan is still a bilingual country, though many people, proudly or stubbornly, speak only either Kazakh or Russian; some writers lament a visible divide in the country's literature between people who read and write in one language or the other. Yet there are cracks in that wall, chiseled out, to a noticeable extent, by women. Fully half the authors in this collection translate literature as well as writing their own, a proportion that would be hard to replicate in any English-speaking country. Translating these stories into English, in turn, is yet another way to honor the work these women do.

A READER'S HISTORY OF KAZAKHSTAN

As we assembled and translated the stories in *Amanat*, we realized that readers who are unfamiliar with the places and events discussed might benefit from a brief introduction to Kazakh history.

Most of the stories in this collection are set in the late Soviet period or since independence, yet Kazakh writers cannot avoid grappling, in one way or another, with a much longer history. People called *Kazakhs* have inhabited the steppes of Central Asia since at least the sixteenth century. Theirs was a nomadic society organized along family and clan lines, the biggest divisions being between hordes, or *jüz*, who occupied various areas of the region at different times. Explorers and military expeditions from the Russian Empire appeared in Kazakhstan early in the eighteenth century and expanded deep into the region for the next hundred years, building forts and forging alliances. Starting in the late nineteenth century, settlers from the European part of the Russian Empire began moving en masse into Kazakh territory, a trend that only intensified after the Bolshevik Revolution in 1917. After several years of relative autonomy during the Russian Civil War, Kazakhstan was officially incorporated into the Soviet Union in 1920, first as part of the Kyrgyz Autonomous Soviet Socialist Republic. The Kazakh Soviet Socialist Republic would come into being officially with an administrative reshuffling in 1936, with its capital in Almaty.

The early Soviet years were a time of upheaval, often with disastrous consequences. Soviet economic policies and social engineering projects caused catastrophic famine in the Kazakh steppes, where agricultural collectivization outlawed traditional ways of life, and civil war and arrests (see "The French Beret") severed family and community ties, frequently beyond repair. Soviet activists and officials moved into the region to supervise economic and educational projects; other ethnic groups were forcibly exiled to various parts of Kazakhstan, some as whole communities (including the population of the village Milochka discovers in "Aslan's Bride"), some as prisoners in the GULAG system. These huge population shifts resulted in the mix of languages and ethnic groups that coexist in Kazakhstan today. Russian was handed down as the language of power and civilization, demoting the Kazakh language and culture to second-class status; soon new generations were being educated completely in Russian, without seeing a need to learn Kazakh at all. The long essay "The Beskempir" explores the personal stories of several older women who lived through these drastic changes in Kazakh society.

As elsewhere in the Soviet Union, the Second World War hit Kazakhstan hard. Men of fighting age were drafted and disappeared, many never to return—"Aslan's Bride" directly addresses this aspect of the long aftermath of World War II. The start of the Cold War brought nuclear testing to Kazakhstan, centered near Semipalatinsk (*Semey* in Kazakh), with catastrophic consequences for the environment and human health. As the Soviet economy began to recover during the relative political stability of the 1950s to 1970s, more Kazakhs moved away from rural villages and into the cities, where they received a Soviet education and worked in modern industrial or administrative jobs. This emptying of the villages had its effects, seen in stories like "Romeo and Juliet." Those who stayed behind in the villages were largely workers at collective farms, as in "Orphan." City life also had its challenges: "Propiska," "Hunger," and "The Lighter" all address the social and economic difficulties faced by Kazakhs who move to or grow up in the big city, while the stories by Zaure Batayeva, Oral Arukenova, Aya Ömirtai, and Madina Omarova explore new types of interpersonal relationships generated by apartment living, modern careers, and urban poverty from the late Soviet period to the present day.

As perestroika gathered steam in the Soviet Union in the mid-1980s, another wave of disruption swept across Central Asia. As the central authorities loosened, then tightened, their grip on

Kazakhstani politics, tragedy sometimes resulted. The unrest depicted in "Black Snow of December" brought ethnic tensions in Kazakhstan to the foreground, and resulted in the ethnically Kazakh Nursultan Nazarbayev rising quickly through the ranks of the Soviet government. Nazarbayev was the top official in Kazakhstan when it declared independence on December 16, 1991. Kazakhstan was the last of the Soviet Union's fifteen republics to do so, and Nazarbayev personified that tendency to cling to the Soviet past: he remained in power for nearly thirty years, reigning over a system of political cronyism, quashing political dissent, habitually running for reelection almost unopposed, and ordering the construction of a new capital city, Astana (renamed *Nur-Sultan* in 2019). Although he recently stepped down in favor of his handpicked successor, he retains the title of Leader of the Nation and is considered the de facto top authority, although the protests of January 2022 made his future less certain.

All this political upheaval caused not just an existential crisis for the country, but immediate practical problems for ordinary people, most of all thanks to the collapse of the USSR and Kazakhstan's abrupt independence in 1991 (see "Hunger"). As the country entered a new post-Soviet era, some writers took the opportunity to revisit Kazakh history and begin a new reckoning with the past ("The Beskempir," "Operatic Drama," "Black Snow of December"). Informed and shaped by this history are the big cultural issues Kazakhstan currently faces. Many of our authors comment on the disparities in wealth that erupted with independence ("Hunger"); others focus on the new relationships now being negotiated between the generations ("Amanat"), between the sexes ("An Awkward Conversation," "18+," and "A Woman Over Fifty"), and between urban and rural populations.

Mostly, though, the pieces we have included in this anthology are not strictly about the history of Kazakhstan. This is our effort to share some of the most intriguing, memorable, and touching stories and essays written by women there in the past thirty years, regardless of topic. There are authors we would have liked to include but whose work was unavailable; there are certainly authors whose work we're not even aware of (yet); and there is more being written all the time. Perhaps those stories will find a home in some future anthology in English. But meanwhile, as you read this volume, we hope that you will gain additional insight into the past and present of Kazakhstan, and begin to recognize it through these women's eyes.

ACKNOWLEDGMENTS

We are grateful to everyone who contributed wisdom, resources, time, and encouragement to this anthology, which is the fruit of many years of work—first by the authors, then by the translators and editors.

Several of the stories have been published in English in other journals and collections, though sometimes as a different version from the one included here. The always-enthusiastic Susan Harris of *Words Without Borders* encouraged us to submit stories for a feature on Kazakh women's writing, a first for that magazine, and published excerpts from "The Beskempir" (here included in full), "School," and "The Nanny" (another excerpt is published in this collection) in January 2018. The worldwide coronavirus pandemic slowed our efforts starting in 2020, but two of our authors, Lilya Kalaus and Oral Arukenova, saw their pieces about experiencing the pandemic in Kazakhstan published in English that year. Zira Naurzbayeva's "The Rival" won a place in the volume *Best Asian Short Stories 2019*.

"Romeo and Juliet" was published by the Singapore Unbound blog in January 2021. Drs. Cathy McAteer and Muireann Maguire of the University of Exeter funded the translation of two stories, "Aslan's Bride" and "Black Snow of December," as part of the RusTrans project on Russian literature in translation, and published an essay about and excerpts from "Aslan's Bride" on their blog in June 2021. Olga Zilberbourg and Yelena Furman read the manuscript and asked to feature Olga Mark's "The Lighter" on their blog, *Punctured Lines*. Finally, we are grateful to *World Literature Today* for including Zira Naurzbayeva's essay "My Eleusinian Mysteries" in their autumn 2021 issue. Thank you to all the editors of those publications who read our translations with interest and saw the beauty in them.

None of the stories here would have turned out as well as they have without feedback from our talented writing and translation colleagues. Shelley had the pleasure of workshopping "Aslan's Bride" with the Northwest Literary Translators and "The Lighter" at an American Literary Translator's Association conference in 2019. Both workshops yielded a few just-right turns of phrase for those tales. Author Anne Charnock also read the entire manuscript and provided copious feedback, providing us a valuable non-translatorial point of view on issues of language and culture. All mistakes and unfortunate choices in the translations, however, are ours and ours alone.

Most of all, we thank the twelve Kazakhstani authors who so graciously agreed to have their work translated in *Amanat*. May this be only the beginning step to sharing their work with the wider world.

ZAURE BATAYEVA AND SHELLEY FAIRWEATHER-VEGA

AMANAT

WOMEN'S
WRITING
FROM
KAZAKHSTAN

ROMEO AND JULIET

BY ZHUMAGUL SOLTY

Translated from Kazakh by
Zaure Batayeva

Regret was eating Alip's heart. Before retiring, he had worked as the director of the district's People's Theatre for a long time, but his lifelong dream of staging something unique had never come true. One day, a young man, lungs in his hands, out of breath, ran into his house and delivered the message that he was urgently expected at the mayor's office. Surprised that the boss, who seemed to have forgotten about his existence, suddenly needed him, Alip took his jacket and went to the office. Even more surprising: the entire district administration was waiting for him. "Hey, Aleke, come in!" said the mayor, getting up and stretching out his hands to him. After a short welcome, the mayor briefed Alip about some upcoming business.

The district was expecting special guests, foreigners, who wanted to come and see the talents of rural Kazakhs. "We pride ourselves on being a talented nation, and it is true that every other Kazakh can sing. So, Aleke, this should not be a difficult task for you. You will be in charge," said the mayor. "By the way, the troupe you formed doesn't exist anymore. It was dispersed after our country's collapse. The youngster that replaced you turned out to be unreliable. We heard that he's living in the city now. These days, every other Kazakh is some kind of merchant. He must be doing something like that, too. We tried to find him but couldn't. That's why we're turning to you."

What could Alip say? This, in a way, was what he had been dreaming of. He did not show his joy, though. Instead he pretended to be worried. "What a pity! I cut my ties with all this long ago. And all my actors have left town. You said yourself that everyone has gone their own way. I'm afraid nothing good will come out of this business, and I'll be the one to face the blame."

"Aleke, you're right," said the mayor. "The regional bosses gave us this task, so we must not let them down. If I'd known we would need those actors, I would've hobbled them all so they couldn't leave the village. If you rescue us this time, we'll be generous. Now the reins are yours. Kazakhs are talented! If you look around, you'll find singers and dancers. If you need anything, just let us know. The thing is to impress the foreigners. Don't forget." Alip understood that he shouldn't exaggerate and made a face as if he had no choice but to agree.

For the visiting foreigners, it would suffice to gather three or four people and throw a feast, but the dream sitting at the bottom of his heart came to the surface again. He didn't give a damn about the public anymore! He wanted to stage a performance that would make him happy.

"Aleke, why do you look so sad? Where are you coming from?" He turned to the speaker and saw it was Egizbay. Now retired, Egizbay used to be a big bird. Maybe he was one of those who could not accept his new dog-like existence. As soon as he saw Egizbay, Alip had an idea. "Ah, I've found it," he said to himself. "This time the solution is not young people, but older folks. They're the ones who'll receive applause from the foreigners and the locals. Why look elsewhere?" He greeted Egizbay, hurried back to the mayor's office, went to one of the mayor's deputies, and reported that he needed a sheep for a small gathering that night. The deputy was quick. The sheep was delivered right away. Alip had the sheep slaughtered and the meat boiled. Leaving the rest of the chores to his wife, he went out again to invite some people to dinner.

After the livestock had settled for the night, the guests arrived at Alip's house. Eating tender meat and rich soup, the guests sweated and relaxed. Alip waited for the right moment, then spoke.

"Today our mayor asked me to talk to you. Thanks to God, we're still needed. We're the elders now. By the way, the mayor said you shouldn't worry about hay. He promised to provide it himself. What else do you need? I told the mayor you might not be in the mood for entertainment since you haven't received your pension money for several months in a row. The mayor said he'd take care of that for everyone who participates in the play. So, you see, it all depends on you. Tomorrow we should meet for a rehearsal. They didn't give us much time. If we manage to produce something good, our words will have influence in the future as well. Here's the list of names I was given by the mayor." Alip put his little notebook on the table. "Hmm, he didn't leave out anyone. Even Ysqaq's here," one guest said, surprised.

After seeing off his guests, Alip searched his bookshelves. What if they tried their hands at Shakespeare's *Romeo and Juliet*, with the twist that it would be performed by older actors? Nobody in the world had ever seen anything like that. Very pleased with himself, Alip went to bed.

Hoping to receive their long-awaited pension money, everyone gathered the next day at the appointed time. Thinking that at most they would be required to sing songs, they were disappointed when they found out they would have to perform *Romeo and Juliet*. Things got even more difficult when the roles had to be assigned. "No way! What will my children say? I'd be ashamed! I don't want to embarrass myself!" Eventually they gave in and were ready to play anyone, as long as it was not one of the two main characters. After some heated discussion, the suggestion was even made to perform the play without the two lovebirds.

"Oh, my God! What an outrageous suggestion!" Alip shouted, blood rising to his head. "Your look is perfect for Romeo," he urged Egizbay. "I'm sure Romeo was no handsomer than your younger self." Egizbay was flattered and silently accepted the role. But, damn it, no Juliet could be found. All the women were refusing as if a fire had caught their skirts. Alip knew them all. He sensed that deep down they would love to play Juliet, but he knew that they were afraid of people's gossip and of their children's reactions. In the end, he gave up. Alip turned to his own wife. Though she was upset, she felt sorry for her husband and agreed. The other parts were assigned quickly. Happy with the outcome, Alip instructed his actors to learn their parts by heart. Alip felt exhausted already. He had never felt as tired as this before.

During rehearsal the next day, the mayor stopped by with his entourage. He generously greeted everyone and, as if agreed in advance, repeated Alip's promises and made all the actors very happy. That visit made Alip's job remarkably easier. Everyone was listening to him now. However, as if on purpose, his wife fell ill and was taken to the hospital. As if that were not enough, the next day it was discovered that Egizbay had left for Astana to visit his son without telling anyone. Alip felt helpless. No one else seemed to be bothered.

Every morning, after driving their livestock to pasture and having tea, everyone, even those not participating in the play, made it a habit to come to rehearsal with their grandchildren and enjoy themselves. Moreover, they would make fun of Alip, who was trying hard to explain the conflict between the two families, the Montagues and the Capulets. "Hey, Montague and Capulet must have had Kazakh origins. Nobody ever outperformed Kazakhs in feuding. Who knows, maybe Montague's real name was Montay and Capulet's name was Qapalbek." Everyone laughed, except for Alip.

Then Alip noticed a woman sitting off to one side. The way she wore her scarf and dress was different. Not only different, she was elegant in her white outfit. She must be that new resident, the younger sister of Kempirbay's wife. Alip felt that he had seen her before but had no time to think when and where. He thought he had found their Juliet. The thought was so strong that he started begging her.

The woman's name was Marzia. Unlike the other women there, Marzia did not put on any airs. Instead, she quickly agreed. "All right, why so dramatic? I will try, of course. I've just moved here, so if you help me with hay and firewood, I'm willing," she said. Now that he had found his Juliet, Alip decided that he would play the part of Romeo himself. Either by being naturally perceptive or by listening to Alip, Marzia settled into the role quite easily, but she was slow on the stage and did not respond to Romeo's romantic entreaties with the same feeling.

The day of the performance arrived. The district's House of Culture was full. Everyone was waiting for the curtains to open. Alip did not see any foreigners except for two women next to the mayor and immediately got worried that the expected guests had not arrived, but seeing the mayor's extreme politeness with the two women, he calmed down. Now he approached the mirror to prepare himself for the stage. What magic power the stage has! It transforms people. Despite being exhausted, Alip looked younger and had a flirtatious gleam in his eyes. Admiring himself in the mirror, he suddenly felt that someone was staring at him. He turned his head, and it was Marzia. The question of why she was looking at him came to his mind, but he was quickly distracted by the applause—the performance had started.

According to the script, the mayor was first supposed to give a short speech. He was already there. Alip had no time to listen to him: he was busy instructing the Montague and Capulet teams about the opening scenes. The day before, Alip had distributed creased old costumes from a pile of long-untouched theatre props. On the day of the performance, the actors had arrived in washed and ironed costumes, some even with makeup on their faces. Now they all were standing in front of the mirror and seemed to have forgotten that soon they would have to go on stage. "If you forget your lines, don't freeze, the prompter will be sitting in that corner," he repeated over and over. No one needed a whip, either.

Everyone played their role. Even those who forgot their parts did not pause for a second and instantly improvised, yelling "Attan!" even if it was irrelevant to the scene. But the audience did not seem to mind. Sometimes the play's lines were replaced by purely Kazakh words that had nothing to do with the play, especially in the feuding scenes. It was clear no such interpretation of *Romeo and Juliet* had ever been delivered on any stage of the world. Alip, observing from behind the curtains, did not know whether to be glad or upset.

Then came the scenes in which he and Marzia were on stage. When Marzia looked at him like a frightened calf, Alip was so confused that he did not notice how he said, "Marzia, I love you and cannot live without you!"

That was it. Marzia smirked and replied, "Hey, may God punish you, what are you saying?" They had both messed up, but they could not pause now.

"I see you everywhere! My love has been growing since I saw you for the first time," said Romeo, and approaching Juliet, he whispered into her ear, "Show some life! Think of your first love or something!"

Juliet understood this in her own way. "That is enough! Don't teach me how to love. I've been in love, too! You forgot, but I didn't!" she yelled, and instead of turning towards him, turned away.

Alip had no choice but to follow her. "Juliet! My desire!"

"All right, don't exaggerate," Juliet answered. "You missed the time when you were supposed to say those words . . . So you forgot about when I was in charge of a herd in Sholaqsay?" Alip hoped that nobody had heard this dialog except for Marzia and himself. Other actors were coming onto the stage. Alip looked at Marzia. She was standing apart, as if waiting for him. When their eyes met, he suddenly remembered where he had seen this woman before. People's eyes don't change. "Oibai," he said to himself. "No doubt, it's her."

They had both been young then. Alip had been sent by the Party to inspect the herd belonging to Marzia's brother-in-law. Circumstances were such that Alip, who was to oversee the lambing, had to stay for several days. Marzia was working as an assistant shepherd. One night, a warm relationship grew up between them. It was one of those evenings when they had returned wet from the rain, running between the house and the barn, transferring young lambs. Until that evening, he had not considered Marzia as someone with thoughts and dreams. They did not notice how the flame of desire had sprung up. He had a wife waiting for him. That was not a real issue. But he had recently become a member of the Communist Party, who had entrusted him with this work. If gossip went around, what would the Party say? No, he couldn't act so giddy. "My God, of all the men, why me?" He argued with himself all night, and by morning, his loyalty to the Party had won.

Back on stage, Alip was distracted, pronouncing the words without making any effort to act. Marzia did not deviate from the script again. On the contrary, she was acting much better now. It was all too much for Alip. When the time came, he approached the dead Juliet and whispered, "Marzia, forgive me. I was not a reasonable person! I was a fool."

Then Alip started to weep. The audience did not seem to notice—the performance received a long standing ovation. The mayor came back on stage and expressed his gratitude to Alip. Journalists from the regional center rushed to interview him. Most importantly, the foreigners were very impressed. But Alip felt unhappy. "Women are sacred. Men who hurt them will be cursed." These words continued to seep into his brain like wet rain.

AN AWKWARD CONVERSATION

BY ZHUMAGUL SOLTY

Translated from Kazakh by
Zaure Batayeva

Guldaria and I get together quite often, and when we do, we put everything else aside. Today, too, we were sitting alone. I noticed at once that lively Guldaria was not really there. She even looked pale. "I've been thinking that it's been a while since my father has gone," Guldaria said. "I often see him in my dreams. He looks at my mum with such unfriendliness. Maybe I've been thinking a lot about him lately." "Why would they quarrel?" I asked, surprised. "Didn't they live together for many years and raise all of you?" "It's a long story," Guldaria said. "To be honest, I don't know if I should even talk about it." But I remained silent, and Guldaria poured out her heart and told her story.

"As the saying goes," Guldaria began, "we appreciate our parents only when we become parents ourselves. As children, we don't pay attention to our parents' states of being. Same with me. I learned to understand my own parents only after I became someone's wife and someone's mother.

"I remember my parents as two oxen toiling under the same yoke. They would leave early in the morning for work and come back late in the evening. I was the oldest in a house full of young-sters. Maybe that's why I matured early. Now, I look back, and it seems to me that I didn't even have a childhood. I was the one taking care of the kettle, cleaning the house, and putting food in front of my exhausted parents in the evening. For me, nothing was more of an honor than when my father's rough palm occasionally touched my forehead. He was mysterious, my father.

"When I try to recall his image, I always see the same picture: he's sitting in the yard, leaning his back against the apricot tree. Who knows what secret it held, but he would always hang around the old tree. My mother didn't like it. Whenever she saw him near it, she would mumble to herself. One spring, the old apricot tree bloomed early, white flowers. We were happy to see that, my dad and me. But my mum was furious. 'How many times have I asked you to cut that damn thing down!' she said, making a fire under the samovar. But my father was so happy that her words passed him by. 'Hey, baibishe, why speak such nonsense? What would you gain by cutting it down? And why blame it for blooming so early? If you want to know, it's called lust for life. You'll see, this year its fruits will be as sweet as ever.'

"'I know, I know everything,' mother replied. 'I see that there is no cure for it; the tree imitates its owner.' My mother was heating up, but then, seeing us, looking astonished, she swallowed the rest of her words. Poor me, I was still too young to understand the meaning of what she said, but I was truly upset with my mum. How could she even think of cutting down the only tree in the yard, blooming and giving so much beauty? What had it done wrong? I couldn't find answers to my questions. However, my mum would soon forget everything, happily serving tea to my father. She was gentle with us as well, petting us all.

"I remember another time. It was midnight. I woke up. My mother was pouring water from a kettle over my father's hands. She sounded upset with him. I pricked up my ears. 'Poor thing, you've got an old man's beard on your face, and you still haven't settled down. Aren't you ashamed?' My father was silent. 'Playing these love games at your age is not becoming. When you were young, I didn't say a word, but now . . . ' Waking up the next morning, I tried to recollect what had happened. Some kind of suspicion settled in my chest. I looked at my mother's face. No trace of last night's anger. She was as happy as a spring day. The dirty clothes she took off my father the night before were already washed and dry. My mother's timidity in such moments surprised me. My father would sometimes shout at her angrily. Mum would just pout her lips and turn away. She wouldn't even defend herself.

"My father had a severe limp, so most of the household chores were on my mother's shoulders. He walked around all day on a heavy wooden prosthesis that looked like a pestle attached to his knee. He only took it off at night, before going to sleep. We would ask about his leg sometimes, and he would just say it was the cruel war's fault. We knew the story our mother told, though.

"They'd gotten married just before the Second World War. Soon my father was sent to fight. When the surviving soldiers came back after the war, he'd disappeared without a trace. My mum waited in vain for his letters but never lost hope. People say she was attractive as a young woman, and some men approached her, proposing marriage. But mum just couldn't believe he'd died. 'I saw him off healthy myself, and I will meet him at his threshold,' she said, and turned down every proposal. Several years later, he really did come back. He was thought to have spent several years in a military hospital. Telling us this story, our mum would say that if someone is destined to live, he wouldn't die even in a forty-year war.

"You know what happened after that. They had ten children. He loved me especially, the first child. He didn't neglect our mum either. Once he came back from the bazaar and tossed a red shawl in front of her. She took his present into her hands, and she hit him with her words: 'Poor thing! Why buy red? Do you want me to pretend to be as young as you do?' His face turned red, but his eyes were smiling. I felt right away that it was part of the same conversation I'd overheard before. On that occasion, one side of the saddlebag remained full. Father made no move to open it and share the contents with us. He nodded his head toward the nail on the wall, and our mum, after hesitating for a few seconds, picked up the saddlebag and hung it on the nail. She didn't even check what was inside. The question of what was in there bothered me. I wanted to know. When I got up the next morning, the saddlebag was empty.

"One day my mum's younger brother died. It hit her hard. She was laid up in bed for several days. It was also a hard time for me because many visitors came to the house, to console her and to drink tea. Unexpectedly, though, I found the key to the questions nested in my chest. By that day, we were getting fewer visitors. A woman appeared, followed by a young boy. At first glance, she was no different from the other women who had visited us, but my mum, when she looked out the window and saw the woman approaching, got nervous. She immediately started putting herself and the bed where she lay in order. The first thing that struck me about the woman was her red shawl. It was the same shawl that my father had recently brought from the bazaar. She must have been wearing it for the first time, because it still had folds in it. The shawl was red, but the woman's wrinkles were visible. It was her big black eyes that showed that she'd been a beauty once. As we say, a good plate may lose its paint but not its quality. My mum behaved as if she were seeing her for the first time. The woman hesitated at the threshold but walked directly towards my mum's bed, bent over, and hugged her. Both were silent. They remained in a tight hug for some time. I knew that my duty was to prepare tea, so I left to make a fire under the samovar. When I came back, they were sitting together. After another pause, the visitor started talking. 'Nagima, please accept my condolences. Don't be upset, I couldn't stay home,' the visitor said, speaking as if she were out of breath.

"'Thank you, Asel. Is there any power that can stop God's will?' My mother didn't know what to say after that. She noticed the boy that was still standing at the door and started fussing about him. 'Oh, your son has grown so big!' she said, not taking her eyes from the boy. 'Come in, my child, come to the tör. Why are you standing at the door? What is wrong with me, letting you stand there! Come, dear, don't be shy. It is your home too . . . Come to the tör.' Mother stood up with unusual speed from her bed, kissed the boy on both cheeks, and sat him down next to herself. That was when I started looking at the boy more carefully. I was seeing him for the first time, but he seemed somewhat familiar. While I was thinking, 'Where have I seen him?' my mum said, 'He must be the same age as my Guldaria. Yes, they look alike, look!'

"The visitor, uncomfortable before, now seemed to calm down but did not say a word. What was my mum saying? I stared at the boy again. Were my mum's words affecting me, or was it true? He looked

13

like me. When I feel awkward, I tend to flush red, and there he was, sitting and burning like a fire. Going in and out of the room to prepare tea, I noticed that the two women weren't able to sustain the conversation. They tried talking about this and that. My mother poured out what was in her heart, even if it was irrelevant to what Asel-apa was saying. 'Inshallah, you have a child . . . ' my mother said at one point. Then she lingered, not able to speak further. After my mother's comment, Asel-apa, who also must have been tired of behaving like a diplomat of another country, started speaking more directly. 'Hey, Nagima, what is in my hand, everything is Allah's will. If you weren't a special woman to me, we wouldn't be sitting here. If I'm guilty of doing wrong to anyone, it is you. Don't curse me. I wake up scared at night, worried that I'll cause lots of trouble for my only child. If something happens to me, I beg you, don't reject him. It's got nothing to do with the child. These days I'm sick quite often. If the poor thing, without any tail or mane, is left all by himself in this world, how will I stay calm in my grave?' Asel-apa dried her tears with one end of her red shawl and fell silent again. She seemed to expect an answer from my mother.

"Whether she was flattered by the compliment or impressed by the weight of her visitor's words, my mum sounded more reasonable than I expected. 'Don't say such things, Asel. May you have the chance to see your child grow up. Don't be upset. If I showed human weakness, don't take it to heart. Our grave is closer than our tör, so it is our duty to talk about it. If you can, forgive me, too. My life is declining, so I decide nothing. You will see, they will find each other.' Sadness is cleaned by talking, as we say, and both my mother and her visitor seemed happy that their conversation hadn't developed into a crisis.

"When Asel-apa indicated she was ready to leave, my mother got up, left the room, and came back with a nice piece of fabric, taken from her collection of textiles for special occasions. 'Asel, leave this house with a white soul. This is for you,' my mother said with a friendly face. The visitor obviously did not expect such a gift, and she stepped back as if she were frightened. She was definitely puzzled. Who knows, maybe Asel-apa understood at that moment that it was my mother's complete sincerity that had tied my father to her all his life.

"The two women were speaking in riddles, but I inferred what I wasn't supposed to know. It was so overwhelming. I stared at the boy who was looking down at his feet, all red. Mother saw my state right away and touched my shoulder. If I had heard about it under other circumstances, I don't know how I'd have reacted, but now I didn't hate Asel-*apa* or her son. Moreover, it was odd to feel that we were tied to these strangers, and no one had any right to cut those ties.

"Several years later, I graduated from school and left home. I studied at university, found a husband, had children. After that, I rarely visited our village. When I did, I didn't stay long. My parents would always be upset, saying to me, 'Why hurry away as if you've come to borrow a matchstick?' They wanted us to stay longer so we could enjoy ourselves, but everyday life didn't allow us to turn our necks.

"Then my father fell ill. When I received a message to come quickly, I put everything aside and went immediately. Father was in bed. He seemed to be in pain, his eyes were sunk deep inside his head, he'd lost weight. It was the first time in my life that I saw my father stuck in bed. It was quiet in the house. All my siblings had grown up and moved out. Mother was busy with the livestock and other chores. When we were alone, it was clear my father wanted to tell me something. Yet he could not be straightforward and changed the subject several times. 'Gulken, is there anything to drink? My stomach is burning,' he said in a weak voice. But he barely touched the cool kymyz that I offered him and returned the cup to me. I could see that he was hesitating, so I said, 'Köke, are you in pain? Would you go to Almaty with me? I'll find you a good doctor.' But father wasn't excited about this at all. 'Oh, dear, what will change if I drag my old boots to the end of the world? I don't even know what's hurting. My whole body's burning. No treatment will help.' My father sobbed like a child. I'd never seen him so weak. I was scared.

"Finally, he told me what he'd wanted to say. 'Gulken, my child, listen to me carefully. You were born when I thought there was no joy left for me in this world. I love all my children, but you've always been special to me. Now you're an adult yourself. What can I do? It looks as if I'm not fated to see the place where you will build your own nest.' This was just the beginning of the conversation. Father turned to me with his whole body. 'My child,' he said looking into my eyes, 'I don't know if you've ever heard about her, but there was a woman named Asel. She passed away. She left a child. As the saying goes, if you're not in touch, you're a stranger. But he is not a stranger to you. Please visit her grave and devote a prayer to her.' His speech was interrupted by a sudden cough. After a while, his eyes turned away, and he said, 'You're smart, you know you shouldn't say anything to your mum. It's not her fault.' I couldn't say, 'Don't worry. I'll do everything you want.' Instead, I started fluffing up his pillow and covering him with a blanket. He must have gathered that he shouldn't worry about it anymore. He calmed down and didn't talk for a long time. The next morning, I found an excuse to leave the house. When I came back, he was waiting for me. He guessed that his request had been met. Father and daughter, we communicated without any words. My poor mum was unaware of all of this.

"That was it. Father did not recover. He faded away. He kept looking at the apricot tree in the yard. Did he want to see its leaves again? The whole village and all his relatives came to say goodbye to him. In the crowd I recognized the son of Asel-apa. He was a man now. Some people were consoling him as well. Whether it was his mother's wish or his own, he was taking care of household chores as a member of the family. There was nothing strange about it. The strange things were still to come.

"The night my father died, it snowed big flakes all night, and the whole region was covered in a white blanket. In the morning, the livestock did not go to pasture. Still, the whole village gathered to say goodbye to my father. 'My master! All my life, I was worried about losing you!' my mother was crying. Did she begin to understand that he'd left forever, or did she think of us, her children, looking at her? Gradually she pulled herself together. She put her hair back underneath her headscarf, washed her face, and turned to her brothers-in-law, who were waiting for her burial instructions.

"'He loved Shyraqjan, with whom he grew up, as if they were two foals. If you remember, when Shyraqjan died, he was inconsolable. "Rest in peace, I will follow you soon," he said then. Let's grant him his wish.' She looked around, as if asking for confirmation. No one was opposed. Father's burial was carried out by the men of our clan. They didn't burden us. Only after the burial did they report to our mum the following: 'Zheneshe, the cemetery was covered in snow. We couldn't find Uncle Shyraqjan's grave and had to dig where we thought it might be.' Now our father had been given back to the earth. Soon all the relatives left, and we were again by ourselves.

Father's usual place at home was like an empty hole. It was hard to accept, but we had to get ready for the seventh day after his burial. My father's maternal relatives, who lived far away and hadn't made it to the burial, arrived on the morning of this seventh day. 'We couldn't bury him, let's put soil on his grave' was their wish.

"So we all went to my father's grave to pay our respects and say our prayers. Nature is strange, isn't it? A week ago, the snow had been packed hard, but now the sun was shining, and the snow had all melted. One of my father's cousins, wanting to say a prayer for Uncle Shyraqjan, asked to see his grave. How could we have forgotten? We looked up and around. Suddenly one of the villagers, who'd come with us to the cemetery, said in a surprised voice, 'Hey, isn't this the grave of Asel-apa?' My mother flinched. She knew where her brother-in-law was buried, at a grave somewhat farther away. But whose was the grave next to our father's? Our eyes turned to the small inscription on the stone. 'Asel, daughter of Suindik' was written there, followed by her dates of birth and death. Astonished, we all fell silent, until my mother fell down on her knees, beat the hard soil with her fist, and cut the silence with her bitter voice. 'Oh, my God! I forgave this bastard everything, but this is too much! This humiliation I won't forget in either life!' We were in shock. My mother was still sitting on the ground, and a strange wheezing sound was coming from her chest. Was it that famous silent cry? My whole body was shivering.

"Seeing my mum suffer like that broke my heart. I felt so sorry for her. She lived with him for almost forty years, had many children with him, but he never belonged to her. In a way, I also understood my father: Loved ones find each other in the end. I didn't notice how I plunged into this kufr thought. I felt so much guilt that my face

18

started burning right there in front of my mother. I'm still carrying that guilt to this day.

"That's it, that's my story." Guldaria forced herself to smile. I'd been eager to hear her parents' story, but now I was so startled that I wasn't able to say a word in support of my friend. We both remained silent for a long time, not able to gather our thoughts.

ASLAN'S BRIDE

BY NADEZHDA CHERNOVA

Translated from Russian by
Shelley Fairweather-Vega

M ilochka Olsufyeva was not a pretty girl, and everyone said it, not pretty, but she was twenty years old, and she dreamed of falling in love, going on dates, and hearing someone speak beautiful words to her, and she would blush, and be shy, and her heart would burst from her chest in happiness. Even now, when she thought about it, her heart beat a little faster.

Milochka worked as a librarian at the children's library. The children came to get books with their mamas and grandmas, and sometimes with their fathers or big brothers. On the street, men didn't look at Milochka, and there wasn't anywhere else to find a husband. But Milochka steeled herself. She bided her time, but her time just wouldn't come. When Milochka turned twenty-five, she started to despair. By then she had been given a room in a dormitory for small families. She collected some nice furniture, she bought a television, she decorated. Now she had everything, but . . .

"What if I move north?" she thought. "They say, there in the north, it's easier to get married." She decided to consult with Antonina, her neighbor.

Antonina rejected the idea at once. "Nonsense! Anyone who can't get married here won't have any luck up there. Maybe someone would amuse himself with you a while, dabble a bit, a month maybe, and then—whoosh! They've all got lawfully wedded wives sitting down south, waiting for their men to come back rich. Any one of them would slit your throat to protect her own! Don't even think about it. Sit tight. Don't be so jumpy."

Milochka didn't have any closer friends than Antonina, and she listened to her, and she didn't go north. But the feeling of despair did not pass. When she came home from work, Milochka wanted her beloved to be waiting for her, someone she could tell all the news to. In the mornings, she turned back to look at the windows of her room. What if *he* was watching her go? She should wave. The lace on the windows shifted a little, as if he were standing right there behind the curtains, seeing her off or welcoming her home.

For a long time she deceived herself, until she reached the very end of her rope. That's when Styopka, who stoked the furnace in the boiler room, came into her life. He drank heavily and was always two sheets to the wind when he came to see Milochka. She pulled him into the room quickly so nobody would see him, but they knew Styopka came anyway. Milochka fed him, washed his worn-out shirts when the grime soaked through, bought him new underwear. Styopka accepted all those things as his due, and he didn't want to get married.

"How stupid do you think I am? I have a wife. I'll go back to her if I feel like it!"

Milochka tried to educate him. She gave him books. Styopka took the books, but he never returned them. One time she found the cover to *The Brothers Karamazov* in his boiler.

"Where's the book?" she asked.

Styopka took a drag from his cigarette and blew the smoke right in her face.

"In there!" He waved a hand at the stove, its scarlet flame rumbling contentedly. "The fire's reading it!"

"What did you do, burn Dostoevsky?"

"Yup! The other ones too. Buncha bullshit!"

"How could you?" Milochka wailed, but Styopka wasn't going to listen. He pushed his live-in girlfriend outside.

"Go on, go scream out there! This isn't a library! This is a serious facility, got it? Authorized entry only!"

She was offended, but later she forgave him, let him in again, fed him pie and fish fillets, poured his wine, and drank right along with him. Then came the sacred moment when they once again went to the fold-out sofa.

Times when there was nothing to drink, Styopka swore at Milochka. She cried behind the wardrobe. He got even madder, slammed the door, and disappeared for two or three weeks. Milochka suffered. She went to the boiler room and begged, humiliated herself. Styopka was stubborn. Finally Milochka would show him the bottle she had hidden in her purse. Then Styopka would relent and come back to her.

Antonina scolded her severely. "You're a fool, Milka! Some knight in shining armor you've found! No man at all would be better than that one. Get rid of him before it's too late!"

"I can't," Milochka whispered guiltily. "It's easy for you to say, you've got a family, kids . . ."

Antonina looked down on her, literally. She was tall, she played basketball. She sighed, feeling bad for her friend.

"Why are you so eager to get tied up like a dog? You poor thing. After all this, there'll be nobody left for you but alcoholics and idiots."

Who knows how long this hopeless affair would have gone on if Styopka had not poisoned himself on homebrewed vodka. That happened on New Year's Eve, 1975.

———————

One day Milochka was looking herself over in the mirror and stared, dumbstruck. So ugly! Dull hair, puffy eyes, gray face, covered with dust. She had nothing left to hope for, and this is what she came up with: she would leave this city forever, go somewhere, anywhere, to some backwoods place where only old people lived, and there she would let time drag by forever and ever. Among those old people, maybe her ugliness wouldn't be so noticeable.

This time she didn't bother consulting with Antonina. She decided all by herself. She sold her furniture and TV. She settled up with the library. She went to Styopka's grave and cried for a while. And then she picked up her little lightweight suitcase and set off for she didn't know where.

She tore along in a train, she suffocated in crowded, dusty buses, she walked on foot, she hitched a jolting ride in a passing cart, she walked some more, she took another train . . . until she was completely worn out.

She stopped at the very edge of the water—and the breath caught in her lungs! The sharp smell of salt and seaweed made her head spin. Any ancient nomad who had crossed the Gobi Desert and the Asiatic steppe and the winter forests of Old Rus' would have been just as dumbstruck at the edge of this endless expanse of sea.

The sea was calm. Shallow waves ran toward Milochka and tickled her bare feet, which weren't used to the earth. She had taken her sandals off right away when she caught sight of the colors of the sky caving in, off in the distance; overhead it was brighter, and at her feet it thickened to gleam like black ink.

Milochka held her breath, and it seemed to her that in a single instant she relived her whole life: the bitter tears at night, her incurable ugliness, the affair with Styopka. And then everything flew away as if it had never been.

———

She walked along the seashore to a village. It was nestled at the foot of some hills. Scorching hot sand. Stone huts with flat roofs, put together any which way, as if by clumsy children. In the thresholds of the open doors stood women dressed in black. Women in black garments walked the streets as well, as if this village was in mourning. Their faces were stern, unmoving. It was impossible to know what these people might be thinking. They didn't look at Milochka. They walked right past. Strange, thought Milochka. They ought to look, if only out of curiosity. All women are curious, but these don't even seem alive.

The steppe reached expansively in all directions, but the village was crowded up against the water, like a herd of sheep wrapped around by the blue backs of the modest hills. They were grown over with sage. A gentle green in April, by midsummer it would turn blue and stink horribly in the heat. After the autumn rains the sage gets white, its venom accumulates, and it starts poisoning the milk of the quick-moving nanny goats. If you don't watch them, they run into the hills and stuff themselves on bitterweed, because the good grass in the lowlands and the sprigs of acacia aren't enough for them. The goats always long for the hills! They leap over the rocky rises, sending out caustic sparks.

The air was dry, even though the sea was so close. The water, gleaming metallically under the sun, looked red-hot as well, and dry. It murmured rather than sloshed, running up on the rustling sand, which never dried here, and it barely rolled up into waves.

It hurt to walk barefoot. Milochka put her shoes on, but soon the hot earth started to burn through the thin soles of her sandals. Her face and bare shoulders had gone red in the sun, and now they ached. She tossed a kerchief over her burned shoulders and went from house to house. She wanted to rent a room, hopefully with windows over the sea, hopefully not too expensive, or at least she hoped the owner wouldn't be mean. Catch her breath for a while, and then she'd be able to see what to do next.

The people didn't understand Milochka. They gave her dour looks and pressed the edges of their black kerchiefs to their lips. "They must be scared at how ugly I am," Milochka thought glumly, and she wasn't angry at these dour people. "They'll probably kick me out, but maybe they'll get used to me."

Finally she found an old man who didn't turn away from her, and most importantly, he more or less spoke Russian. She asked him if anyone had a room to rent, not holding out much hope now, and not knowing where to turn. And to tell the truth, she didn't want to go anywhere anymore, she liked it here so desperately much. She didn't want to be separated from the sea, from these untamed hills, from the call of the goats and the cry of the seagulls. She even thought that maybe sometime, in some past life, she might have lived here, and now she was recognizing with joy this scenery so dear to her heart.

Like everyone else, this old man was sitting at the stone threshold of his home, on a low bench, but he was not idle. He was working, slowly. He had put an enormous shoe made of thick buffalo leather on an iron stand, and he was replacing the sole. The old man smelled of Chypre cologne, as if he had poured a whole bottle all over himself.

Short of stature, he had such a sizable nose that it was strange the nose didn't bend his whole frail body double and topple him over onto the ground. The old man reminded her of a solitary eagle, sitting on a heap of rocks. Especially because his hut looked like a messy pile of lumpy stone.

He also had an eagle's gaze, sharp, but his neck was thin and wrinkled just like a turkey's, covered in remnants of gray fluff. It was a funny combination, and Milochka barely kept herself from laughing out loud.

The old man's outfit was comical too. He had wrapped himself tight in two shirts, one pink with little flowers, one coarse calico in white. "What a sloppy old slob!" Milochka giggled to herself. "Now that's a sight!" The old man's thin, striped cotton pants were tucked into thick wool socks with big red patches darned on the heels. For shoes he had soft, well-worn slippers.

His graying curls burst exuberantly out from under a beach cap with dark blue anchors. That cap only emphasized the old man's awkwardness, and Milochka, though bashful by nature, felt superior to him. The old man looked Milochka over too. Then,

27

shrugging his shoulders and muttering something in his own language, he walked away into the hut. He brought his guest a yellow folding chair. She sat down and felt embarrassed to still be taller than the old man: he had perched on his low bench again and was now at her feet. But he wasn't bothered in the least, as if he had sat at her feet his whole life long, smelling of Chypre. The scent made Milochka's head hurt, not to mention the lavender blowing in from the steppe.

Milochka hadn't made up her mind yet to repeat her question about the room, and the old man seemed to have forgotten all about it. He was busy working, holding brass tacks between his lips.

Behind the old man, inside the half-lit hut, Milochka could make out colorful pictures on the smoke-cured wall, torn from magazines: alluringly beautiful women, brightly made up, hair curled; the Indian actor Raj Kapoor in a straw hat, with a handkerchief knotted at his neck; Fidel Castro and his black beard and beret; and in the most prominent place of all, the obligatory mascot of all shoemakers, Stalin. That was a magazine illustration too. Georgia's native son, in a white jacket and boots, holding an elderly Georgian woman by the arm. She was dressed in black and looked like the women in this settlement. His mother, apparently.

What a mess, Milochka thought, with another look at all the pictures on the wall.

The old man pounded on the sole, whittled it down with a file, and looked it over, satisfied, giving it a pat with his small, brown palm. Finally, Milochka made up her mind to speak again.

"Who has a foot that big? Like a giant!" She nodded toward the shoe that was ready. The old man put it down near the door and picked up the next one.

"These are Aslan's shoes!" he said gently. The old man used pliers to coax the gleaming nails from the sole of the second shoe, and put them down neatly, side by side on the threshold.

Milochka felt braver now, encouraged by his friendly tone.

"And who is this Aslan?" To herself, she wondered if he might be a young man, and a possible boyfriend.

"Aslan is Tomiko's son. He's at the war."

"What war?"

"What war do you think? The one they had . . . That's where he is." And the old man nodded toward the sea.

Milochka had no idea how to respond. She wanted to ask what he meant. The war was long over, thirty years now, and if someone hadn't come back yet, that meant he was dead. So why mend his shoes? She was disappointed. Aslan could not be her betrothed. By now the old man had removed the shoe's yellowish sole and put another one, just as new, in its place, and he patiently explained things to this Russian woman, who was not so pretty, as he had noticed straight away, but was to all appearances harmless.

"Tomiko thinks of it like this. She didn't get a paper saying Aslan was gone, that he died. So he's still alive. And she has his shoes mended every year, whether he wears them or not."

The old man slipped a nail into the existing hole and gave it a few taps with his hammer.

"She'll bring them again a year from now. I'll take off these soles and put on those," he said, nodding at the ones he had just taken off. "That's how I keep myself busy. You said you needed a room? You can rent one from Tomiko. Why should she live all alone? She'll come check on me soon. She has a big house. Not like my old shack. Why should she be alone?"

Milochka felt more alert now, and she waited anxiously for Tomiko to arrive, but so as not to seem impolite, so the old man wouldn't think she was tired of him, she asked, "Why is it that all the women wear black here? In this heat! Are they widows?"

The man brushed leather shavings off his lap, moved the iron stand away, and shot a sharp gaze at his guest again.

"They are and they aren't. Sure, they're widows. But it's something else, too. Our girls wear light colors, but soon as you're married, you put on black. It's the law. What's your name?"

"Milochka . . . I mean, Liudmila Olsufyeva!"

"I'm Costa."

"What's your patronymic?" asked Milochka, embarrassed. But he just smiled merrily, baring his big, healthy teeth.

"Who needs a patronymic? Just Costa! Everyone calls me that, so you should too."

This is going to be awkward, thought Milochka. I can't call him that! It's one thing for those old ladies, but I don't fit in, not here or anywhere.

While they were talking, a tall old woman appeared in the alley. She looked dry as a bone, and she was dressed all in black but for a brown cashmere wrap tied around her tightly, despite the murderous late-afternoon heat. The sun had begun to slip down toward the sea, but it stopped halfway there and snoozed, and its white rays hit hard, right on her face, through the hut's tiny windows, the door, and the stone walls already heated by the day. Costa looked straight at the sun, not shading his eyes with a hand. Tears leaked from his eyes and ran down along both sides of his mighty nose, but he still looked at the intolerable brilliance of the smooth sea where the sun had stopped and not at all at the woman coming toward him. Such indifference filled his face. Fat chance!

The woman in black came closer, and Milochka realized she must be Tomiko. Like a mind reader, without turning toward her, Costa nodded his head in affirmation.

"That's her!"

Tomiko walked up. She nodded gravely to Costa and Milochka, her red face steaming from the heat, burnt by the sun. Costa and Tomiko started talking in their throaty, incomprehensible language, like two big birds. His nose got redder. And a little bigger, too, it seemed. Costa clucked like an eagle. Costa gesticulated like a madman. Tomiko yelped out her words, like a black seagull.

Milochka turned away demonstratively to face the sea, so she wouldn't bother them. But they didn't even look at her. They didn't talk for long. Suddenly they both stopped. Costa's nose turned pink, then olive, like before. Finally Costa handed Tomiko the finished shoes. He clicked his tongue, regretting something. Tomiko examined his work carefully, running a finger over the newly attached soles, tapped a split yellow fingernail against the brass tacks, and was satisfied. She reached deep into the folds of her black dress and took out a tiny pouch, and from that she took some coins and dropped them in Costa's child-sized brown hand. Without counting them, Costa slipped the money into his pocket.

When the transaction was finished, Costa nodded at Milochka and said something to Tomiko. Tomiko stared at the stranger as if she had only just noticed her, as if when she said hello before she had been talking to an empty chair. Tomiko walked all around Milochka, and Milochka thought sadly, "She'll never let me stay with her!

Look at her stare. She's never seen such an ugly mug." Milochka got angry and glared at Tomiko, wolflike. "Well, never mind! I'll go somewhere else."

Tomiko finished her examination of the strange young woman. Suddenly, she smiled broadly and spoke in Russian.

"Let's go!"

Tomiko walked off without looking back. She had the huge shoes clasped under one arm, their soles shining new and bright as egg yolks. The brass tacks Costa had hammered in and the fancy heels reflected the rays of the dying sun, blinding Milochka. She kept trying to turn to escape the glare, but it never worked. So Milochka squinted her eyes as much as she could and trotted along after Tomiko, who walked over the scorching blue gravel with a man's long strides, her heavy dress hiccupping along. Following Tomiko, Milochka could see that the back of the old woman's dress had scorched in the sun, turning gray and thin, and she could make out her sharp ribs underneath, trembling either from her quick pace or from a soundless weeping. Tomiko's face never once turned to Milochka.

Without exchanging a word, they reached a stone house. Tomiko opened the door with one sweep of her arm. She nodded to Milochka. Timidly, Milochka walked in. It was surprisingly cool and clean in the house. Tomiko brought her into a small room, recently whitewashed, with windows overlooking the sea. That made the windows blue.

As soon as Tomiko shut the door, leaving Milochka alone, Milochka darted straight to the wide couch, covered with a red carpet, and collapsed. She was so tired. Her body softened, bit by bit, her damp dress now pleasantly cool, but her face was still burning. "It would be nice to freshen up," thought Milochka. But she didn't feel like standing up and didn't want to have to explain about water to her new landlady. Tomiko didn't understand a word of Russian.

"How are she and I going to live together?" she wondered next, but instead of concentrating on that, Milochka's thoughts lazily wandered to ponder how nicely she had gotten herself set up, and her sleepy eyes wandered over the low white, almost bluish, ceiling and empty walls. Only an awkward-looking table, and a chair just as heavy and rudely made, stood between the two sea-blue windows. There was no other furniture in the room. And without even noticing, Milochka fell asleep.

When she woke up, it was dusk. She didn't know where she was at first. The moon shone through a window like a polished brass heelplate. Somebody had opened the windows. From the sea came the smell of salt, the briny aromas of southern plants that came alive at night. And from the slightly open door came the smell of foreign food, apparently cooked with exotic herbs. Tomiko was making noise with a metal tool and speaking with some man in a monotone. Milochka recognized Costa's voice. That made her feel calmer. Her fear of her landlady passed.

"Costa is here, so I'll be fine!" She stretched, luxuriating, to her full height, then shrank down again. In the moonlight she could see how dirty her dress was. She couldn't go out to join Tomiko and Costa like this. She groped in her suitcase and found a knit shirt with a low neckline and an unwrinkled skirt made of a gleaming synthetic fabric. She changed quickly, with one eye on the door, and sighed with relief. It would have been nice to look in a mirror, or turn on the light, but she had noticed that afternoon that there was no electricity in this room. "Fine!" Milochka sighed. "The moonlight is nice, too."

She slipped carefully through her door and found herself in a bigger room where Tomiko fussed around the table, feeding Costa. She took one look at her tenant and froze, stupefied, as if she had walked out naked. Milochka covered her neckline with her hands, embarrassed. Tomiko shook her head disapprovingly and said something. Costa laughed.

"Don't listen to the old lady! Let's have some dinner."

Tomiko handed her a ceramic bowl she had filled with yellow porridge from a big cast-iron pot. Costa was eating that porridge, licking his wooden spoon with pleasure, picking up every yellow lump that dropped on the table. His nose was suffused with scarlet from the effort.

"Corn grits!" he told her, seeing how uncertain she looked. "Do you like corn?"

"I think so," Milochka said, blushing, and she smiled wanly, ashamed of her own awkwardness. Costa poured some warm liquid from a tall bottle over her porridge.

"There. Eat up! Don't worry, it's houndberry syrup. It'll taste good!"

Milochka took a shy taste and raised her thin eyebrows: it really was good! They both laughed happily—both Costa, regaling their guest, and Tomiko, who was observing her warily.

Suddenly Milochka felt much better and more at ease here, with these two old folks, at this planed and pitted table, as if she were feasting not just on their food, but on the spirit of this land, the one her feet had carried her to.

There were flat cakes, too, made of cornflour, and the landlady served a big white mug of goat milk to wash it down, still warm and steaming.

After dinner, Milochka moved to wash the dishes, and Tomiko let her, after she poured hot water into a big copper basin. Costa sat with them a while and spoke with Tomiko in their language—simply, monotonously, the same way old people probably speak everywhere in the world: will the dry spell last for long, will there be a good harvest, what helps most for radiculitis, what's in the letters from the children who live in the big cities and never darken their parents' doorsteps. There was plenty to expound upon, after all, for two old people who had lived near each other for ages and knew everything about each other, down to the last drop.

The kerosene lamp started to smoke and go out. Costa took out a tobacco pouch and held a pinch to his nose. He had shaken that tobacco out of the Cuban cigars his daughter had once given him. He waited for it to take effect, but it took a long time for the tobacco to explore the far reaches of Costa's cavernous nose, and it didn't seem to be in any hurry to work. There was nothing to be done. The old man rose to his feet with a grunt, ceremoniously exchanged good-byes with Tomiko, and shuffled off to the door in his slippers. At the threshold, he turned around, and in the weak light Milochka caught his sly brown face, his watchful eyes, and his blinding, even teeth.

"Well, Tomiko likes you!" he told Milochka. The old woman started at the sound of her name, the wrinkles on her forehead tensing as she tried to catch the sense of Costa's Russian words. But she couldn't. She stared helplessly from her corner, where she was putting away the dishes Milochka had washed in a handmade cupboard. Costa said something to Tomiko, and she relaxed. Then he winked at Milochka.

AMANAT

"Tomiko says you're fair and beautiful. There's nobody like you anywhere on this coast. When her Aslan comes back, he'll marry you. She'd like to call you her son's betrothed."

He repeated that, word for word, in his own language, and Tomiko responded immediately, nodding her little birdlike head, which was wrapped tightly in a brown kerchief, and she looked at Milochka with maternal tenderness. Milochka was embarrassed, and she blushed, but Costa cheered her up.

"It's fine, it's fine! It would be a sin to offend Tomiko. She doesn't have anyone at all. Be her future daughter-in-law! What could it hurt, eh? Maybe Aslan really is alive! Who knows . . . She says you didn't come here just like that. God sent you."

Milochka shrugged, and the sunburnt skin on her shoulders made her regret it. She gave the old woman a sympathetic look. Tomiko was standing straight and thin, all in black, waiting patiently for her decision. Costa went on.

"She says now that you've come, Aslan will soon be home."

Milochka swallowed feverishly, and it came out like an involuntary little nod of the head. Tomiko turned to her son's portrait on the wall and started talking to it, with feeling, pressing her thin hands to her breast.

Again Costa took out his tobacco pouch, stuck a pinch of tobacco into his nose, and waited to see if the long-anticipated sneeze would find its way out this time—but it didn't. He walked outside quietly toward the low nighttime stars, and Milochka slipped out after him. She felt on edge, and she didn't want to be left alone with Tomiko, who was all mixed up, talking with her son, dead in the war, as if he were alive and well. As if he had just stepped out, and any second now he'd come back and put on those

36

buffalo-leather shoes, so nicely greased and resoled, that he had never worn.

The sea smelled fresh, and under the crescent moon the sand glowed a gentle blue. Everything seemed unreal, shot through with fantastical currents. Sky, earth, and sea combined into a single enormous space with the tiny village sculpted into it, and there was Milochka's body, a lonely white spot hovering inside it. The sea churned heavy masses of water, rumbling and conversing with heaven and earth. The sky answered with a twinkling of close-in stars, but Milochka couldn't hear its voice. The earth responded with the metallic shrieking of cicadas, the calls of some nocturnal bird, and the strangled, eerie cry of a hunting weasel.

It occurred to Milochka that she didn't understand the language of nature, but she lived right beside it, and that was fine, it didn't bother her. So why couldn't she live with Tomiko?

The bluish darkness of the night was suddenly split by Costa's muffled sneeze, so surprising that Milochka physically recoiled.

"Well!" she thought, recovering. "The tobacco has finally made it through him! What a nose that Costa has!"

In the morning the old lady got Milochka out of bed soon as day broke, chattering away in her own language. Milochka followed her without complaint. The old woman helped her wash up, pouring water from a gray pewter jug over her hands. Then they breakfasted on last night's cornmeal porridge and houndberry syrup, served with warm goat milk. The old lady added a handful of orange fruit to the meal, sour cherry plums. The plum tree grew up against the wall of the house, bent and crippled by the wind from the sea.

They finished their food and got ready to go out somewhere. Tired of explaining things to Aslan's mute bride, Tomiko took it upon herself to wrap Milochka's head in a white kerchief so the sun wouldn't bake her. She handed her a hoe, and they set off for the hills, taking a herd of goats with them, which the old woman drove along the narrow path, shouting and waving her cane.

Just past the hills, they came to a cornfield. Green amidst the scorched white earth, it could have been an island, washed up here from another galaxy. A haze of morning heat was strung along the rows of tassels, while the green island trembled and swayed, as though hanging in the air. Any moment now it would lift off and start to float, rise higher and higher over the hills, over the sea, over the whole wide world. Milochka laughed at what she had imagined. Tomiko gave her a look, but she didn't say a word. Her face was focused and stern. She obviously had her own attitude about this field and what she was planning to do next. Here and there, Milochka could now see the brown kerchiefs of other women. "She'll make me pull weeds or hoe!" thought Milochka, with distaste. She had no experience with farming. "I'll broil out here. Aslan's betrothed!" she mocked herself. "I've really made it! Unbelievable!"

But Tomiko was all business. She parted the long cornstalks and stepped into the sweltering thicket. Milochka pushed her way in after her.

———

Every day, Tomiko found a job for Milochka to do, figuring that it would not be right to keep Aslan's betrothed away from the housework. She would be offended.

Costa often looked in on them, to check on Aslan's shoes, as he said. He was lonely on his own in his little hut. His sons lived in the city, and his daughter all the way off in Moscow, where she worked as a stewardess and was always flying to Cuba and back. She was the one who had brought those cigars to her father on one of her rare visits and pasted all those pictures from foreign magazines on his walls. Only Stalin was really Costa's. She gave him the cap with the anchors on it, too. Costa wouldn't let that cap out of his sight. He only took it off to sleep. His sons came to visit even less often, which was silly because they didn't live too far away. They sent money instead of coming themselves. Costa kept the money in a metal cigar box, so it smelled faintly of overseas tobacco. When the kids needed to buy something in a hurry, he gave them a hundred or two from that box, and it made him very pleased to have that capital and to be able to help.

Costa's wife had passed away quietly probably fifteen years ago. An apricot tree was growing out of her now. Costa the widower went around sighing over Tomiko, whom he had liked ever since they were young. But he was afraid to bring up his feelings. She was very stern. She might stop talking to him altogether, and he wouldn't be able to live with that.

Costa loved fixing shoes. But the thrifty old ladies didn't have their shoes mended very often. They bought the kind that would last the whole rest of their lives.

"They used to know how to make them!" they said, and Costa agreed.

The other villages nearby had their own cobblers, so Costa never had much work. He waited excitedly for the time when the incomparable Tomiko would appear in his doorway with Aslan's shoes. That was a real holiday. On that day he dressed up, usually, and spritzed himself with a strong dose of Chypre.

———————

Milochka was glad when Costa came to visit Tomiko. She dropped what she was doing and sat herself next to him. Tomiko gave Aslan's betrothed a disapproving look: what a frivolous girl! But as always, she kept quiet, stirred the cornmeal porridge, shelled the beans, or strained the goat milk.

Milochka wanted to know more about Aslan. What was he like? How did he walk, and talk, and laugh? Costa nodded understandingly, blew his nose like a bugle into a big checkered handkerchief, and began a leisurely tale.

"Aslan was a good boy. They don't make them like him anymore. Sometimes the kids would go out carousing, but he was always hoeing the corn, helping his mother. His father died early. Aslan was strong like his father. Was he ever strong! He could move a hut by setting his shoulder to it, or push over a tree.

"Once we lost our collective bull. Back then, before the war, we had our own dairy here in the village, lots of young people working here, a blacksmith pounding away, jigits galloping around on horses. Lots of fun, lots of noise! Now it's quiet, though . . . All the doings got moved over to Big Farm, and now there's nobody to do the work, nobody but old folks. The thistles took over the blacksmith's shop. The cowsheds rotted. Weasels live there now. But back then everything was alive . . . Well. We had lost our bull, like I was saying. The poor heifers were in mourning, as you can imagine. What could we do? We allocated some funds from the collective farm and sent our agronomist, and Aslan along with him, to Big Farm to buy a bull.

They had a market there Sundays. Still do. A trading village, always has been. The agronomist picked out a hulk of a bull, a real beaut! Dark thunderclouds roll in over the market square, blocking out the sun. The agronomist and the seller shake on the deal for that bull, they put a rope around its horns and give it a tug. But no! That bull isn't going anywhere. He plants his horns right in the ground, his eyes go all red—he won't budge. The agronomist tries this, tries that. No luck. Now what, eh? He's snorting, nostrils flaring, head down. One look at him and you can see he's a bad seed! Now the people come to laugh at them. They're watching, they think it's funny. 'Clumsy oafs!' they say. 'Buying him is the easy part! You still have to take him home!'

"Aslan has been watching the whole thing. He takes a deep breath, he squats down under the bull, and he lifts it up on his shoulders. You should have heard them all gasp! And the bull can't figure out what's happening, he just shakes his big head and drools in long ropes. Aslan carries him all the way to the village and tosses him down next to the communal corral: 'There!'

"Everyone was afraid of shaking Aslan's hand. If he really put his heart into it, your bones would splinter. That's how strong he was, even though he was still young, just seventeen. But he laughed like a little boy. That laugh just poured out of him! One look at him put everyone in a good mood. And he was so kind. He always used to say, 'I'll never leave you, Mama. I'll stay and live with you.' She told him, 'You'll get married and move away!' And he said, 'No, I'll never get married! I'll always be with you!'

"He felt sorry for his mother. She didn't have any other children. Just him. Before the war, he worked in the smithy, like his father. His father worked himself to death early on. Tomiko put all her hopes in

Aslan. She put everything on him . . . Hey, Tomiko! I'm telling the truth, aren't I?" And he repeated it all in their language, throaty and full-toned.

Tomiko looked sadly toward the sea and froze, probably remembering her boy. The wool she had been plucking at since she finished the kitchen work dropped from her hands. She wanted to make some winter socks for Aslan's betrothed, warm and white, the kind everyone had, from downy goat wool.

———————

Milochka stayed and lived in the village. Costa got her a job as a mail carrier.

Before, Tanzilia had been the mail lady. In terms of years, she wasn't all that old, but she had run out of steam early, and now she looked almost just like all the old crones in the village.

Before the war, just a girl, she had run around with a thin leather pouch on a strap, carrying the letters. Whenever an envelope came for Tomiko, from her older sister or father-in-law, Tanzilia always figured out a way to deliver it to Aslan, just to get one extra look at him. Everyone knew young Tanzilia was secretly in love with him, and Tomiko knew, too. Any time the girl managed to casually come across Aslan, Tomiko appeared in an instant, swooping down like a vulture on the poor mail carrier, and she backed away from her young man, blushing and silently cursing Aslan's ever-present mother. Nothing ever happened between them. Aslan didn't care one way or another about Tanzilia. He only loved his mother. Tomiko was proud of that, and she didn't like Tanzilia, who was painfully plain. Tomiko wanted an extraordinary bride for her only son, the kind of woman nobody had ever seen.

Just as soon as Aslan turned eighteen, the war began. He left for the front, floating away on a barge. Tomiko was left on the shore. Every night she walked to the sea and waited for him to come back. Tanzilia also kept running to the sea, hiding from Tomiko in the houndberry thicket.

A heavy burden fell on Tanzilia then: she had to carry the notices of death. She made widows of them all. Though the women understood that Tanzilia wasn't writing those terrible letters herself, they still blamed her, to this very day. She handed out all the notices, and only kept one of them secret. That was her sin. But nobody knew about that sin, though they did wonder why it was that one day she fainted right there on the street. Somebody poured some water on her. They figured it was from hunger. But she was strange after that, as if touched in the head. She wandered the hills, singing wild songs, and sometimes she howled, loud and long. Who knows why?

The war was hard on people. Take Tomiko, such a strong woman. Once she could milk twenty cows a day. Now she wasn't herself either: she had that peculiar habit with Aslan's shoes . . .

Now it was harder for Tanzilia to carry the mail. Her legs swelled. She could barely drag herself from hut to hut, calling the names in her trembling voice.

"Faina!"

"Shazina!"

"Kama!"

"Nutsa!"

The women looked through her as they took their newspapers and occasional letters. Their lips were clamped shut sternly, their black clothing was grim. The widows of that village were as impregnable as the stone walls surrounding the place. Those walls had been built long ago, and they had defended their ancestors from their enemies. Walls and towers at the edges. Here and there, they were ruins now, overgrown with juniper and relentless sage. People had hauled some of the rocks back to their huts. Rain and wind were doing the job on the rest.

Tanzilia the mail carrier always lingered for a while outside Tomiko's house, though she never had any mail for her. Why would she? Everyone Tomiko knew had died, and she couldn't read the newspapers. Tanzilia watches Aslan's unspeaking mother, takes a deep bitter breath like she wants to tell her something, but never makes up her mind to do it. Tomiko brings her something to drink, as if that's why Tanzilia has stopped at her door. The mail carrier drinks, then shuffles off to her own house in a sulk. She sits on the warm stone steps, her legs, throbbing from all that walking, stretched out before her in their thick stockings. Tiny tears roll along her brown wrinkles toward her soft lips. Tanzilia licks them with her sharp catlike tongue, licking quickly, out of habit. She doesn't even notice she's crying. Her eyes tear up of their own accord. They're tired of the whole world. But if Milochka walks by, Tanzilia jumps to her feet, shouts mean-sounding words, and throws rocks at her. Milochka doesn't understand her anger, and she complains to Costa. Costa shakes his head.

"Well, now, she's jealous!"

"Why? Why would she be jealous of me?"

"Because of Aslan!"

"That's crazy!" she says, but her cheeks spark red. She is Aslan's bride! She is, not Tanzilia!

Now Milochka collected the mail over in Big Farm, the place from which Aslan had once carried the stubborn bull. She went on foot through a field of purple lavender. The floral scent soaked through her dress, and when Milochka walked into the village, a lavender cloud came with her. She distributed the mail to each village house. There was never too much of it. Milochka had time to run to the seaside, shirking the many instructions handed to her by Tomiko, who never sat around idly and wouldn't let her do so either.

Milochka tossed off her dress and splashed into the warm water at the shore. The sea recognized her, tossing curved waves to meet her. Milochka squealed and hopped away from the churning foam, but the waves chased her, grabbed her salt-whitened heels, splattered her face and bare chest with spray. Milochka yelped and covered herself with her hands, laughing out loud. Then she and the sea got tired. Milochka sat near the now-calm water, her thin arms wrapped around her pointy knees, looking out over the receding plain of the sea, the white gulls, the distant cresting of diving dolphins.

She felt like a girl again, fifteen years old. In the city, at the library, she was never brave enough to use her real age. But here by the sea she didn't need to hide, and she loved it. She felt she must have always lived near the sea. She had been swept by the wind to foreign lands, she had taken on some stranger's ugly face—and now she had returned home.

In the evenings, running past the mirror in Tomiko's room, she saw her new reflection. Her face was tanned but still full of light, her hay-colored hair looked blonder now, and the tilt of her head had the grace of some wild creature, running free. And her eyes shone with the glorious light of love that has been transforming faces for a thousand years or more. Milochka saw for the first time that she had clear blue eyes and a classical nose like the Greek goddesses in the *History of the Ancient World* book Aslan had left behind. Tomiko took very good care of that book, and she would place it carefully in Milochka's hands when she asked for it.

The sea lazily tossed up pebbles decorated with fantastic patterns that looked like some forgotten alphabet. Milochka loved to examine the magical runes on those flat stones—pink, yellow, pale green, white, and bluish black. What had nature written on these stone tablets? Maybe it was the key to immortality, or the history of the universe. Or maybe it was a trove of knowledge never revealed to humankind!

Milochka collected handfuls of pebbles, dried them on the beach, and arranged them before her, sorted by pattern. Just a little more and she thought she might be able to read their clearly written formulas. She could understand Tomiko's language now, after all. Just a little, but she could.

———

In the evenings, the two of them sat for a long time together. Milochka paged through the *History of the Ancient World*, squinting next to the kerosene lamp. The book was written in crisp lovely letters that looked like the patterns on the pebbles. Milochka couldn't read them. But she remembered some of the ancient Greek myths, and she told them to Tomiko from memory.

Tomiko listened solemnly. But most often, they didn't speak. Milochka daydreamed about Aslan, and Tomiko rummaged through her old trunk, where she kept sundry treasures: a wedding dress with a multitude of tiny buttons and such a small waist that Milochka was astounded, looking at it from the corner of her eye: how had Tomiko ever fit in a dress like that? Her husband's black tunic with its sewn-in strap for cartridges still smelled of powder and tobacco. Next to it lay a sheepskin hat and leather belt decorated with silver. Her father-in-law had worn that belt.

One time Tomiko pulled from the chest a white silk shawl with long tassels. From its long rest in the trunk, yellow stains had crept over the shawl here and there, and it smelled of dry herbs and something else, too, something harrowingly sweet. Tomiko shook out the white shawl carefully, admired it for a moment, and then draped it over Milochka's shoulders.

"This will be yours! Aslan likes it. He always asks me to wear it on holidays. He'll see you and give you compliments!" Tomiko said, and Milochka understood almost every word. The important thing was that Aslan would like it.

Now Milochka had a portrait of Aslan on the table in her room, exactly the same picture that was on the wall in the big room, but smaller, the size of her hand. She had asked Tomiko for the photo, and Tomiko had approved. Milochka glued the photograph to a firm piece of cardboard, attached a little stand to it, and set the portrait where she could always see it, next to a bouquet of wildflowers. A fresh bouquet every day. Those bouquets were a new development. Marat the postal clerk gave them to her. He was a short man, pock-marked and very shy. The girls laughed at him, but Milochka never did. Marat thought she was of unprecedented beauty. He never said anything, just blushed at the sight of Milochka, and she blushed and didn't say anything, either. They always stood like that for a few seconds. Then Marat handed her a bouquet of daisies or lavender, got on his motorcycle, and drove off.

Tomiko always waited in the doorway of her hut for Milochka, staring suspiciously at her bouquet.

"Where'd you get that?"

"I picked them in the field!" Milochka always lied.

Tomiko thought sadly, "She's leaving me." But Milochka was already running to the kitchen, singing, setting the table, even though she always dropped a fork or a spoon or spilled the water when she poured. "She's leaving," Tomiko grieved, and she covered her lips with the hem of her kerchief.

Milochka's bouquets stood next to Aslan's portrait as if he was the one who had given them to her. Aslan never took his rapt black eyes off Milochka. It seemed to her that he missed her terribly in the far-off lands he was traveling through and couldn't get enough of the sight of his betrothed. Milochka spent a long time staring at Aslan, too, always finding something new and dear in his features. Sometimes he smiled at her: he forgave Marat, though he didn't want to look at the flowers, and Milochka moved them away from the portrait and put them on the windowsill. That is how they lived. She never thought about how if Aslan returned, he would be like Tanzilia. Old. Time had gotten jumbled in her heart. She was fifteen years old, and her young man was seventeen.

———

Before bed, Tomiko and Milochka would walk to the sea, crunching through the silence across the coarse dry sand. Every grain of sand was visible. The moon was full, making the water white. The hills stood out too, white, as if covered by a smooth coat of snow. In the bright moonlight, Tomiko's face changed. Her wrinkles and natural duskiness disappeared. Tomiko was young, bright of face, just like the young Aslan, and Milochka gazed upon her with joy.

They stood there a long time at the brim of the living sea. A tall, silent woman, all in black, and a smaller young one who kept her thin arms and rough elbows tucked behind her back. They were waiting, just in case the barge that had once carried Aslan away to war appeared on the horizon.

ORPHAN

BY AYAGUL MANTAY

Translated from Kazakh by
Zaure Batayeva

His real name was Nurseit. But his sisters-in-law called him Urseit, observing the Kazakh tradition of finding a cute nickname to avoid pronouncing the real names of the younger brothers of their husbands. His father, already old, mistakenly gave his nickname to the authorities, and his official name became Urseit. His sisters-in-law joked that they were not allowed to call him by his official name and that they would call him Murseit from now on. Our mothers called him Murseit-qainaga, and we, the children, called him Murseit-ata. He himself used to gently scold us, offended by the liberty we took: "Little rascals, why do you call me by my name? You are like my grandchildren."

Urseit-ata's hut was located close to the river Zhalbyz, which took its name from the wild mint that grew there. In spring, when the apple trees blossomed, his little hut would completely disappear in flowers. Passersby were stunned by this natural beauty. All summer we would swim in the river and steal the old man's apples from his garden. As soon as the little apples appeared on the trees, we grabbed the unripe fruit, breaking the branches. We ate the apples as we picked them, ran back to the river, and threw the cores into the water. Upset with our wild behavior, the old man would call to us: "You little bastards, why not wait until they're ripe? There's nobody at my house to eat them. I would give them to you anyway. Why are you so impatient that you need to break the branches? Why don't you just pick the fruit?" But he always forgot quickly and became like a child himself: "Hey, you rascals! Let's have a race! I will buy ice cream for the winner, the first to cross the Zhalbyz!" We were children and did not understand that he was lonely. But even adults would not understand why a white-bearded old man would play with children. Perhaps he was ashamed of his hunched back or had never played with his peers when he was a child himself.

One day he even swam with us. He played soccer with us. Then he braided my hair. He even wiped the nose of Satpaq's whiny daughter and braided her hair as well. That day he did not call me "yellow girl" as usual, but asked my real name. He called Satpaq's whiny little girl by her real name, Beibitgul. He asked each of us, "Hey, little rascals! What are your real names? I'm so old, I forgot them all."

The next day he did not come to play with us. We heard that he had been taken to the hospital that night and died there. When the people of the village pooled their money and buried him, nobody really wept for him. People just said that the "poor old orphan" had been a nice man. "Can an old man be an orphan?" we wondered. Soon we children forgot about our oldest friend. Now, though, every time I visit our village and wash my face in the river's water, I remember the hunchbacked old man.

Back then, the adults were always warning us that the weeds were full of snakes, and if we made too much fuss in the water, we would anger the snake king. One day we were playing in the river and Masaqbay's boy Kokkoz, running away from another boy, hid in the weeds. The snakes, scared by a human presence right in their midst, came up to the surface of the water, entangled with each other. We were horrified. Kokkoz could not speak for some time. We rushed to the shore and ran without looking back. That was the first time we realized that it was the hunchbacked man who had always been there before, guarding us and protecting us from all kinds of trouble.

We did not swim in the river again for a long time. That left the way open for the children of the smaller, neighboring kolkhoz, the one called "Communism." We were not happy about that at all. "Hey, you kolkhozes! What are you doing swimming in our river? Why are you crossing the border and coming into our village?" We attacked them with those words because the people of our village felt *we* were the real citizens. How could it be otherwise? As the biggest collective farm around, we were the ones who had a two-floor school, a House of Culture, a hospital, and a park. "We are kolkhozes, but so are you! Did you forget where you live? Zana Turmys is a kolkhoz, too! Want us to remind you?" they shouted back. "*We're* the kolkhozes? *Us*?" we raged, and Gopher showed them his little fist.

Why should we listen when they said the Zhalbyz belonged to both villages? We would never allow that. Angry with such unfair treatment, they made a new demand. "Your dead people lie in our cemetery! If we cannot swim in your river anymore, then you take away your dead bodies from our cemetery!" "We will! We will not allow our ancestors to stay in your cemetery!" we declared in chorus. "When? Take them today!" they threatened us. "What if we don't?

53

What else do you guys have in your village except for the cemetery? Your village has nothing cultural at all!" we argued back. "Hey, why are we fighting about the cemetery? We'll all go there one day," someone shouted.

We all fell silent for a while. The thin dark-skinned boy with broken lips smiled, happy that his words had affected us so much.

Zharabas, who got this nickname for his never-healing sores, broke the silence. "Hey, jerk, who told you that?" "My grandpa. My grandpa is a mullah!" said the dark-skinned boy, then licked at the greenish snot horse running from his nose. Zharabas, who immediately withdrew his claws after the dark-skinned boy's answer, was bewildered and scratched a sore on his elbow. Back then we did not understand the words on the cemetery gates: "We were like you, you will be like us." I hated the dark-skinned boy. Whether scared by our silent reaction or scared that one of us would beat him, he sat down on the ground and started to cry. Nobody tried to console him. Nobody teased him either.

I still remember that day, how I cried myself, all alone, in the corn field. Afterwards, I tripped and fell on my face while I was running home frightened. I stayed like that for a long time, glued to the ground, afraid to get up. Exhausted, I came home only in the evening. My mom, already upset that I was so late, got even more worried. "Who beat you?" "She would not let anyone beat her! She is the one who beats others," smiled my father. "Look, she's been crying, and she hurt her face!" said my mom. "Did you really cry?" my father asked, surprised. "Papa, why don't people live six hundred years?" I asked, and my father caressed my head with his big palm.

HUNGER

Excerpt from *THE NANNY*

BY AIGUL KEMELBAYEVA

Translated from Kazakh by
Zaure Batayeva

When the time comes for spring to sink into summer, I will receive my diploma and leave Moscow. Then I will forget about coming back every year to this blessed nest, like a migrant bird. It will be difficult for me to part with Moscow, but Almaty is a beautiful city. To admire a city is a strange and inappropriate thing for a Kazakh nomad like me. The multiplication of meaningless items in such a big, settled place makes the world too crowded.

When life changes as fast as evil, there is nothing you can do. It was becoming quite clear to me that I had never been taught to step outside my beloved literature and look at the real world. Now the real lessons were beginning. At first I was too startled to really grasp it. In a cruel trick, a money order arrived at the dormitory, my student's heart rejoiced, and I rushed to the post office to cash it. In the palm of a post office employee that weighty sum evaporated into thin air. "This transfer is unauthorized," she said. "We no longer hand out money from Kazakhstan. It will all be sent back." Her words sounded like a court sentence. What nonsense was this? Thinking that she must be joking, I showed her the piece of paper and my passport again. When the clerk refused to take my passport, the words flew off my tongue. How come? Why not? This was ridiculous! What right did she have to deny me the money that belonged to me? But it was very clear, soon, that this situation had nothing to do with the post office clerk.

What was to be done? Who was to blame? Terrible, rebellious queries stuck to my throat and started sucking my blood like a leech. You can't survive in a megalopolis without any money. That blatant reality grew stronger every day. Soon after, the same cursed post office denied me 30,000 rubles sent by a telegraph, then 90,000 rubles transferred conventionally, and then, in the middle of November, 50,000 rubles that my mother sent, hoping her third attempt would finally work better. Suddenly I felt like a character from Kafka. Society had adopted an anti-utopian model, and its slogan was: no more transfers from Kazakhstan to Russia. Kazakhstan was a foreign country now, and it was going to print its own currency, the national tenge. Maybe it had already started! Apparently the world's bureaucrats, sitting in their offices, had decided that the student community should die of hunger.

As my hardship began, I received a letter from my mother. It felt devastating that I could not afford a drink of kefir while milk was flowing in rivers in my own village. But there was no way I could write the truth to my mother, that I was close to starving and my poverty was wrapping around me like bindweed. That would only break her heart and trouble her mind. As the Kazakhs say, a young wolf does not show its thinness, but lets its fur bloat instead. In this giant city, nothing is for free, and it never will be. So the thought about my mother giving out milk free of charge, right and left, got stuck in my mind. All I could do was ask God to give me patience, sabyr. I received another letter from my mother, who wrote that the post office decided to stop accepting parcels going to remote cities or other republics. They consoled her by saying it would all be worked out after the New Year.

Every day after class I looked for a job. Like a sardine getting dumped from a barrel, a wave of the crowd pushed me forward off an escalator. I left the metro and walked down the street, one phrase constantly on my mind: *Wash a donkey's ass, if you must, as long as you earn some money.* Now I felt as if Abay himself was leading me through the streets of Moscow. Those words were not fading in my mind; on the contrary, they were growing brighter and bigger with time. I felt as grateful as ever. When your feet are tired and your mind is wandering, it helps to feel there is no shame in great words. The only problem was that I could not find a donkey. No office wanted to hire me. Everyone waved me off as soon as they heard that I was a full-time student. A small book stall seemed to show some interest, but they offered so little, it was no help. I would sit there all day with no break and get paid worse than a slave. Not long ago, a third-year student paid someone else 3,000 rubles to write his term paper. As Abay said, a lazy man is good at wasting money. Last year I wrote a paper on Don Juan for a girl, but I was not paid; she asked me to help her, so I did. At that time, money was not yet my goal.

Sometimes the thought comes to my mind that I have no shelter except for my umbrella. But those are the moments when we forget about God. I do not want to walk all the way past Chekhov Street to the metro, so I go to a trolley stop. There is a bread stand right behind it. I go in and buy a bread stick. The shelves are full of baked goods, no empty space at all. They have everything but bird's milk. There is nothing like the smell of fresh bread, is there? Lately I haven't been able to think of anything but food. When you eat nothing nourishing, when you are deprived of meat, your empty stomach has no interest in other things. In the mirror, I don't look emaciated. I have lost weight, but I look younger. I feel the lightness in my body. But my belly is tight, and I have started feeling dizzy and exhausted.

I had lost the desire to read the books I needed for my exams. My mind was succumbing to fatigue. Books began slipping from my hands. I was tired of eating fried buckwheat and potatoes with bread every day. I fell into a type of madness in which I searched out passages related to sweet, tasty food in all the books and stories I had ever read. It was like stumbling on a flat road. The tortuous days seemed to have no end. I started threading together all my favorite writers' tales of hardship in their novels and stories. Was it a trick to assert that I was not alone, that I was their spiritual heir? Was it my way to console myself? But what point was there in trying to figure that out? How could I cope with the long, drawn-out suffering of hunger?

As I underwent the torments of Tantalus, I understood why Knut Hamsun wrote *Hunger*. I remembered my short visit to my sister in Qaraghandy during winter break of my first year at the university, when I was treated like a customer at a resort. I thought of the huge goose that she cooked in the oven. When I asked her if she liked going to the movies on weekends, she told me that she preferred to stay home with her family and cook something delicious. Henry Miller turned the hardest period of his life into a classical novel. When visiting a friend, he could hardly restrain himself from stealing a chicken leg from the hands of a child sitting at the table. Right now I feel it would be difficult to find anyone else in the whole world so willing to understand such a confession.

I started looking in the mirror more frequently. My elongated neck, and my sharpened nose and cheekbones, were the result of hunger, but my eyes looked more acute. Nothing unusual was visible from the outside. This thinness seemed nothing more than the beauty of youth.

I was acquiring a weird habit of perceiving books by smell, like an animal. Now, for me, Hemingway was associated with the smell of fried fish and freshly caught trout. I swallowed my saliva as if I could truly smell that fishy odor coming from his nourishing stories, as if I could see with my own eyes the reddish-brown color of a cooked fish fillet. When I thought of those fish being pulled out of clean mountain waters, my hunger only increased. Ever since I was a teenager, I loved reading Gogol. Now I associated Gogol with the delicious scent of street fairs and the generosity of gourmet cooks.

At night, in the twilight of my room, unable to sleep, I imagined the jam described at the wedding of Emma Bovary. It popped into my memory, and I craved something sweet. I remembered how Uzbek Robinson Crusoe was, and I wept: he had a herd of goats on the island, and he dried grapes into raisins. Don't be so greedy! Share a handful of raisins with me! Pushkin, my closest relative, rejoiced by saying that he drank honey at a wedding. His words had the magical power of exciting the appetite. Why didn't I go with the poet to that wedding? If only I could taste just a morsel of real peasant food with Gerasim's spoon, as Turgenev describes it. I bet that Cervantes's stomach was making noise, that he was hungry himself, while he was describing the pie that Sancho Panza ate. I was a prisoner of thoughts about food, and it was becoming impossible to tell if I was ashamed of it.

Human beings are born destitute; we fear nothing more than an empty dish. Only God needs nothing. All I could do was repeat more Kazakh sayings. *The end of endurance is pure gold. A lamb of God will not be eaten by a wolf.* There was always a way out of any crisis, so really, there was no use despairing. And patience was golden, of course.

Lilya from the translation department was already working as a nanny, but while she worked, she hadn't touched her thesis, and now time was pressing her hard. She could no longer do the job every day and needed a partner to take turns with her. Close to February, Lilya took me to the apartment where she worked, so I could get my first glimpse of the new era. The whole metro ride there, I felt sorry for myself, astonished by my situation, feeling like my free head was suddenly locked in a halter, that there was no way I could break loose. But I also knew that if the owners of that apartment saw me as a stranger and would not hire me, then I would continue starving, destroy my health, and have that burden for the rest of my life. I was stuck: if I pulled one way, my bull would die, and if I pulled the other, my cart would break. The idea of being enslaved by strangers in the long days of winter was depressing. But, as they say, in three days a person can get used to anything, even the grave, so I had to hope for the best.

When Lilya rang the doorbell, my heart was in my mouth. A pale young woman with a long bob opened the door. Her face seemed so familiar—she was a Kazakh, and her name was Jamal. But that did not make me happy to have come. Lilya had told me the woman of the house was not pretty. That meant Lilya's understanding of beauty was wildly incorrect. This woman was a little over thirty, with a straight nose, hazel eyes, and beautiful eyebrows. Her body was petite. But she looked tired. She was wrapped in a long blue gown with white stripes that went down to her feet, as if she were cold. Lilya must have told them she was bringing me, because she greeted us indifferently and cheerlessly, gesturing that she had a headache. Just then, a little girl jumped out from behind her like a kid goat. Her eyes were shining, and her carefree childhood was smiling cheerfully on her face. "Rita, turn off the TV. Haven't you finished watching your cartoons?" said the mother to the daughter. "Go and do your English. Your father will quiz you tonight." She said a few words to Lilya about some household chores and then went back to sit at her computer in the bedroom. You could see from her pale, exhausted face that she worked constantly, even on Saturdays.

That day, it was my job to clean the room where Jamal was sitting. Even though it was not a pleasant feeling, I soaked a dust cloth in a bucket of water and started wiping up dust. Finishing quickly and escaping became the most pleasant thing I could imagine. While dusting around Jamal, I tried not to look at her, because the unhappy, annoyed mood of the young woman staring at the computer was easy to sense. It must have been discontent with the heavy weight that fell on her fragile shoulders, too much difficult work. But just then I was having a hard time paying attention to other things—I was obsessed with myself.

Grief is an abyss: you may fall and sink. Do not burn your coat because you are annoyed by lice. Even roses have thorns. If you want to taste happiness, then come to your senses. This new voice tried to console my suffering heart. If I had been a slave in ancient Rome or Egypt or in a world ruled by some kind of tyrant, my situation would not have seemed so odd. But the haughty look of this woman, using me as slave labor here in this modern time, made me angry. "Damn you, you bourgeois fool! One day I will be a world-renowned writer!" I thought to myself. But I knew that was the whimpering puppy of powerlessness talking, and a more kingly soul would be more forgiving.

What can I say? I was experiencing mixed feelings—pity and sorrow for myself, joy at having found a way to make money, shame and surprise at having my leisure stolen from me. In the meantime, it seemed unspeakably odd and humiliating to be crawling around on all fours, up and down, now with a wet cloth, now with a dry cloth. Who knew that earning money by washing a donkey's ass could look like this? In two hours we made that two-room Moscow apartment shine like a mirror. We had scrubbed every tile in the bathroom, and the clean sheets and Rita's freshly laundered clothes were hanging on a rope over the balcony. We had ironed the laundry that was already dry. Why did people call such cleanliness "German"? Was cleanliness the attribute of just one nation? The world could really use the cleanliness of the nomads. When those chores were done, Lilya and I started taking care of lunch in the kitchen. We warmed up some borscht we took from the fridge, and Lilya, apparently right at home here, put butter, bread, cheese, and jam on the table. That must have been the first time in fifteen days that I had decent food. After the meal, I remembered what my grandmother used to say: God creates every person with his own share in the world. But feeding myself in someone else's kitchen still bothered me.

When Jamal's husband opened the door and walked in, we were drinking tea. Lilya quickly jumped up and took two of the three bags that he was holding. "Hello," he greeted us softly. He was a friendly man about the same age as his wife. He was tall and had typically Russian features. Compared to his wife's slimness and fragility, he was much healthier and showed no traces of tiredness. "Papa! Did you bring the movies?" shouted his daughter from the other room. "Yes, Rita. Here, come and get them." Rita rushed in and immediately read the titles. They were Walt Disney cartoons. What except *Tom and Jerry* could interest a nine-year-old girl? Lilya was still putting away the groceries the husband had brought home. It was obvious that he had chosen only the best fruit. The rich color of the oranges, the size of the green apples, big as bowls, the peels on the bushel of bananas—everything indicated deliciousness. Clearly, all the fruit was for Rita.

After lunch, Jamal let us go early. Still wrapped in her fleece robe, as if all her young energy had been sapped by her computer monitor, or as if she simply never got enough sleep, her face sad and suffering, she handed 5,000 rubles to each of us. "Girls, I was supposed to spend 5,000 per day for a maid," she told us wearily. "Today I'm paying 10,000 rubles. From now on, I'll need you to come one at a time." "Thank you," we said.

No doubt that she was obeying her Kazakh nature when she accepted the extra expense that day. I won't lie, those bluish banknotes made me feel dizzy. For months, all sources of cash, except for my student stipend, had been blocked. And I was wasteful by nature, because there is nothing more humiliating than counting change. Right after high school, I won a literary contest, and my story was published. I received a big award and decent royalties. But I wasted that money, with complete irrationality. A big portion of the award my mother distributed among relatives as suinshi, and the rest was spent on the feast we gave to celebrate. I spent the royalties myself, buying expensive clothes for my sister, who was getting married. I could have saved that money and bought a small apartment on the outskirts of Almaty, but I was not able to see into the future.

I wondered if I should be worried about the unattractive way in which I was now earning money. It was the first time in my life that I had to take a job as an actual laborer, cleaning someone's floor and washing their dishes. I had never undergone any hardship, never experienced despair, so to me, my new situation seemed insane. My soul was whining like a wolf cub, crying like a camel calf who had been fooling around carelessly and finally stepped into the fire. But the texture of that blue banknote seemed to have the magical power to heal the wounds in my soul and erase all my whining and complaining before it poisoned me. Sabyr nested in my heart like a swallow. Sabyr would carry me to my goal.

With my daily wage of 5,000 rubles and the free food, this miserable, dependent life would help me survive until I got my diploma. I could also read and study at work when I had the time. But the moral burden was enough to discourage my soul. When I went up in the elevator my first day there on my own, I met two old women. They must have been neighbors and probably knew that I was Rita's sitter. They greeted me in friendly tones as if we were acquainted. If only they had known that I was dragging myself off to prison. I felt inferior. The hope that all this was only temporary helped to clear away the uncertainty, and it saved and protected me.

It was difficult to value what I held in my hands. Especially with the economic crisis still emerging, and our formerly huge country dissolving and disintegrating into separate states. Alongside a new pauperism, a new group of the wealthy had appeared. At the end of the century that had started with a revolution, everything had changed quickly and diabolically. Wealth and poverty were truly separated, now, and they definitely did not want to see each other again. At that time I was far enough removed to think of myself as somebody who did not belong to either group, somebody who would be able to earn money purely with the knowledge in my brain. I would be a bohemian, I thought, hungry one day, full the next.

PROPISKA

BY RAUSHAN BAIGUZHAYEVA

Translated from Russian by
Shelley Fairweather-Vega

The city lay at my feet. It hung its buildings all around me, sprayed me with its fountains, hit me in the nose with the smell of barbecued meat, lured me down its cool, shady avenues. But it was not my city. In the year, more or less, that I had spent far away, the city had become a stranger, gotten its back up, shrunk away from me with one cold, forbidding word: *propiska*. As I wandered its streets restlessly, searching for refuge, I learned envy. I envied everyone who lived there, the ones with every right to hurry about on their business, or rest on the benches in the squares with monuments, or have an ice cream on the run, adjusting the bonnets on babies in their prams. I envied all the dogs and cats, even the strays. Their beastly lives may be short and stupid, but they never ran across that most terrible of words.

At the start of the second month, when I realized I had outstayed my welcome at my uncle's house, I moved in with other relatives. My ties with that family were so distant as to be almost invisible, but the atmosphere there was simpler. Three girls, the oldest of whom was twelve, surrounded me with chitchat, reminding me of my own sisters. They were actively intrigued by the contents of my makeup kit, they adored my white Czech purse with its gold buckle, and they loved going to the movies with me.

My aunt was pregnant, expecting a boy, and that general feeling of expectation put a certain tension on her face, as if she were afraid of failing the most important examination in her life. Her husband, my Uncle Chingis, a strong, handsome man, took good care of her, anticipating her every desire. But despite the kindness around me, I still felt stuck, hanging between the earth and the sky. There was never even a hint of my long-awaited propiska, the official document which would give me authorization to get a job and then a place in a dormitory. Every so often, despair would send me images of inglorious defeat. I'd travel back to my spot in the collective farm's technical school, to my colorless, dull existence as a drawing teacher for teenagers with empty eyes, for whom that subject was absolutely incomprehensible, like life on Mars.

One morning the doorbell rang, and the house quickly filled with happy voices. Guests had arrived: Uncle Chingis's cousin Amangeldy and his wife Yulduz.

She was Uzbek, and her name meant "star." My aunt and uncle pronounced her name the Kazakh way, though: Zhuldyz. Amangeldy was of medium height. He moved briskly and had light skin, flashing brown eyes, and a hearty voice. And she . . . she was such an awkward match for him, she might as well have been a chance acquaintance. Yes, she had enormous black eyes under a canopy of thick lashes and sable brows, but her wide, flattened nose and thick lips negated all that elegance. Yes, her teeth sparkled like two strings of pearls, but her low, hoarse voice, and her strange laughter, made you forget that bit of perfection. She was already stout for her thirty-two years, with a protruding belly. This visitor spoke in a mixture of three languages: Uzbek, Kazakh, and Russian. And her short, curly hair was haphazardly styled. The most horrifying thing about her, though, was her outfit: a Crimplene pantsuit in a venomous green color.

Amangeldy was a military man. He was not much older than his wife but had worked his way up to colonel.

My aunt and I set the table in the living room. They mentioned that the girls had gone to the countryside to visit their grandmother.

"Everything's so cramped and crowded here!" Yulduz exclaimed as she took her seat at the table. "In our place in Moscow, everything was twice as big, wasn't it, Aman?"

Her husband disagreed gently.

"Maybe it seemed that way. Bigger, sure, but not twice as big."

My ears perked up at the word "Moscow," and another pang of envy struck me, perhaps the most painful one yet. Even the fact that Amangeldy and Yulduz had recently returned from Moscow to Dzhambul and were waiting for new orders could not soothe it.

"Well, Starlight, where are those gifts you brought?"

Starlight, he called her! I felt like a target into which these guests were shooting arrows. They hit the bull's eye every time. Yulduz gasped, slapped herself on the hips, and shimmied back to the front door. From there she brought back a ceramic bottle of Bulgarian wine and a box of candy and put them on the table. Then she draped a Pavlovsky Posad shawl with fancy fringe over my aunt's shoulders. She was pleased with her present, and everyone sat down to eat.

I moved to excuse myself, but the colonel turned to me as he poured the wine.

"Where are you off to?"

"Sit down, sit down, girl!" said Yulduz, grabbing my arm.

My uncle joined in, and I sat down next to my aunt.

"This is Raihan," my aunt told them. "We're second cousins."

Amangeldy, sitting at the head of the table, was across from me, and every time I raised my eyes, I met his gaze. Suddenly a tiny space opened inside my tortured heart, and every glance from his laughing brown eyes injected something exciting into that space, as if at the end of an endless, dull corridor, a door had unexpectedly swung open, and I couldn't wait to get a good look inside.

After breakfast I washed the dishes. The women talked in the bedroom, and the men were off somewhere by themselves. The colonel's face stared at me from the bottom of every bowl, but Yulduz, in her garish getup, kept grabbing him away.

My aunt came in to stew some horse meat.

I got up my courage.

"Where did those two meet?"

"They've known each other since they were children. They grew up playing in the same courtyard. When Aman was serving in Germany, his mother was afraid he'd bring home a German girl. He came back on leave once, and she married him right off to her best friend's daughter."

"That's terrible!" I said before I could stop myself. "How could he agree to that?"

My aunt smiled. "I can tell you don't like her. But we're used to her. She's a good woman. And her mother, Auntie Zulfia, is so kind, she'd share her last crumb with anyone."

She left the meat with me and went out shopping with Yulduz.

The men had turned on the fan and were setting up a card game.

"Want to keep us company, Raihan?" asked Amangeldy when I walked in, meaning to dust an already sparkling-clean cabinet.

His eyes expressed nothing in particular. This was just an ordinary invitation.

But I was still embarrassed and shook my head. "No, no! I don't know how to play!"

The two men laughed.

"Why so frightened?" asked the colonel with a smile. Then he sniffed. "Mmm, what a heavenly smell! It's been a hundred years since I ate horse meat."

"Bring us some beer, Raihan?" my uncle asked.

"Sure." I hurried out and spent a long time searching the refrigerator for beer.

I found it in the bathtub, bottles of Zhigulis lying in a row in the cold water. Some of them had already shed their labels.

I was equally torn between the living room, where the men were playing cards and kept bursting into laughter, and the bathroom mirror. I gave my haggard face a critical look, then carefully went over my eyebrows with some tweezers and put on a little eyeliner. I didn't feel brave enough for anything bolder. But that was enough to make me feel victorious over the colonel's awkward wife. I turned on the radio in the kitchen. They were playing "Bésame Mucho," and the tune added a punch to my already romantic mood.

I didn't know what to do with myself, so I mixed up some dough for noodles, to make beshbarmak. My aunt seemed happy about that when she and Yulduz returned, laden with shopping bags. They called me into the bedroom to show me what they had bought. Yulduz had found a mink manteau from which I could barely tear my eyes. It had a dark brown sheen reminiscent of some other life, one dashing with expensive automobiles, rivers of champagne, gentlemen going down on one knee before ladies to kiss their hands. Though as far as I could tell, Yulduz didn't fit into that picture at all.

"I found this at Beryozka!" she said, modeling for us. "And we got your auntie some nice shoes. Come on, try them on!"

My aunt slipped into some fall shoes from Czechoslovakia, with buckles.

"They're so comfortable!" she smiled. "Like my feet can sleep! Thank you, Zhuldyz."

"How many times are you going to thank me?" The colonel's wife laughed and slapped herself on the hips. "Your state department store's pretty worthless, isn't it?" she added, disappointed. "In Tashkent they're better equipped."

Then she showed off gifts for her hosts' daughters, bright summer dresses, each prettier than the last.

With every minute I was feeling more like the poor relation, looking wistfully at the lives of the benefactors who had taken her in. There was something childish about that feeling. I missed my home unbearably, and my mother, and the delicious layered bread she made in the cast-iron qazan, which you could tear off in big clumps and soak in cream. I missed the smoky aroma of tea from the samovar and the clucking chickens in the yard. And that sweet moment when my mother would suddenly exchange a look with my father and say, "Listen, daughter, we've bought you something new. Here, try it on!" My eyes clouded over, and afraid I'd start to cry, I hopped up and hurried to the door.

"Where are you off to?"

I turned at the question. Yulduz was handing me some sort of package.

"What is it?" I asked, trying not to be caught looking.

"Open it up!" my aunt said, and smiled.

I unwrapped the paper package. Inside was a sarafan with broad shoulder straps and three big buttons on the bodice, stitched in my favorite style, à la Natasha Rostova. Pink tulips that would never fade were strewn across a field of milky white. The cool, sturdy cotton caressed my hands, and the label had the magical inscription "Made in Hungary."

"What are you waiting for? Try it on!" said my aunt.

"Is this . . . for me?"

"Of course it's for you, girl!" said Yulduz, and she laughed her hoarse laugh.

"But I can't." I was upset. "I don't have any money right now . . ."

"Money? It's a present, I'm telling you!"

"Put it on!" my aunt said encouragingly.

"Thank you," I stammered, feeling my heart fill with an uninvited love for this woman in the monstrous pantsuit.

When I had dressed myself in that sarafan, before me in the mirror stood not the poor relation, beset by insecurity, but a slender, confident young woman with gleaming eyes.

"Wow! Gorgeous!" exclaimed Yulduz with a click of her tongue, giving me a thumbs up.

"Yes, it's just perfect for you," my aunt agreed, and added proudly: "I'm the one who picked it out. With your darker skin, that color lights you up."

"Well! Wear it in good health!" said Yulduz, waving a hand and chuckling.

Just then, Amangeldy appeared in the doorway. His eyes swept the room and stopped on each one of us, lingering just a little extra on me.

"I'd call this painting *The Four Seasons*. Only I can't find spring."

We looked at ourselves and laughed.

"That's true! The four seasons!" Yulduz giggled like a little girl. "I'm winter, you're summer, and your auntie is fall."

"There's spring, too," said my aunt, winking at her guest. "Where are those shirts you brought?"

Yulduz slapped her hips again and rifled through a big bag. She pulled out two men's shirts.

Then there was a lavish lunch with slices of zhaya that melted in my mouth and amber links of sausage atop the thinnest slices of square noodles. I sliced cucumbers and tomatoes, and my aunt opened her last jar of preserved summer squash.

And again I found myself sitting across from the colonel, but this time I was wearing my magical sarafan. When they offered me red wine, I did not refuse.

Logically, this sarafan should have been an impenetrable wall between me and our male visitor, extinguishing the sparks of my wayward feelings. By giving me the dress, Yulduz had in a way paid me off, putting me in her debt. It was clear as day that she had bestowed this luxury upon me purely out of generosity and her own expansiveness of spirit. She probably had not an inkling of the threat I posed to her. But that didn't change anything. The only way I could escape this danger zone would be to refuse the gift. But that would have been awkward, and I didn't have the heart to do it. I was simply enamored of the quality and beauty of that dress. In that swampy expanse of the Stagnation, an item like that could only be gotten illicitly or on the last day of the month, if you stood in a kilometer-long line. And then only if you were lucky.

In other words, logic was obliged to retreat, knitting its brow.

And everything, wondrously, changed.

All my priorities had shifted, and now Yulduz was not my competitor, and I did not suffer constant jabs of jealousy and envy toward her. Now she was my kind relative, and I no longer noticed her shortcomings, the same way I wouldn't notice them in a sister. What's more, her connection to her lawfully wedded spouse seemed somehow completely insignificant, or erroneous, as if she were still just his old childhood friend, a girl with whom he had played hide and seek or stolen apples from the neighbor's tree. That allowed me to receive those scintillating looks from Amangeldy as something that rightfully belonged to me.

After our filling feast, the guests wanted to lie down for a rest. Their nighttime bus ride had worn them out, too. My aunt and uncle put them in the bedroom at the end of the hallway and also went to nap in their own room. Soon I could hear my uncle's loud snoring.

I flitted about in my sarafan, clearing the table, hauling the dirty dishes to the kitchen. That glass of wine wasn't making me sleepy. Instead, it had woken me up, and filled every part of my body with a bubbling energy. And my heart! Something was singing in my heart, a liquid melody, full of sparks. It was the only melody I needed. I could sense the sleeping colonel, very close by, just a dozen or so paces away, and I felt ready to protect his sleep—so that later, when he awoke, I could bring him a glass of cold beer. And bathe myself in his gentle brown eyes and listen to his laughing voice. And Yulduz . . . Yulduz was simply a well-meaning star who shone on us all with a motherly love. Even their two children, who were off at a

Soviet summer camp just then, were young stars, barely twinkling in the vast starscape of life.

Soon all the dishes were washed and drying on the table. I sat down on a kitchen stool and looked outside. Ordinary summer life was underway out there in the city, where at this time of year, there are two kinds of people: those who have already finished their vacations on the beach at Issyk-Kul or Kapchagay or the Black Sea, and those who were eagerly looking forward to them. The nightmarish word *propiska*, which was usually present everywhere, like a watermark, had vanished.

My aunt walked in, holding her stomach. She settled heavily on the stool across from me, poured herself some water from the pitcher, and started to sip.

"You should take off your sarafan. You'll get it dirty."

I shook my head, frightened. "No!"

I thought that if I took it off, I'd lose this magical power over life.

My aunt smiled. "You're like a little girl. One time we bought some little sandals for Bakhytka. She wouldn't even take them off to go to bed."

I laughed, feeling solidarity with little Bakhytka. Neither of us spoke for a while.

"We're out of tomatoes and cucumbers," I said.

"Would you go shopping?" my aunt asked. "It's the evening bazaar. You can get everything cheaper. Grab a kilo of grapes, too. And don't forget lettuce."

All the merchants at the bazaar wanted to serve me and offered me laughably low prices. I made my way home feeling like an intoxicating Little Red Riding Hood, bringing treats to her granny. The resemblance was reinforced by the basket I carried, where a gigantic cluster of Muscat grapes lay like a still life over green leaves, cucumbers, and tomatoes from the local dachas. And just like that naive girl from the woods, I had not the slightest idea of what lay ahead for me. On top of that, I could barely recognize the city! Previously arrogant and aloof, now it was friendly again and smiled at me gently from every shop window, showered me with droplets from its fountains, winked craftily from its traffic lights. I felt like singing. So I did—the love song, "Black Eyes," only I made them brown.

Amangeldy opened the door for me. I was surprised and stopped in the doorway, stunned by the sight of him.

"Who's this? A forest sprite?" he asked, quietly.

I said nothing, but my heart spoke eloquently for me, pounding away in my chest under the sarafan.

"Oh, no—you're a fairy from the melon fields," he said, as softly as before. He tore off a grape and popped it in his mouth.

"That hasn't been washed!" I said, looking up at him.

"So? Are you afraid I'll be poisoned?"

I nodded, then shook my head. I was confused. Something was whispering a warning in my ear, that this was a practiced routine by a habitual flirt. But I . . . I was willing to listen to him forever.

"Who's there, Aman?" My aunt walked out of the kitchen, wiping her hands on her apron.

"Your assistant!" Aman announced, loudly now, and he took the basket from me and went into the kitchen.

"Did you get everything?" my aunt asked in her everyday voice, which clashed horribly with what had been happening just a minute before.

I nodded without speaking and slipped away into the girls' bedroom. From the mirror, an unbelievably gorgeous young woman looked out at me, with crimson cheeks and radiant eyes. I was completely enraptured by her when that warning voice hissed in my ear again. "Shameless! All your feelings are right there on your face for everyone to see. Get control of yourself!" But nothing could make me obey that voice.

I held the bunch of grapes under the faucet and turned the fat, juicy fruit in my fingers, seeds glowing through the soft pulp, until all the dirt had been rinsed from the surface. Then I carefully rinsed them again, this time under icy cold water. Usually I'm not as careful with jobs like washing fruit. Now I felt conscientious as a saint. And my whole ritual was for the sake of one person. Yes, I was afraid he'd be poisoned, get sick, even die, God forbid. At that moment, that man was the center of the world, my everything. A concentration of all the most wonderful things I had ever known about life, my savior, the one who had pried me from the talons of failure and despair.

At dinner, it was just the colonel and me. All that was missing were the candles. Unexpectedly he turned down vodka and decided to drink wine with me . . .

At dinner, everyone was there except me and the colonel. My uncle and Yulduz drank vodka, and my aunt drank mineral water . . .

I felt like singing. I felt like dancing. With him. But they sent me into the kitchen to wash the dishes. The rest of them sat out there, playing cards.

But, as I dealt with the endless dishes, I sang anyway and danced. With him. Then I turned off the light, sat by the window, and looked outside. The streetlights and headlights glowed brightly, so it was light in the room.

The door opened, and Aman walked in. He sat down across from me at the table.

"Would the lady mind if I smoked?" he asked, in that same confidential tone that had twisted my heart around before.

I nodded permission, stood on my tiptoes, and opened the ventilation window.

"Where is everyone?" I asked, listening to the silence.

"They're asleep," he said, and he held his arms wide.

"Asleep?" I didn't believe it, and I turned to look at the door.

"Yes. I put them to sleep," he said with a shrug.

"What?!"

"It was easy. I slipped some sleeping potion into the tea."

I laughed. It was so funny.

"So now what will we do?" I asked, not the least astonished by my own boldness.

"This," he said. He put out his cigarette and, bending over the small table, reached for my face and kissed me on the lips . . .

"Raihan!" It was my aunt's voice. "Go and lie down in bed."

I blinked and looked around, dully. My neck was aching from its uncomfortable position on the table.

Yulduz walked in, laughing.

"What did you do, girl, fall asleep? You're tired, I can see it. Go and sleep." She yawned. "We're going to bed too."

"Ugh, I'm so swollen everywhere!" said my aunt with a sigh, examining her feet. "The sooner this baby comes . . ."

Yulduz said something in response, but I was no longer listening. I wanted to get back to that interrupted dream. To bring that dream to life, at that moment, I would have given the most valuable thing I had: the gold earrings my parents had given me for my twentieth birthday. But I didn't know who to go to with the sacrifice. And all night I lay there with my eyes open, listening to the muffled noises in the sleeping apartment. My cheek still remembered the warmth of his hand. My lips still felt the gentle touch of his lips. Sometimes, in a dream, everything is brighter and more distinct that in real life. And worse torture. I only fell asleep as morning approached.

"Get up, it's eleven o'clock," said my aunt when she peeked into my room.

The apartment felt dead. Something in it had changed, and that change spawned a vague worry inside me.

"It's like that sarafan has attached itself to you!" my aunt laughed as she poured me some tea. "They called Chingis into work. They won't leave him in peace."

"And where are . . . your guests?" I asked, sitting at the kitchen table and trying to make my question sound casual. "Have they left?"

"No. Zhuldyzka dragged Aman to the park for a walk. They're leaving tomorrow."

Tomorrow! They were leaving tomorrow! The news made my heart ache, filling me with pain. She *was* dragging him—away from me!

"Maira called," my aunt reported, taking a bite of candy. Maira was my other uncle's wife. "They're flying to Sochi tomorrow for their vacation. They asked you to come and stay with the kids and their grandmother. Oh, and I almost forgot! She said your uncle found you a propiska!"

A propiska . . . Three days ago, I would have been jumping for joy, kissing my aunt, and galloping around the room like a wolf. But instead, the first piece of news overshadowed the whole rest of the world. It knocked at my temples, beat at my diaphragm, and made my whole body feel weak.

"What's wrong, aren't you happy?" My aunt was surprised.

"No, I'm happy, of course I am."

She looked at me closely, her eyes dark as the deepest water. She said nothing.

I moved to wash the dishes, but she stopped me.

"Go and pack. I'll do that. They're having guests for lunch, and they need help."

Those words sounded like a prison sentence. I took off my sarafan and folded it into my bag. The dress had lost its magical power. Then I stole a minute, slipped into the other room, and found Aman's shirt, hanging over the back of a chair. I knew I would never see him again, just as if he had died or moved far away. That shirt was only a thing that reminded me of him. But it held the scent of his body, and I snuggled up to it greedily, for a moment, in farewell.

As it turned out, I never did see him again. My aunt stubbornly kept mum about him, and I was never brave enough to ask. She and I saw each other very rarely. We were only distantly related, after all.

But my heart . . . Oh, my implacable heart! It still cherishes the memory of those days, and it gets excited every time they play "Bésame Mucho," as if it were all just yesterday.

THE BESKEMPIR

BY ZIRA NAURZBAYEVA

Translated from Russian by
Shelley Fairweather-Vega

INTRODUCTION

The roar, filled with anger and a hot wrath, changed into a long, sad howl. My horror was quickly replaced by doubt, because that scream had sounded on a sunny summer day in Academgorodok, some-where among the brand new, pink-seashell-trimmed buildings of the academic institutes and the housing units for the people who worked there.

I came here fairly often after class and during breaks to help my mother fill in her daily data on the ten square meters of peach graph paper that lined one wall, help her plot out every new data point and connect the dots in pencil. This dreary job, which demanded not just precision, but also constant strain on the eyes, was too much now for my mother, who was only working a quarter of her former hours. Her sense of responsibility and her pride prevented her from rejecting this hellish burden altogether, and her bosses, all yester-day's graduates whom she had nurtured herself, tried not to notice.

That was why I was at the institute and heard that shriek through the open window.

I looked at Mama. But, contrary to her usual habit, she offered no explanation right away. She looked down, guiltily, somehow, and did not speak. The woman who shared her office did not speak, either. The scream came again. Now I knew for sure it was a person screaming. Mama winced so noticeably that I couldn't ask my question out loud. I went on working on the graph paper, sorting out possible explanations in my mind. A cry of sorrow? The weeping of some alcoholic, in the heat of delirium? A domestic quarrel, some scandal or fistfight? Someone who was just plain crazy?

That evening, when it was just the two of us on the way home, Mama finally found the strength to tell me. It turned out it had been a Kazakh woman screaming, in the apartment building across the way.

The woman's grown daughter worked at the Institute of Biology and had been in line to be assigned an apartment, and in order to get a bigger one, she had registered her mother as living with her, though the old woman actually lived back in the aul. A lot of people did that back then. Just to be safe—in case the committee showed up unexpectedly or someone reported her—she talked the old woman into staying with her there in Almaty for a while. Her elderly mother was in a hurry to get home. She was lonely in the city, she wasn't used to it. But her daughter talked her out of it, telling her she needed to stay a little while longer. What if one of the neighbors decided to file a statement? They'd take the apartment away again. After putting up with it for a while, the old woman made her preparations to go home for good. But by then, she had nowhere to go. Her daughter wanted a new lifestyle to go with her new apartment, and on the sly, she sold her parents' house in the old aul and used the profits to buy some furniture. What was the big deal, she thought? Why should the old woman live in poverty all alone in that distant village, stoking the oven and lugging buckets of water around? Let her live with her daughter in this apartment in the city and enjoy all the comforts and conveniences.

What else could she do? The old woman agreed. Academgorodok was located, back then, in the middle of an uninhabited green space. Below was the Botanical Garden, to the right were the vacant grounds of the Kazakh State University campus. Since the old woman was used to moving around all day, and being closer to the earth, she started to go out for walks. But problems arose. All her life she had lived in one place, in a tiny aul on the steppe, and now, in her old age, she could not possibly learn to get her bearings in a new, unfamiliar location, among these thick groves of trees and multistory buildings, which all looked identical to her. She got so lost, a few times, that the whole building went out searching for her. They almost called the police. Finally her walks were restricted to the courtyard of the building.

Then there was a new tragedy. In the far-off aul, where strangers were extremely rare, she had never once locked the door, and that meant that here in the city, too, she was always forgetting to lock up or leaving her key somewhere. Her daughter finally took her key away for good. When the daughter left for work in the morning, the mother walked out into the courtyard with her, sat down on the bench, chatted with people walking by, and kept at it until her daughter came home. The neighbors felt bad for the old woman, and invited her in for tea. But the daughter didn't like it that her mother was going in and out of the neighbors' places like some homeless beggar, so now when she left for work, she left her mother shut up alone in the apartment.

At first the old woman still wandered the courtyard in the evenings, but the new climate and the new way of life had its effect on her health, and she grew weaker and weaker. Climbing the stairs to the fifth floor was becoming too difficult. When winter came, she stopped leaving the building. Her solitary confinement in the stone box clouded her mind. Now, from time to time, she walks out onto the balcony of her apartment, and she stares at the far-off mountains and the gardens all around her and the people going about their business below. And she wails.

In the Almaty of the 1960s and 70s, the older generation in Kazakh families was represented, almost always, by a sole grandmother, an azhe or apa, widowed by the war. If the husband had survived the war years, then the old folks usually lived out their lives together in the aul. But their grown children tried as hard as they could to get the widowed old women to move to the city, mostly to help raise the grandchildren. There was also love, of course, and a desire to avoid being accused of leaving an old woman all alone.

It's only now that I understand how hard it was for our grandmothers to settle in this strange city of stone, where a completely different set of morals rules, where you needed to stand in a suffocating line of people for hours on end to receive a two-kilogram bundle of bones wrapped in cellophane, where your grandchildren might not know a single word of your native tongue.

City life itself was more than just unusual to them. It went against their traditional upbringing and their sense of decency. We knew a man who came from my mother's village. He was a colonel in the KGB, and when *his* mother came to visit, he used to have to escort her to the bushes, right there in the center of the city, early in the morning and late in the evening, because the idea of handling any physiological needs inside the house was shocking to her. "God forbid my son or my daughter-in-law or my grandchildren hear any gurgling!" she would say. It was a comical situation, in a way, and just one example, but essentially it was a collision of worldviews.

The psychologist Erik Erikson described how Native American girls educated in boarding schools often developed depression due to the differing concepts of cleanliness in their own families and at school. For the girls' mothers, the ritual cleanliness of their daughters was very important, while for the white teachers, the essential thing was sanitation and hygiene. As a result, the teenage girls felt dirty in both places. The native people also believed that excrement needed to be exposed to the cleansing effects of sunlight and wind, and they were horrified by the white people's habit of burying their filth and letting it rot in one single place. We city-dwellers can easily imagine what the white people thought about the Natives. But the first redesigns that Kazakhs made to their urban apartments, when that became possible during perestroika, concerned the lavatory. They tried to move the door to the lav, so that it would open up into the entranceway, rather than into the same little corridor as the kitchen. In more recently designed apartments, the doorway to the guest toilet is often in the line of sight of anyone sitting at the table in the big room off the main hallway. That still bothers people who retain the rudiments of their traditional upbringing.

The colonel's mother never could get used to the city. She moved in, plunged into depression, and began calling my Azhe, my mother's mother, and asking her to come visit. My Azhe tried to straighten her out. *Sure, this place can turn your stomach, but it's not as if I can arrange a proper welcome feast for you. Come now, your son's at work day and night, your daughter-in-law's in the hospital, think of your grandchildren, let's at least go to the store and buy some groceries.* But the crowds in the store and the need to make the rude saleswomen understand what she wanted in Russian were terribly frightening to my grandmother's friend. She left, while our Azhe put down roots here in Almaty. But only she herself knew what that cost her.

In the late 1980s, she and I watched a TV show together, about a Turkish village holiday with horse racing and everything. Azhe's reaction took me by surprise. She sighed and summed up everything she had seen by saying, "Look how lucky they are, living on the flats!" She herself, in her younger days, had occasionally given in to her son-in-law, a public instructor in tourism, and went off on hikes in the mountains with us. But the stately beauty of the Alatau turned out to be less than inspiring for a native of the flat steppe.

Deprived of their old way of life and everyone they had known since childhood, our Kazakh grandmothers tried to re-create their world in the city. Children and grandchildren were all well and good, but Kazakhs consider their peers their own people, while younger generations are like a lesser, stranger tribe who have come to settle in an abandoned camp. An old man who has outlived his friends is a person who has been accidentally left behind when his clan moved on, forced to live as a guest with these new settlers. This is the constant face of a traditional culture.

Picking up and moving to the city to live with their adult children cut these old widows off, both socially and psychologically, and they often ended up the hostages of their children, whom city life had turned cruel. Pride prevented them from going back home to the aul and admitting, publicly, that things weren't too good with their children.

When I was little, and even in my teen years, Azhe was the most important person in my life, so I judged people almost exclusively on the strength of their relationship with my grandmother. I saw how a coddled city teen who caused his parents endless problems could be perfectly happy to squat on his haunches to help his azheka put her shoes on and lead her out to the courtyard and ring her friend's doorbell and then bring her back up to the fourth floor, say, and how he could do that every single day. I saw my own Azhe returning shamefacedly to our place after trying to express her sympathies to the family when one of her friends had died. She was ashamed because that family was experiencing no grief and needed no sympathy. But it was the old grandmas themselves, each and every one of them, who were most interesting to me.

One of my lifelong friends told me, recently, that in a lot of ways, I was still a child. "But at the same time," she said, "you are much older than I am. Sometimes you seem ancient to me, older even than my mother." That is probably true. I remember that when I was a teenager, I preferred spending time with little kids or ninety-year-old women rather than with my own peers. But there are still things I could tell you about the world which had already begun to disappear. Almost none of those Kazakh azhes now remain.

I have called this portrait cycle *Beskempir*, which in Kazakh means "five old women," because it is an idea quite widespread in Kazakh folklore and also in geographical names. Quite a while ago now, some scholar or other determined that the Kazakh word *kempir*, "old woman," was etymologically derived from the two words *kam* and *pir*, where *kam* means shaman and *pir* refers to a spiritual teacher or a supernatural benefactor. Presumably, the word *kempir* originally meant a benevolent master of the elements and other natural phenomena in the guise of an aged woman. Later the meaning lost its loftier connotations and became what we have today.

Indo-Europeans have their male thunder gods, like Zeus or Thor, but the Turkic peoples have a kempir, what we might call a "thunder grandma" today. Kazakh scholars have noted this sort of matriarchal orientation in Turkic and proto-Turkic mythology. The Turks— hunters, herders, and warriors all—bowed down before their mothers. All this means that "Beskempir" could well be the title for some sort of ancient pantheon of goddesses.

One basic element of this mythology is the custom of taking newborn babies, born to families where the children frequently die, and passing them between the legs of three or five old women. Now this custom is explained as a way to confuse death. The original point, though, was to show that the child had been born of these "masters of the elements" and shared their strength. The first Kazakh Olympic champion, Zhaqsylyq Üshkempirov, got his last name from this tradition.

Here in Almaty, our Kazakh azhes did not feel like goddesses, or even first wives or matriarchs, but their fates, at the end of their lives, were inextricably woven into the enormous tapestry of city life. Sometimes it scares me that, in the fuss of everyday life, they might be finally forgotten, and I repeat their names, or actually their nicknames, since they rarely called each other by their true names, in an echo of an ancient taboo. Nyanya-apa. Astarkhan-sheshe. Sary kempir. Öskemen kempir. Oficerdyn kempiri. There are others who we lost earlier than our Azhe, and I remember them poorly; in their lifetimes, for me, they were just her friends. Those who outlived Azhe, the ones whom I invited to her wake, lent their warmth and their respect for our grief to help me through the darkest period of my life. When the last of them departed, the quick-witted, boastful Oficerdyn kempiri (by then I had learned her real name: Nurganym), my door to that world closed.

NYANYA-APA

Nyanya-apa was our nickname for the old woman who was my nanny from the age of three months, when my mother's statutory maternity leave ended, to three years, when it was my turn to start nursery school. There were very few Kazakh grandmothers in Almaty back then, and the staff at the Institute of Mathematics passed them around to each other by turns.

I don't know Nyanya-apa's real name. She had her own little house near the Mir movie theater. As far back as my memories go, I remember walking with her around her tiny front yard, gathering up broken twigs she could use to stoke the fire under her samovar. When I was little, I could tell by how the tea smelled whether it had been cherry or apple tree twigs that had fueled the fire to make the water boil. We drank our tea at a low, round little table, sitting on very strange little stools, which resembled enormous wooden spools for thread with a hole through the center. Of course, those stools were upholstered in brightly colored fabric, and I loved to turn them on their sides and roll them back and forth. They were probably my favorite toys.

The origin of those stools was a real mystery to me for many years. I never saw anything like them anywhere else. Then in grade school they took us on a field trip to the cotton factory in Almaty. There were enormous bobbins full of thread spinning on the machines there, and I thought that maybe they had once used those huge wooden spools there, instead, and that those had then ended up somehow in Nyanya-apa's house.

I also remember the cotton batting that we put between the panes of the windows in the winter, which we decorated with snowflakes we cut out of tea foil and other decorations for the New Year. How that batting and those decorations ended up between the window panes I had no idea. After all, her house had the same non-opening double-paned windows as houses in the aul did.

So we sat for hours drinking tea and eating the fried dough treats called baursak and other sweets, and Nyanya-apa told me stories, taking little interest in whether I was old enough to understand them. Later she read what the Sufi master Inayat-khan wrote about how the best way of educating children was to tell them legends and life histories they could grow on.

Nyanya-apa's brown, wrinkly arms were laden with silver brace-lets, and she wore two or three rings on each finger. I looked at them while she held her cup, and after tea time, I loved to spin those rings around on her fingers. She used to show me, "You see? This ring doesn't come off. It's grown into my flesh. When I die, the flesh will melt off my bones, and then the ring will come off. I'm going to leave this ring to you." Those words terrified me. At the time, or maybe later on, I imagined those bones going bare in the tomb, and I imag-ined people opening up the grave and slipping that ring off the skel-eton's hand for me.

One time my cousin, who was a university student, took her ring off and left it by our sink. It was too big even for my thumb, but I put it on, squeezed my fingers tight together so it wouldn't slip off, and went out into the courtyard to play. I completely forgot about that ring, and at one point I was terrified that I had lost it—but, fortunately, it was still there on my finger. But my finger . . . It was terribly swollen and blue, and I couldn't remove the ring. I had to tell the grownups what I had done. Now a new image frightened me: I was lying in a coffin, my bones were shining white, and the ring, finally, slipped off my finger. My cousin soaped up my finger and was able to twist off the ring. But today I don't even wear a wedding ring. I have some sort of phobia.

Nyanya-apa kept up our acquaintance even after I began nursery school. By that time my Azhe had moved in, and she had a good deal of respect for Nyanya-apa, who was her elder. Once she told me that Nyanya-apa was a local, an Almaty native. Azhe also said she had an arqa, meaning an ancestral spirit helper who gave her special talents, and for that reason, people were always going to her when they needed some extra assistance. I was not quite sure what those words meant back then. I only knew that Nyanya-apa's son, who worked as a driver, tended to drink a lot and get mean, and for that reason, she stopped inviting me to visit her.

When I turned eleven, we moved from Dzhandosov to the university neighborhood. Soon after, they knocked down Nyanya-apa's house, and they gave her and her son an apartment in a new neighborhood called Taugul. She came to see us less and less, eventually only once every few years. But those visits were like nothing else. She went to the bus stop near her building, climbed aboard the first bus that stopped, got off again at a stop that looked interesting to her, and asked people walking by where I was. When she arrived at our building, she was always outraged. "What's wrong with these stupid kids around here? They don't know anything! I ask them where Zira lives, and they shrug their shoulders. There I was just walking down

all the streets. Finally one of them dredged it up. 'Oh, Altay's big sis
ter is named Zira.' How would anyone not know you, huh? Why
don't they know you?"

After questions like those, I felt somehow at fault, as if I hadn't lived
up to my nanny's hopes, hadn't become a city-wide celebrity that
everyone and his dog knew well. Apparently, she just could not com-
prehend how much the city had grown since she was small. Or perhaps she had simply never left her own neighborhood. Now I
understand that she might have set out to visit more often than I knew,
but perhaps her search did not always bear fruit. I also think that
Nyanya-apa's grandchildren and the children she nannied may have
grown up on stories about me and may have universally hated me.

Her last few visits were strange. Once she showed up in an old
man's suit jacket and told us, incoherently, that her children had
locked up her house and hidden her clothes, and she had barely
escaped. Another time she appeared and was frighteningly thin and
dark. She asked to put a jar of cold water into our freezer, and then
she drank the icy concoction, saying that food and tea weren't going
down anymore. She wasn't wearing any rings that time, so I suppose
she had managed to take them off. I thought that might be the last
time we would meet. But she came again about two years later, looking much healthier and happier. She accepted some money from
Azhe, enough for two geese, so she could treat us. Why geese, exactly,
and why she had finally decided to invite us to her place, nobody
could understand.

I walked her home. It was the early 1990s then, and what seemed
at the time to be a very heavy flow of cars was driving down
Timiryazev Street. Nyanya-apa never even thought about going to
the crosswalk. Without a single glance around, she cut right across

the street. I held her by the arm, trying to navigate between the cars. She had her head wrapped in three warm scarves, which meant her ears were covered in nine thick layers of wool and she could hardly hear a thing. When we made it safely to the sidewalk, I asked her, "Nyanya-apa, aren't you afraid of cars?"

"They're the ones who are afraid of me!" she answered. Then she launched into a lecture. "Are you getting married yet? Well, good, they're all idiots. You're supposed to become a big boss . . ." Her bus came, and she rode away.

At home, I told Azhe about my old nanny's confusion, and Azhe, who was dreaming of great-grandchildren, said what she truly thought for the first time. "Senile old woman! What does she mean, they're all idiots? Just wait till she invites us over for those geese, and I'll tell her." But we never saw Nyanya-apa again, and my Azhe, too, died soon after that.

THE ALGERIANS

Our father did not smoke, and he did not permit guests in our home to smoke, either. But he made one exception. Very occasionally, several old women got together at our place, and they smoked Belomors and drank vodka and swore just like Russians. I used to escape to play outside, but in those instances, I always worried a little about Azhe, who was left in the midst of all that, in her white kerchief, pouring tea.

Much later, after perestroika began, we learned that those women were the widows of Kazakh men who had been repressed, former inmates of the prison camp everyone called Algeria, for the Russian abbreviation of its name: the Akmolinsky Camp for Wives of Traitors to the Motherland. As it turned out, during his student days, our father had made friends with someone named Arystan, who was the son of Sultanbek Khodjanov, a famous Kazakh political leader from the early twentieth century. Arystan had grown up in an orphanage for children of enemies of the people, changed his last name, and went to university to study math. Arystan Khodjanov died young, and my father, as a sort of legacy, inherited the status of adoptive son of his mother Gulandam and adoptive brother to his sister Ziba. For our father, who had also grown up in orphanages, these relationships were extremely important, and he went to spend the night at his adoptive mother's house whenever she felt unwell; Ziba lived in Moscow and was a psychiatrist, well known in the Soviet Union. But we only found out about that after the fact.

One member of this clique was the widow of Mağjan Jumabayev, called Zlikha-sheshe. She came to visit us later on, after we learned of the role she had played in preserving her husband's poetic legacy. Jumabayev had been rehabilitated, and his collection had finally been published. Only then did Mama tell us how hard this woman had worked, how she had survived on a miserly pension and traveled from archive to archive, reassembling her husband's verses bit by bit. I don't know for sure whether she did time in Algeria herself, but she certainly seemed at home among the former inmates.

In the late 1980s, Zlikha Jumabayeva gave up her one-room apartment near the exhibition grounds to the state, and she moved to Petropavlovsk to live with Mağjan's relatives. She spent the night before she left with us. I'll always remember how she carried her own gravestone with her, probably out of her habit of relying only on herself. We had a small carpet hanging on the wall over the children's bed, and she asked if she could have it to use as a prayer rug. They didn't sell them in Kazakhstan, yet, in those days.

No one from our family had suffered during the repression. My grandfathers and great-grandfathers died in rebellions and wars, or they died from hunger, but only my father's older brother, Qaldyqoja-bapa, ever went to prison. His was a typically Soviet fate. He buried his parents when they died of starvation, he grew up an orphan, he took care of the younger children. He got called up to join the Red Army and was just about to be discharged when the war against Finland began. He fought, then stayed on to serve longer, and then the German war began. He fought some more, was captured, worked as a stable hand on a rich German man's estate, then was liberated—and was sentenced to ten years in the camps for having been a prisoner of war. But none of us ever served time for our politics.

Still, though, those "Algerians" gathered at our apartment. We were neighbors with the Seifullin family, and many of my oldest friends had parents who had grown up in orphanages full of the children of enemies of the people. A large portion of the Kazakh people were directly affected by those repressions. When we speak about the consequences of hunger and Stalin's terror, we always must remember that those cataclysms sent half of the Kazakh population to orphanages. My father grew up in an orphanage, and so did my uncle. I am grateful they did not let them die and contented themselves with serious attempts to remold them in the proletarian spirit.

MAFRUZA-SHESHE

"Then, that night, a light turned on inside the sofa, and the ogress emerged from it, the monster who drags people into the sofa while they sleep!"

Olga finished her story, and my little sister and I, trying to huddle as close together as we could, walked home. Finally we made it through the dimly lit courtyard and apartment building entrance-way. It was nice and light at home, full of people, and almost not scary at all. I had just about calmed down when I learned that tonight I would be sleeping . . . on the sofa! Alone!

Our family of six had a setup that was perfectly good in those days, a two-room, Khrushchev-style apartment in a building erected by the Academy for its young employees. It was rare that we ever had an evening with no guests spending the night.

Very often, Mama made up five or six extra beds on the floor for visiting relatives and then drove off with Papa to meet them at the airport. When they came back late at night, they found all those spots already occupied, so more beds were laid out. Then in the morning, it would be revealed that our cousin the university student had stayed out too late with his friends, and since they wouldn't let them back into the dormitory after 11 p.m., he had brought his whole gang to spend the night at our house. All that was perfectly normal for those years, when not many Kazakhs had their own place in Almaty, and family ties were strong. Depending on the situation, we kids might find ourselves in sleeping bags or under the table or just out in the kitchen. In the summer, when prospective students were in town to take their entrance exams, we usually slept on the balcony, where my father rigged up a bedspread into a cozy tent. The men carried folding cots out into the front yard or took over the benches in the gazebo outside. It wasn't easy housing half a dozen aspiring college students and their whole team of fans.

That particular evening, we were not overflowing with guests. Only an old friend of Azhe's, Mafruza-sheshe, was spending the night. The two of them hadn't talked themselves out during the day, so she had decided not to go home, so they could go on chatting all night long. After some complex reconnoitering, it was decided, for one reason or another, that I would sleep on the sofa in the living room, and the two old girlfriends would sleep on the floor next to the sofa.

I lay down and listened to their endless reminiscing. It could have been something out of the Book of Numbers: Karabala begat Bekbolat, and Bekbolat begat Samat, and Samat begat Myrzahmet . . . Occasionally a car drove past the building, and its headlights wandered in an arc across the ceiling. I was too scared to fall asleep. Finally I convinced myself that when the sofa-book opened, the Monster from the Sofa would see before her the white, plump, nice-smelling Mafruza-sheshe, and so she wouldn't pay any attention to a bony little girl, and plus, I reasoned, when the ogress emerged, the cushions would swing open and hide me from her line of sight, as if I were standing behind an open door. I told myself those things over and over again, snuggled myself deeper under my brand new körpe, and fell asleep to the sound of the old women whispering.

Somebody was pulling my quilt off me, slowly but insistently. In the nighttime quiet, all I could hear was heavy, wheezing breath. I froze in fear. As if that terror were literally holding me down, I couldn't make a peep, much less wriggle. The körpe was sliding away, slowly, inch by inch . . . Suddenly something enormous and dark rose up from below, moved close to me, and whispered in my ear: "Let's switch quilts! Mine's too heavy, it's pressing on my heart, I can't sleep."

It was Mafruza-sheshe!

In the morning, the old women drank as much tea as they could hold, and after they chit-chatted through their goodbyes, our visitor finally got in a taxi to ride home. Only then did I tell Azhe about the events of the night before, skipping over the part about my fear and my calculations. Azhe laughed for a long time.

"Ah, what a silly old lady! I showed her those quilts yesterday, the ones I made for my grandchildren, and she begged me to give her one of those for the night, but I said no, those are for my grandchildren. So then she waited till I was asleep and did what she wanted to anyway! She always was a spoiled one. Her father spoiled her, then her husband did. After her husband died in the war, she went to live with her twin brother, who was a big boss somewhere, and he adored her and catered to her every whim. Now, that Jaken is spoiling her. Too much time on her hands, that one!"

So the whole reason behind my nightmare was my brand new körpe. The year before, Azhe had ordered a bale of camel fluff (not wool, mind you!) from the aul. She washed it, dried it, beat it, and combed it thoroughly. Mama helped her buy silky cut-outs in scarlet and navy blue for the top, yellow satin printed in a fine pattern for the back side of the quilt, and some gauze for the lining. Only then did she get down to work on the quilting. She spread out the gauze on top of an old sheet she used to cover the floor. On top of the gauze went an even layer of fluff, then another layer of gauze on top. She attached those three layers together with a tiny stitch. When she quilted the fabric covering on to that three-part inner filling, her stitching was no longer just meant to attach the layers. Now she made patterns, different designs on every körpe. Sometimes when her eyes grew too tired she called us in to help, to thread several needles at once with thick string almost as long as we were tall. Azhe concentrated over every tiny stitch, whispering something to herself. She kept at it all day long, taking breaks only to cook, sitting there on the floor, her back absolutely straight, her legs stuck out in front of her. It took her about a month to finish each quilt. She made two in dark blue for the two grandsons and two in dark pink for the granddaughters. When our little brother was born, much later, she made one for him, too, in green.

Azhe made the lining out of gauze, so the quilts would be lightweight. The gauze in my körpe crept to the edges over time, and the fluff started to bunch up in places after twenty-five years or so, long after Azhe was dead. I thought about having it repaired but changed my mind. I opened up the seams and fixed it as well as I could myself. I had neither the time nor the patience to sit and work at it like Azhe had, and on top of that, my little daughter decided it was great fun to roll around on the opened-up blanket. To replace the gauze in the lining, I used some cheap cotton we had lying around the house, and sure enough, the hastily requilted körpe turned out very heavy. But my little girl still loves to hide under it when it's cold in the house.

It was my duty to accompany Azhe around Almaty when she went visiting, and I always liked going with her to Mafruza-sheshe's place. It was a fancy apartment downtown, and usually nobody else was home. All sorts of rare and yummy things were on the table, and the bookshelf was full of titles that came by subscription only. You could lie down on the leather sofa, read medieval novels or science fiction or Sir Arthur Conan Doyle, and sheshe fried a new batch of her sumptuous, airy baursak every hour and brought it out with small mounds of chocolates. The old ladies themselves drank tea in the kitchen, where Mafruza-sheshe would tell a story about how her favorite grandson gave her a "back massage" before she went to bed, and Azhe would not know what that word "massage" meant, so

Mafruza-sheshe would explain, and on they would go talking, a conversation with no end.

Mafruza-sheshe's children were at work or on a trip, and her grandchildren were always in class or on vacation somewhere with their parents. That situation suited me just fine. I needed a break from the busy family ruckus at my house once in a while, and anyway, I didn't like the female head of her household, Auntie Clara, who had been my mother's classmate in school. When they came to visit us, Auntie Clara always tossed a critical glance at our creative disorder and very rudely, we thought, set about straightening us out. Maybe she was just expressing concern for my mother, her friend, who was not as lucky as she was in life, but we didn't like it. However, we all loved Jaken-ağa, who was just as fair and slight as Mafruza-sheshe. They even looked alike.

A child always has her own idea of the relationship between people, and often those perceptions remain with you your whole life. I knew that Azhe and Mafruza-sheshe were from the same village, and that Mama and Auntie Clara were from the same class, and that Jaken-ağa was from some far-away, completely different land. When she was young, stubborn Auntie Clara had been too snobby to go to the theatre to meet Jaken-ağa's relatives from the provinces when they came to the city, so the furious young Jaken convinced one of his fiancée's best friends to go with him for this demonstration. The relatives adored Jaken-ağa's "fiancée", and when the wedding happened later, there were all kinds of sitcom-like misunderstandings. The strange thing is that even knowing all of that, I always assumed Jaken-ağa was Mafruza-sheshe's son, and I never doubted it.

Jaken-ağa had a good career, and his household lacked nothing, but he left us early, almost the first to go from my parents' circle of friends. Only after his funeral, when I heard Azhe commenting that it was a good thing Mafruza had left us before Jaken because it would have been hard for her to live with just her daughter, did I finally realize Jaken-aǧa was sheshe's son-in-law, not her son by birth. I remembered the three of us eating an excellent cut of horse meat in that spacious kitchen, and Mafruza-sheshe quietly complaining to my Azhe about Auntie Clara. She was always cooking borsch and city food like that, but the sheshe didn't want to eat those twigs and weeds. She cooked horse meat on the sly, and she was happy when Jaken filled three refrigerator-freezer combinations with meat. But Clara scolded him, and one time she even dumped a whole pot of stewed meat down the garbage chute. Azhe added to the picture that was finally taking shape in my head: "One time Jaken couldn't restrain himself, and he yelled at Clara right in front of me. 'I should have divorced you a long time ago, but I would feel too bad for your mama! You don't even give her room to breathe!'"

Kazakhs love to tell the same jokes about mothers-in-law that Russians do, but when it comes down to it, in most Kazakh families the son-in-law treats his mother-in-law almost with reverence. Many of our friends wanted their wife's mother to live with them. One reason for that could have been traditional Kazakh ethics, but there was another explanation, too. A mother, as a rule, lags behind her daughter's generation when it comes to family relationships, so most often she demands that her daughter spend more time fussing around her husband, and the mother then spends her energy creating a comfortable atmosphere in the house

Mafruza-sheshe's grandson, by the way, was a serious young man. He tinkered with radios as a little boy and graduated with honors doing something with radio technology in Moscow, then became a successful businessman. But he loved his azhe and probably would have spoiled her, too, if she had lived a little longer. Some women are just like that, fragile-seeming, the kind men always want to spoil.

THE COMMUNIST AND THE MULLAH

I'd like to step away from my central topic, Kazakh grandmothers in a Russian city, because I've just remembered a funny episode—the time two crazy old men both took a shine to my Azhe and almost came to blows.

Azhe was invited to go and celebrate Eid with some friends from her old village who were living, at the time, in the Kazakh Institute of Agriculture building. When we arrived, the neighbors were already seated around the table—some old women and two old men, both in Russian-style, store-bought suits, who even had medals pinned to their chests. Maybe the village's almost rural location was enough to explain the extravagant way those two male representatives of the older generation presented themselves.

Whatever the case, our hostess sat Azhe at the head of the table, with the two old men on either side of her, and she put me a little further away, past the one sitting to Azhe's left. I was used to Azhe being given the seat of honor, and of course we had come from far away, and Azhe had been friends with our hostess's parents and the hostess herself for a long time. Still, though, I found the sight of Azhe sitting above those two old men a little odd.

Soon it became clear that the hostess had plenty of reason to separate the men, because they each stood proudly on the podium of a different worldview, and by all appearances these two were local inveterate polemicists. One was a devout communist, maybe even a Stalinist, and the other, with a skullcap on his shaved head, was a

Muslim, a genuine Kazakh mullah. He might have been a religious neophyte, though I wasn't sure; in Soviet times, men usually took up religion only after they retired. Kazakhs in general, like the Emperor Constantine, figured that it was best to think about God and saving your soul in your old age, when you had less opportunity left to sin, and they even frowned on an excess of religion in the young.

As a mullah tends to do, this one tried to preach and tell us stories to save our souls. It was Eid, after all, so it seemed the proper occasion. And the communist cut him off at every sentence with a comment about the "opiate of the people." Eventually it became obvious that this long-standing debate had taken on a new aspect: competition for a woman's attention. Azhe always did have the posture of a younger woman, and she knew how to dress herself with good taste. The color and texture of her big traditional kerchief complimented the crepe-de-chine dress she had made herself, she was wearing size 33 dress shoes I had brought back from a business trip to Moscow, her silk slip peeked out from beneath the hem of her skirt—in a word, when I accompanied Azhe on her visits, I always felt like I was a page or lady in waiting to a queen. She was a new face in this crowd, too, and her place in the seat of honor, above those two old men, endowed her with an even queenlier status.

The hostess's decision to use Azhe as a buffer between this pair of ardent bickerers turned out to be a miscalculation. Their discussion was heating up now in a way that had stopped being funny, and as they polemicized, they kept addressing their remarks to Azhe, as if calling on her to pass judgment over their eternal argument. Throughout the tirade, one or the other of them would be placing choice morsels on Azhe's plate with all the gallantry of old age. Each one peeled and cut up fruit in nice shapes for her, shelled nuts, and laid all these offerings in a crescent moon around Azhe's dish. My grandmother ate and listened, her face serious, pretending not to notice the competition, but I knew that she was taking a sly pleasure out of the spectacle of these two roosters pecking at each other. She did not really have time to enjoy the irony, but she understood better than anyone how funny the situation was, and once in a while she almost winked at me, before going back to keep an eye on each of her two suitors.

Suddenly the old man sitting next to me came back down to earth for a second and looked around at all the other women at the table, who had been forgotten in the heat of the debate and were completely bored. He pressed a paring knife into the palm of my hand and ordered me to get to work. "Why are you sitting there doing nothing? Take care of these guests!" Then he turned back to Azhe. Though they had been abandoned by their beaus, these old women still had no objection to eating fruit and nuts, so after that, I had no more time to monitor the head of the table. It's no easy task feeding a dozen old grannies. That's all I did until the feast was over. I peeled and sliced apples, separated oranges, cracked nuts and shelled them. I didn't have time to eat a single bite myself.

The logic of life gave the last word to the mullah, who was assigned to recite a prayer and a blessing at the end of the event. He did so, and tried his best to draw us away from our earthly problems.

ASTARKHAN-SHESHE

The way she recited the Koran, with her drawn out assssshaytani rrrrrajimi, will probably always seem like the standard way, for me, as someone with no particular knowledge of that art. She was the one who recited the prayers around the feast table at our house on holidays. Azhe singled her out especially from among all her friends, for her age, for the fact that she had memorized the entire Koran, for the difficult fate she had lived out and learned to make peace with— "täube" was what the Kazakhs called it. Plus, she was from Astrakhan, which we all pronounced the old way, As-TAR-khan, and she belonged to the same clan as we did.

Not only was she a widow like all the others, but she had outlived all her children, thirteen in number, and behind her back, some people called her a jalmauyz, a type of monster known as a bottomless pit. She lived with one of her grandsons, who had twice been divorced due to his wives' lack of interest in catering to their ancient grand-mother-in-law. The third time he married, he decided not to tempt fate, and he traveled back and forth between two homes, taking care of his ninety-year-old grandmother himself. Sometimes he broke down when he had something to drink, and in a drunken rage, he'd blame her for the fact that he was only just becoming a father at the age of fifty. At times like those, even his grandmother's piety infuri-ated him, and she refused to answer him, just praying silently for him instead, looking at him with those gray eyes misted with age, which seemed swollen behind the thick lenses of her glasses. In fact, of course, he was a wonderful grandson, and with him taking care of her, she lived to be almost a hundred, never wanting for a thing.

It was the 1990s, and Astarkhan-sheshe's age made me think about how human life measured up against history. Not only had she been born before the October Revolution; she had been a grown-up young woman, by the standards of the time, when it happened. Her lifetime covered the civil war, collectivization, World War II, the Thaw, and God only knew what else.

Astarkahn-sheshe was tall and thin and could no longer walk unassisted (although she kept her own house and rolled out the dough with her own veiny hands), and when her grandson wasn't at home, they usually sent me to fetch her to our house for a visit. It took us about fifteen minutes to walk over from the building next door, and she told me all kinds of stories while carefully feeling her way with her cane. When Azhe left us, I brought Astarkhan-sheshe to our home for the wake, and after that, on Fridays, I went to see her so she would recite from the Koran in her memory. She and I sat at a table near a window, and she told me that my Azhe used to come by on Fridays just like this, and when she was going home, she always turned around in the courtyard outside and waved goodbye. The sheshe lifted her bony hand and showed me exactly how Azhe had waved to her. For some reason, it was very important to her, and she told me about that every time I saw her.

Sometimes Astarkhan-sheshe demonstrated a truly childlike naivety. Once she told me of a dream she had. Her mother was standing there, dressed all in white and waving a hand, summoning her. "What do you think that dream might mean?" she asked me. Then she went on. "I don't even remember what my mother looked like. She died a long time ago, before the revolution, and her image has been washed from my memory. But I know it was her. I was angry at her, you know. When I was little, there was a terrible infection in our aul, and all the children in our family died from it, except me and my little brother. One evening Mama tucked me into bed crossways, at my brother's feet. By morning he was dead, but I survived. I could never forgive my mama for that." After that dream, the one where she saw her mother calling her, Astarkhan-sheshe lived several more years.

SARY-SHESHE

She was a pale-skinned, red-haired woman with greenish eyes, big boned and heavyset, completely uncharacteristic of her generation. She didn't know where she had come from. Somebody had found her near the Karaganda train station, in the hungry years, and delivered her to an orphanage. Sitting at a table for a feast, she always smiled somewhat sheepishly because she couldn't hear very well and couldn't take part in the general conversation. Her son had occupied some high position. But after he died, her daughter-in-law and grandchildren gave Sary-sheshe the cold shoulder, because her younger children, born when she married her husband's brother after her first husband died at the front, were trying to get their hands on the separate small apartment her first-born had given her.

I barely knew Sary-sheshe, but for some reason, several years after Azhe's death and hers, I dreamed of her several times, her and one other old woman whose name I forgot as soon as I woke up and could never remember. In those dreams, she was blessing my newborn daughter, trying to protect me from making mistakes in this life.

ÖSKEMEN-SHESHE

This dark-skinned grandmother, fairly tall and thin, was a native of Eastern Kazakhstan. She lived alone with her grown son, fussed around doing the housework, and did not talk with women her own age too often. One day Azhe came home from her usual walk with her friends seeming a little depressed, and she told me, thoughtfully, "Öskemen-sheshe told us how hard it was after her husband died on the front, how rudely all the activists in the aul treated her. I didn't believe it, but everyone else said it was true. Where we lived, in

Jambeyty, it wasn't like that. When they notified somebody of a death, an official from the administration brought the letter, not the postman, and they gave their condolences and helped you arrange the wake and supported the bereaved family as best they could. You know, now I think that maybe your grandfather set it up like that, in our aul, before he went away to the war. So much depends on what people decide to do."

At the one-year anniversary of Azhe's death, I wanted somebody to recite from the Koran at her grave in Kensay. Things like that had been important to my Azhe when she was alive. Ever since I was little, I had gone with Azhe on her trips to visit the grave of her son, our uncle. In the 1970s and into the early 1980s, you only needed to wait by the grave site for half an hour before an old Tatar man would show up, one of the people who spent all day puttering around the neglected tomb stones, reciting prayers for those whose loved ones had forgotten them. Azhe knew him, and they said hello, and then he recited a verse from the Koran. Later he stopped showing up in Kensay, and we started seeing a younger mullah sitting at the entrance to the cemetery, who would walk to the tomb with us if he was invited. This next generation of mullahs wanted to make money the easy way, sitting at the gates, so they put new regulations in place, which seemed to say it didn't matter where you recited from the Koran. Azhe had no respect for them, and often she walked right by without paying any attention to their sales pitch, and she recited the prayers over her son's grave herself, in a whisper.

I couldn't bring Astarkhan-sheshe to Kensay, especially because that winter was a cold one with lots of snow piled up everywhere. I got up the courage to ask Öskemen-sheshe, whom I hardly knew, and she seemed very happy to do me the favor. The taxi dropped us off at the gates to the cemetery, and we walked in on foot. Past the office, the snowy path had not been cleared at all, and we crept up the hill, wading through snow almost up to our waists. I was ashamed to be torturing this 80-year-old woman this way, but the sheshe responded very calmly to every inconvenience. The way back was no easier. By then it was dark, we couldn't catch a taxi, and finally, cold and wet, we got a ride on a very full bus and even had to transfer. I'll never forget the warm look Öskemen-sheshe gave me when we parted at her front door.

Soon her son moved the two of them into a less expensive apartment, and later the news came about the terrible way in which the sheshe had died. She perished in the bath tub, scalded by hot water. Her friends, without saying it out loud, suspected her son of murdering his mother.

OFICERDYN KEMPIRI

She was the only married woman in the crowd, a fact reflected in the nickname they gave her: the Officer's Old Woman. But she could easily have been a widow, like all her friends. During the war, her husband was gravely injured and declared dead. They were already filling up the communal grave with dirt when they noticed his hand twitch. They expected him to die again in the 1980s, when a motorcyclist knocked him over in the usually quiet Markov Street, which was practically untraveled in those days. The old man's children decided death was obviously his fate, and they felt bad for the young Ingushetian man on the motorcycle, and they were happy to sign a statement waiving their right to prosecute.

Oficerdyn kempiri was a noisy, talkative, happy, entrepreneurial woman who loved to brag. I remember that Azhe even wondered whether her friend's character might be due to the fact that she had spent most of her life alongside her husband. But probably she was just born that way. She was an Argyn, one of the big ancient Kazakh clans, and she loved to remind us of that. Her children inherited their parents' good luck and high energy, and her family was better off than many others.

In contrast to most elderly Kazakhs, Oficerdyn kempiri took to the market system enthusiastically in the 1990s, and she answered the president's call for everyone to go into commerce (only the lazy don't do business, I think is how he put it). Öskemen kempir, for example, used to stand at an improvised little bazaar at the corner of Al-Farabi and University. Her son made her do it; he was a doctor at a health spa and used to obtain certain goods at the facility where he worked. She was terribly ashamed of her business, so we had to make sure to avoid passing by that intersection. But Oficerdyn kempiri went to work at Nikolsky Market of her own free will, and any time somebody she knew popped up in her line of sight, she used to start shouting, calling them over at full volume to her little stand. Her children had mixed feelings about her business breakthrough, but her attraction to commerce was truly irresistible.

I remember that one winter she came to see us and asked us conspiratorially, "Do you need any rice? I was just doing a little business nearby, and they've cut the price twice now, but we have plenty of rice at home. And my kids will yell at me if they see a sack of it, because they don't let me carry heavy things. Take a cart, and you go buy it instead of me. You don't know how to do business." I really did buy rice at a good price that day, and she even tried to help me pull the cart home, telling me all the way about how successful her children and grandchildren were and what a rich life they were leading.

Her bragging was delivered with such good humor that there was nothing annoying about it. "You know, I sold my oldest son for qazy-qarta. I didn't like that fiancée of his, but her folks turned out to be from Kökshetau, and they fed us such nice horse meat. . . . I thought to myself, no matter who my son brings home, I won't like her, but at least this way I'll get plenty of good Kökshetau sausage!" And she burst out laughing.

I went past her courtyard once after my own wedding and stopped to say hello. First she asked me about my husband and congratulated me, reminding me that there was a reason the Kazakhs say that a girl who stays single too long will eventually find her place. Then she let me know that her feelings had been hurt—though out of politeness, she blamed my father, rather than me. "Your father is a scoundrel! He didn't invite me to your wedding, and your Azhe and I were so close, we ate from the same plate!"

I was distraught. We truly had forgotten to invite her in our hurry, and it was worse because she had outlived all her girlfriends, she was lonely, and she had started spending more and more time at her youngest son's house rather than her own place and inviting herself to her other children's homes as well. I began to mutter my apologies. "Sheshe, I'm so sorry, forgive me. Any time you like, we're always so happy to see you . . ."

She interrupted me haughtily, in a sly mix of languages. "I'm not the kind of old woman you can just tell to 'zakhodite-prokhodite' like those Russians! I need a proper show of hospitality. I need a special invitation." But she couldn't keep it up, and she giggled.

She was well past eighty when, despite her declaration, she came by our apartment one day with no special invitation at all to pay her respects when my little girl was born. She brought a present, a thick red mohair cap she had knitted herself, the kind we used to wear when we were little. "My eyes don't see so well anymore, and I had trouble with the loops, but I did it. This is your Azhe's first great-grandchild, after all. May she always be happy."

THE RIVAL

BY ZIRA NAURZBAYEVA

Translated from Russian by
Shelley Fairweather-Vega

B y the time her husband came home from work, she had already put their daughter to bed. He stepped inside and handed her a plastic shopping bag. The neck of a dombyra stuck out the top.

"Could you take this to my study?"

She switched on the light in the room, crowded with piles of books and magazines and wood scraps. Then she pulled the instrument out of its bag and propped it securely in the far corner, so that her husband, with his poor vision, wouldn't accidentally knock against it.

"Want some tea?"

"No, unless you want some. I ate at Sultan's. Let's get to bed early. I have a busy day tomorrow and that concert tomorrow night."

She was cleaning up the kitchen for the night when her husband, fresh from the shower, looked in. When he spoke, his tone of voice was so insistent that she immediately sensed his indecision.

"I'm fed up with her nonstop antics. Sometimes she speaks like a living being, other times she won't stop mumbling. On stage, she stammers. I asked Sultan if I could borrow *his* dombyra for the concert tomorrow." He paused. "Why aren't you saying anything?"

"I don't know. Sultan's dombyra is fine, of course. But it's just average, really. For a performance on stage . . ."

"No! His has a nice timbre, and she's even-tempered, reliable."

"Maybe your dombyra just needs more attention. You know how she is."

"But what can I do?" he objected. "This mindless translation work is killing me. I never feel like playing. If I could have it my way, I wouldn't even go to that concert, but they won't leave me alone."

"We have the apartment now. You don't need to take translation jobs anymore. You could write something of your own."

"That again!"

"All right, all right. Should I get your suit ready?"

"No, I'll just put a light-colored shirt on under the jacket. That will be fine. Should we go to sleep?"

"When I'm finished cleaning up."

———

As she gathered dirty dishes, she suddenly recalled cleaning up late at night after their wedding, several years ago. Of course, that had been a much bigger job. And standing in the corner of that big room, as big as this one but filled with tables and chairs borrowed from the neighbors, had been Azhken's dombyra. Back then it was not yet decorated, and its sounding board had been attached only loosely with handmade wooden pegs. Her husband had wanted to work on the dombyra's sound some more, whittle out the sounding board in places.

It had been years since an instrument maker Azhken knew had brought him the cedar plank from Khakassia. Azhken meant to carve an instrument for himself out of that board because he had given his old dombyra to a student who had moved out to the countryside. But during his years of unemployment, when he earned his livelihood making dombyras, an instrument every day at times, and gave them away to everyone he knew, he kept putting off the project, and he only returned to it when they decided to get married.

She always enjoyed visiting his studio, seeing how a rectangular piece of wood was transforming into a musical instrument. For some reason, the most amazing part, to her, was not the process of creation. It was how the surface, scraped repeatedly, became smoother, silken to the touch, how the curves took on the rough, raw beauty particular to a thing which has been reliably built.

Even before he attached the neck to the soundboard with those temporary pegs, Azhken had begun taking the dombyra for test runs. "Kazakh dombyra makers don't know what their instrument is going to sound like until it's finished, lacquered and strung, and all the frets are in place. But the Japanese masters taught me differently. I test every detail separately and create the timbre I need," he used to brag. This dombyra truly did sound extraordinary. Orders began coming in from more successful musicians and the wealthier conservatory students. Someone even wanted to buy the unfinished dombyra.

"It's a good price. We need money to get ourselves set up," he tried to argue.

"No. You've been making that dombyra for yourself. You're a musician. You should have the very best one."

"There's always a risk that a finished dombyra won't sound the same as it does at first. We do need the money." The debate continued right up to their wedding day.

A year after, he was still taking the dombyra apart, now the sound-board, now the neck, redoing this or that, sanding it all again, telling her fascinating stories about the lines of force that carried the vibrations of various frequencies, about how they X-rayed Stradivarius violins. Later he abruptly became disillusioned with theory and started talking about the overblown fame of the luthier from Cremona and about how the problem wasn't in the instrument itself, but in its strings, and that a genuine Kazakh timbre could only be obtained from gut strings, not the fishing line they used these days.

Without noticing how it happened, she got more involved in his endless experiments, helping to brew up "dragon's blood," the secret ingredient of the lacquer Stradivarius used to buy ready-made from the apothecary in Cremona, and she scoured sporting goods stores for the specially woven strings used in badminton racquets.

One morning, she felt someone's gaze upon her while she was getting dressed. It wasn't an angry gaze, just an interested one. An almost rapt gaze. Physically palpable. She looked. The door was closed, and as always, the curtains were drawn over the first-floor window which looked out over the road. The room was so small nobody could have been hiding in it. And yet someone was watching her. Suddenly she realized that the gaze was coming from the place where the dombyra hung on the wall. It was the dombyra looking at her. The sensation was so pressing that she gave no thought to the absurdity of the situation, just gathered her clothing up in a bundle and went to get changed in the bathroom.

By evening the experience was really getting to her, she didn't want to run down the hall to the bathroom all the time, and she turned the dombyra around so that it faced the wall. When she did, she felt free, for the first time all day.

"Who turned my dombyra around?" her husband demanded when he came home from work that evening.

"I did. All day long, I had the feeling it was looking at me."

"Aha! That means you've sensed it."

"Sensed what?"

"Last night the goddess Qoybas-ana came here. Legend says she's the protectress of all dombyra musicians. She blessed my dombyra and gave it a soul. You'll get used to each other soon enough. But don't turn the dombyra toward the wall anymore. That's what they do when a musician dies."

A new life started for the three of them. She remembered how, in the mythology of the Siberian Turks, a musical instrument was considered to be a branch of the Tree of Life bestowed upon a chosen person, a shaman or a musician. And in the other world, it would become the shaman's trusty steed, and not just that—it would be his sexual partner, too, his wife in heaven. So she started jokingly calling the dombyra her rival. The dombyra was her toqal, the junior wife in their family.

Azhken's students used to stop by their room in the dormitory once in a while, the ones to whom he taught the fine points of the old ways of performing, skills which had been almost banished from the conservatory. One time she witnessed a student practically glowing when he finally heard the nuance in the sound of Tattimbet's iconic kuy *Kökeykesti*, played with an extra quarter tone. Inspired, Azhken began playing the kuy from the beginning. And suddenly she finally heard the kuy, too. She, who even as a child had accepted she'd never be able to tell if a melody was an octave higher or lower! She heard all the beauty of the shades of the timbre. She heard the savage grief of the kuyishi who had lost his beloved, and his delight in the idea that love had ever existed. It seemed the whole world stood still with her, listening to the music, and she realized—no, felt physically— why it was the Kazakhs called that kuy the whisper of Tengre, the whispering that only a Chosen One could hear and retell to other people.

She sensed a column of light appearing over her head, vibrating in sympathy with the dombyra's sound. And suddenly she understood that while her ears were hearing the kuy as they always had, this wondrous sensation was coming from somewhere lower, from her belly, where, finally, a long-awaited infant was stirring.

That was the beginning of the strange days and months when the ordinary gray world, suffocating in Almaty's summer smog, suddenly stood before her beautiful and brilliant, and she realized that was how the world looked to their unborn child. But it became difficult for her to ride public transportation or to walk by outdoor cafés because now she understood what her husband meant when he talked about foul musical themes. It was true: foul, filthy words and voices, timbres and tunes, crowded tightly packed in what the Greeks had once called the celestial ether. The foulness made her belly hurt, feel as if it were being torn apart, as if the baby were being tortured.

Her only break from the pain came in the evenings, when her husband took the dombyra in his hands. But that started happening less frequently. Her growing belly scared him more than delighted him.

"I don't want to bring a child into this world. I don't want my child to grow up wandering homeless, like me. Look at our friends! Their children were born in dormitories, they grew up there, got married, had children of their own there. That's not what I want," he said. The harshness of his words was frightening, but when she saw how the young pregnant women in the dormitory had the habit of settling in to live in a corner of the grimy common lavatory so they'd always be able to reach the toilet, she understood her husband. But she also understood that neither one of them was young enough to put off having a child to better times.

Her husband had always brought work home with him, but now he began toiling over translation and editing jobs on the side, never lifting his head from his work. When she woke up at dawn, he was already working. When she tried to fall asleep, late at night, he was still at his desk, a lamp on next to him. His poor vision kept him hunched close to his papers. Sometimes he would lean back in his chair and rub a hand over the right side of his abdomen and complain about how his liver felt like a rock under his ribs, as if his ribs were chafing against it.

The birth of their daughter changed their life very little. Their enormous joy was soon plastered over with new worries and fears and an even greater sense of responsibility.

"Our daughter is a lucky charm. The orders are flooding in!" Azhken crowed, bringing pennies' worth of translation work home with him. There truly were more of those translations every day. She was impressed with her husband's amazing capacity for hard work. "When I'm working," he said, "I see the eyes of my daughter. She is going to have a home of her own."

She had to keep a hand on her growing daughter at all times. Anytime she was distracted even for a moment, the little girl would crawl to the table, pull herself up, hold on to the edge, and peer over, trying to see what her papa was up to. That made him laugh. "I think I see two stars shining at the edge of my table! But those are my daughter's eyes." Then he would pick his little one up in his arms and take the dombyra off the wall. He composed a kuy for their daughter, gentle and playful. But those moments were rare, and more often he was annoyed, not wanting to be distracted from his work.

Sometimes he didn't touch the instrument for weeks or months. The dombyra's voice grew thick and dull. Its sound was always changing, and it became unreliable. The dombyra's disposition had changed for the worse. She noticed an odd pattern. If her husband courted the dombyra, changed the frets, adjusted the pegs, or just wiped the dust off it, the dombyra instantly responded to that care and sounded like it used to. But not for long.

Once a musician they knew, a tall, handsome man with a well-kempt mustache, came for a visit. After tea and a chat, he bit his upper lip nervously and asked to borrow Azhken's dombyra for a week. "I took a leave from the bank just for this, Azhken. Please? I've dreamed for ages of playing your dombyra." Her husband smiled and handed him the dombyra.

When their guest left, she started to grouse about it, but her husband laughed off her concerns. "It's not a problem! Let her get some air, have some fun. Mirzatay will give her some youthful energy. And that guy knows what he's doing. He could become a wonderful dombyra player."

The dombyra returned home not one week later, but two. It really had changed. Now just one touch of the strings, and the instrument sang, practically of its own volition. Her husband laughed. "Shameless girl! All day and all night in the embrace of that young musician, weren't you!" But time passed, and the dombyra's voice grew dull again. One time she asked her husband why Mirzatay had stopped coming to see them. "He's been ill. There's something strange going on with his hands. When he touches a dombyra's strings, he feels as if he's getting hit with an electrical shock. He can type on a computer and drive a car, but he can't play. He's very worried. He's been seeing different doctors, but nothing has helped. I feel terrible for him."

So the years went on. They saved money in every possible way. The time came when they had saved enough to think about buying their own place to live. Luck smiled upon them, real estate prices collapsed—and instead of a one-room apartment at the far edge of town, they managed to buy something nicer, better than they had ever dreamed of, not far from the center of the city. Wandering all those rooms, they missed each other, at first, having been so used to always being in the same small space.

But theirs had not been a cloudless happiness. Once they had reached the goal they had worked toward all those years, her husband was demobilized, in a way, and one by one, the illnesses set in. What's more, he had grown used to putting aside everything he loved, everything he wanted most. He still talked about his plans but did not dare to put them in action. There was always something in his way. Just as before, he rarely picked up the dombyra, and the young musicians came to see them ever less frequently. The conservatory students they knew graduated and moved away. And the new generation of students never came to visit, sensing a certain distance.

———

The phone rang.

Her husband picked up and, as usual, turned on the speaker phone. They could both hear an excited voice on the line: his childhood classmate Kulzipa. Her words came in a flood.

"Azhken? I'm sorry to do this to you, but Aytqali is on his way to see you. I couldn't help it. He was here at my place for two hours and demanded your address. I told him you're in poor health, you've got a schedule to keep, you're not the same kind of person we are, and he can't just drop in on you. But he's as stubborn as a bull. You know how he is! His older son and his daughter and his nephew are with him. His younger son's getting married, and he's here to get things ready for the wedding. And, Azhken? He's drunk. He was already in that state when he came to my place. Then he drank up all the raw alcohol I had. He said, 'If you don't have any vodka for your old classmate, then bring me plain old alcohol! You're a doctor, you must have some!' Don't be mad, okay, Azhken? I don't think he'll stay long."

"Don't worry, Kuleke. I'm not mad. I haven't seen Aytqali for almost thirty years."

"Good. Anyway, I warned you. Bye now."

Her husband hung up.

"Did you hear that? Do we have anything in the house?"

"There's an unopened bottle in the fridge. I won't have time to cook any meat."

"That's okay. It's his own fault, not giving us any warning. Maybe fry up an omelet? Should we put the kitchen table in the family room? No, we don't have enough chairs . . . We'll put a spread out on the carpet."

In her bedroom, their daughter started to cry. Her husband went to check on the little one while she made preparations for their midnight guests. She put the teapot on the burner. In the family room, which seemed enormous in its emptiness, she spread a tablecloth over the new carpet and set out piles of quilts and pillows around it. She brought out shot glasses and tea cups and things to eat with their tea. The omelet she'd leave for later. Deep in her soul was a glowing hope that their late-night guest would get distracted and end up somewhere else.

But no. Heavy footsteps and loud voices sounded outside. *What will the neighbors think? We've barely moved in, and already we're causing a ruckus at night*, she thought as she walked to the door. Her husband came out of the bedroom. He opened the door before they rang the bell.

"Azhken! Look at you!"

Bursting through the doorway was a big-headed, buzz-cut, thick-set, long-armed man in a leather coat who managed, surprisingly, to just stay upright. Not only that, but when he embraced his host, who was almost a head taller and twenty kilos heavier, he lifted him right off the ground, and more than once. Her husband was not exactly a featherweight. She watched, astounded, as Azhken's feet swung in the air. Two young men and a teenage girl stood frozen in the doorway, eyes open wide.

A curious little toddler nose stuck out of the bedroom door.

"Is that your oldest? Your only?" Their guest snorted. "My oldest grandson is bigger than her!"

He snorted again and turned to look right at her.

"Is this your wife? A city girl?"

He snorted yet again and turned to the figures standing in the doorway.

"Come in, come in! This is Azhken. I told you about him."

The guests found seats around the dastarkhan. She went to steep the tea. Soon their guest's daughter came into the kitchen, embarrassed, and handed her some paper money, one big bill.

"A gift. For your daughter. I'm so sorry. We won't stay long. We'll try to get father out of here soon. Auntie Kulzipa explained things to us. But he was so excited about getting together. He almost never comes to Almaty. He's tried to find your husband before, but . . ."

"Oh, that's all right. It's hard to find a person when he doesn't have his own place to live."

"Can I help?"

"No, thank you, there's not much to do. Let's take the kettle and go back."

In the family room, she saw the bottle had already lost its top, so to speak, and the elixir for laughter had already been poured into the glasses.

"Hey, is your wife from our part of the country? The Lesser Horde, out west? Where'd you find her?"

The guest snorted, again. But there was nothing offensive about his snorting and sneering. Her husband had said his old classmate worked with horses. His snort had something equine about it, a sniff followed by a long "pr-r-r-r."

The omelet she cooked earned another snort and a new question.

"Hey, is she younger than you? Get outta here! We were seventeen when we got married. Still live with the same old lady, too."

Their guest suddenly pulled up a corner of the rug, cleared his throat noisily, and spat on the bare floor. He did it so naturally that all she could do was let her mouth drop open. The rug, bought using her husband's honorarium for a concert in Paris, was the most expensive thing in their bare apartment.

The visit went on. It seemed there would be no end to the memories. But ever since she was little, when she used to pour tea for her mother and grandmother, she had been used to hearing stories about people she had never met and probably never would. The eldest guest went on raising his glass and tucking into his eggs, and his children went on pretending to drink their tea. Her husband poured their guest more vodka, and she wondered how he'd feel tomorrow, deprived of his usual early bedtime. Suddenly their guest covered his glass with one hand.

"This is not what I came for. Where's your dombyra?"

She cast a questioning look at her husband.

"Could you bring the dombyra out? My dombyra."

The guest, snorting as usual, took the instrument in his hands and turned it over to examine it. He gave it a pat, for some reason, and passed it back to its owner.

"Play us something old."

Her husband tuned the dombyra and began playing, a very old kuy.

"No, no!" the guest interrupted. "Play Tattimbet."

It was so strange to watch this rough horse wrangler gradually relax, his gaze growing distant, as he listened to the kuy that the young Tattimbet had played back in the 19th century, along with sixty-one other tunes, back to back, all so a man who had lost his son could weep and give expression to his grief. Now their midnight visitor was listening to the song, listening and nodding, as if openly agreeing with something in himself, or with himself. She stole a look at their other guests. They clearly felt this had little to do with them. The daughter had nodded off listening to the music, curled up on a pillow like a kitten.

"Your grandfather died, shirkin, may the earth be a pillow for him, and you went away, and nobody is left to play for us. Remember when we were eleven? You played that kuy, and old lady Mugulsum grabbed us, and whacked you with her stick, and let you have it?"

"I remember. I had to tell my grandfather everything. He laughed so hard when he heard I had learned the *Zar Qosbasar* without telling him, and he asked me to play it. Then he laughed and laughed and said I was too young for that one. Right before he died, he taught it to me again."

"And do you remember when Mugulsum chewed out her son for disrespecting you, and she kissed your hand?"

"Was that when we stopped by their place for a drink of water, during that construction job? Sure."

"Play one of your grandfather's kuys."

Their guest listened to the tune, the tale of a wild goose who hid his crippled love from the relatives who meant her harm and then died of grief when she perished despite his care. When the kuy was over, the guest sat still, his head bowed.

"Father, we need to get to the station."

"Now, sing," said Aytqali.

"You're not going to make me dance, too, I hope," Azhken laughed and retuned the dombyra. As if purposefully suppressing his voice, restraining it, he sang the old song almost inaudibly. This one compared a girl to a silver mirror and to the tail of a battle-lance flag fluttering in the wind. She already knew that this song was a tanbaly, a landmark kuy, and that its performance demanded a surpassingly powerful voice and exemplary technique, and so it had almost been forgotten. Kazakh had a strange word for the reflective surface of a mirror, she thought: *deneker*, meaning an intermediary. A mirror shows a different world, doesn't it? One that opens up for warriors riding off to battle. And the girl, the young bride, is a creature from that other world.

"Father, it's time for us to go."

Their guest took the dombyra from his host's hands and touched the strings with one calloused finger.

"Did you make this dombyra yourself?"

"Yes."

"You got any other dombyras you made?"

"No."

"So. My youngest daughter, the eighth grader, is in a song contest. Traditional songs. I promised her I'd bring her a dombyra you made. Will you give this to me?"

She had just decided to finally take a swallow of her cool tea. Now the cup nearly dropped from her hands. The young guests might not have thought twice about the request, but Aytqali knew. Asking a kuyishi for his dombyra was like asking a Kazakh for his horse while he was still in the saddle. And what if that was his only horse? In the nineteenth century, there was once a bard named Musa who gave his horse away and then had to travel on foot from village to village. After that, everyone called him "Walking Musa."

"She's yours." His voice was calm.

"You won't miss her?"

"No."

The visitor pulled his host into a rough embrace, then just as abruptly stood up.

"All right. Time to go."

She and her husband, not used to sitting cross-legged on the floor, stood up much more slowly, coaxing their stiff legs. Everyone walked to the door. Aytqali's daughter hung back from the rest and took her aside. Looking abashed, she took out more money, a smaller bill than last time.

"A housewarming present. For your new apartment."

At first she didn't realize what she found so funny. Ah, yes. Surely the girl must have seen the lacquered, lavishly decorated dombyras they sold at the bazaar, the ones Azhken said they sold by the bundle. This one, in contrast, was roughly shaped, with a fat neck and no fancy patterns, painted unevenly with wool dye. So she must have thought it was worth less but was still trying to compensate them appropriately for what she certainly thought was a rude gesture by her father.

One more bear hug in farewell, one more time heaving him off the floor, more invitations to his son's wedding, and their guest, flocked by his offspring, finally tumbled out into the hallway. Her husband closed the door and smiled at the racket they made walking away. "It's as if someone set a herd of horses loose out there. I'll put the little one back to bed." Then he turned to her. "You put the kettle on—we'll sit a while, just the two of us."

"Don't be upset at Aytqali," her husband told her as he sipped at a fresh cup of tea. "He liked you. That's just how he behaves. I cleaned up the floor there, where he was sitting. He was too drunk to remember he was in somebody's house, not a stable, where it's okay to spit.

"You know, the last time I saw him, we were still students. My university years were a struggle. The dean hated me from the start, and after the first semester, I didn't have a place in the dormitory or a stipend. In the winter, the guys and I worked nights unloading freight cars at the train station, and in the summer, we went out to the village to work construction. I went back during summer vacation once, saw my old classmates, had some good times, but I didn't see Aytqali the whole summer. He was off with a herd somewhere far away. I worked construction jobs that whole break. When the break was over, I had to go back to Almaty. I was riding the bus to the station when, all of a sudden, the driver hit the brakes. Two men on horseback had rushed up to the bus and started riding in circles around it, slapping the windows with their whips. Just like in a Western. One of the men climbed in the front door and stood there, swaying on his feet. Then he headed straight for me. It was Aytqali. Like a good cowboy, he had instantly picked me out of the crowd on that bus. He walked up, barely able to stay on his feet, gave me a hug, pulled some kind of bundle out of his pocket, said 'Open this in Almaty,' and walked away again. That bundle had three hundred rubles in it. You remember what a huge amount of money that was in the late seventies. Especially for a student like me.

"I sent my mother back in the village a telegram. She took three hundred rubles from the money I had set aside and went to Aytqali's house. He had been married practically since tenth grade and already had four kids at that point. Mama told him, 'Oh, Aytqali, bless your heart, you must have gotten drunk and mistakenly given Azhken your whole salary. You've got your children to think of, and I've come to give that money back.' Aytqali took offense. 'What are you saying, apa? I know what I'm doing! I'm here among my own, but Azhken is a student.'

"Later, Mama died, my sister sold the house in the village, and I lost my reason to go back to visit. In the nineties, everyone else who still lived there moved away, some to the city, some closer to the highway. Aytqali's children bought their parents a little house outside Semipalatinsk. But you can't keep horses there, so he wants to go back."

"Will you go to the wedding?"

"No."

"He'll be offended."

"What can I do, though? The way the train rattles will set my liver off again, and it will probably be freezing. I'll send a telegram. He can decide whether or not to be offended. Did you get his daughter's address?"

"Yes."

"Let's go to bed. You can clean up in the morning."

"Oh, no, that's not how I do it. You go ahead and lie down."

———————

Now there were more dirty dishes to gather. And she realized, suddenly, that the dombyra which had been with them through all those joyful and difficult years, the one who had become a member of their family, had left them. She was on a train, riding off somewhere far away, with strangers. *How oddly things have turned out,* she thought. *Azhken brings someone else's dombyra home with him, planning to take it on stage with him, and then an unexpected guest appears in the middle of the night with an unbelievable request.*

Perhaps the dombyra had chosen her path herself. *How will it be for you there, among strangers?* How will a teenage girl handle a dombyra used to the strong hands of a real kuyishi? Or will she be ashamed of her unlacquered dombyra with no pretty decorations and toss it in a corner?

Forgive us. Be happy, my rival, my toqal.

AMANAT

BY ORAL ARUKENOVA

Translated from Kazakh by
Zaure Batayeva

B edridden for several months, Maira woke up at dawn one day and called for her youngest son Zhalgas. It was her eldest son, Baltabay, who came to her bedside instead. "Where's Zhalgas?" asked the old woman in a hoarse voice. "He'll come soon," Baltabay consoled his mother. "Will he? Is he all right?" Maira, instantly worried, grabbed her son's hand as if asking him to stay.

"Zhalgas will come soon, I've just spoken to him," Baltabay said, taking his phone out of his pocket. Baltabay called a number and spoke loudly while holding the phone to his mother's ear. "Hello? Zhalgas? I've given the phone to Mama." "I've already told you, I'll come by this evening!" an angry voice shouted back, and the connection was cut.

"I heard his voice, thanks to God," said Maira, tears flowing down her face. She gathered strength and addressed Baltabay. "Son, I have an amanat," she began. "What are you saying, Mama! You will recover!" Baltabay replied, caressing her hand. "Don't interrupt me," Maira said, and had to rest for a few moments before she could continue: "Build a new house for Zhalgas. Find him a nice Kazakh girl and save him from that albasty of a girlfriend he has." Maira died that evening.

After the men had buried the deceased, they returned to the family's house, where the women had stayed behind, consoling each other. Zhalgas arrived late, with a companion. Baltabay stopped him at the gate and took him aside. "Why did you bring her? This is shameful, take her away." "None of your business," Zhalgas replied brusquely. Zhalgas took the woman inside and found a place for both of them at the top of the table. Everyone could see that the woman, white-skinned and heavyset, was much older than Zhalgas.

Maira's friend Tazhilgul, seated at the other end of the table, started to cry. "Dear Zhalgas, may Maira's soul rest in peace, she had no other worries but you. It was her dream to see you married and have children. She would always say she had no other wishes." "Auntie Tazhilgul, I am married. Here's my wife, Raya," Zhalgas replied. "Is she? I was wondering who was sitting next to you, looking so much like Maira!" Baltabay intervened. "No, he's teasing you! Next year, after the one-year anniversary of our mother's passing, we'll organize a big wedding for him, and you'll meet his wife." "Aaah, that is a good way to do things! Bless you, son!" said the confused Tazhilgul.

After the guests had left, Maira's children and grandchildren gathered at the table. Only Zhalgas was missing. He had already left, upset with Baltabay. "According to our mother's amanat," Baltabay began, "this house belongs to Zhalgas. I'll bring him here tomorrow." "Oibai, what are we going to do with that albasty?" asked one of his younger sisters.

After a brief pause, Baltabay answered, "For the time being, your task is to look for an appropriate bride." "Correct! Sounds like a good plan!" the other relatives agreed. "I don't know about that," his youngest sister Alma argued. "He's been with Raya for ten years. He's refused all the girls we've shown him. Why don't we accept his Raya and leave him alone? It's his choice, let him be happy! Let him bring Raya here and live with her. Why interfere now?" All remained silent. "No way!" Baltabay said firmly. "We've got to fulfill our mother's amanat!"

Soon Zhalgas returned to his parents' house to live there by himself. His sisters took the opportunity to introduce him to new girls. Zhalgas did not seem interested. Hopes were raised when his sister Alma stopped by, accompanied by her friend and her friend's younger sister Qaraqoz, a psychologist who had just graduated from university. Whether it was because of her profession or because they were truly attracted to each other, Zhalgas and Qaraqoz got along quite well. Alma was so glad to see this improvement that she called Baltabay to deliver the good news. "Strike the iron while it is hot," Baltabay thought. The next day he went to talk to his brother. He mentioned Qaraqoz, and Zhalgas did not deny that he liked her. "After the one-year anniversary, we will go to her parents to ask for her hand," Baltabay said. Zhalgas sniffed. "We'll see," he said and looked away. To Baltabay, this sounded like a guarantee. Within a week, he had announced that he would build a new two-story house for Zhalgas, demolished his parents' house, mercilessly crushing its strong foundation with a bulldozer, and moved Zhalgas into the summer kitchen in the yard. After the remnants of the old house had been cleared, two trucks arrived and unloaded construction materials. "It will be ready by autumn," Baltabay promised.

On a nice day in June, Baltabay, about to start construction on the new house, on his way to see Zhalgas, called his brother several times on the phone but could not reach him. When he arrived at the site of his parents' house at dusk, he was happy to see that the light was on in the summer kitchen. He left his car at the gate and walked into the yard. Passing by the stacked bricks, he smiled at his own thought: "Mama's amanat will be fulfilled by autumn." But when he opened the door of the summer kitchen and crossed the threshold, first he saw Raya, peeling potatoes, and then, next to her, Zhalgas, happily playing his dombyra. Baltabay shot his brother a dark look and turned back without saying a word. The next day the trucks reappeared and took the construction materials away.

PRECEDENT

BY ORAL ARUKENOVA

Translated from Kazakh by
Zaure Batayeva

Kulaisha knocked at the door with the plaque that read "Dina Kaden, Lawyer." She was happy to see the Kazakh name. Some Kazakhs who had come to work in Atyrau did not even speak Kazakh. The locals called them mankurt. Wretched people. "Hello! Come in!" Kulaisha was relieved to hear no Russian accent.

"My name is Dina, and I'm a company lawyer. And you're Kulaisha, correct?"

"Yes. I'm a cook."

"And you have brought charges against Luigi Falconi, your boss and a chef, correct?"

"Yes." Kulaisha said, immediately becoming emotional. "He cursed at me for half a year. He didn't have any right to do so. He came to our land, and now he's making money and insulting us. Moreover, I'm a woman."

"Yes, indeed," the lawyer replied. "Please, calm down. Would you like water, maybe a cup of tea?"

"No, thank you. I had lunch recently."

"You see, Kulaisha, you, Luigi, and I—we're all employees of the same company. And usually these conflicts are resolved within the company, internally."

Kulaisha interrupted her. "I've been warned you would say that. Don't even try. I won't withdraw my complaint."

"Can you tell me which words he used to insult you?"

"*Porca Eva*, *puttana*, *cazzo*, and some other words."

"And do you understand the meaning of these words?"

"In the beginning I didn't. Now we have a new assistant to the chef, Katira, and her daughter knows Italian, she's an interpreter, she explained everything to me. This word *cazzo*, what it means! Maa, I'm a married woman, a mother of two kids. What right does he have to say such things to me! And then he makes his fingers like this!" Kulaisha continued, connecting her thumb and index fingers. "Ugh! If you knew what that means! When I learned, I almost died of shame. Maa, and then he adds something indecent to it!"

"Kulaisha, do you know these words are not considered curses in his country? Even the prime minister uses them in public sometimes."

"Maa, at home they can do whatever they like, but why don't they respect our traditions? Why spit in the well you drink from?"

"Please, calm down. I understand you. Now, can you explain what you want from Luigi?"

"What do I want? You ask me what I want? I want him to appear in court and be judged by the law!"

"Yes, he will, but the problem is that he's a citizen of another country, and the court will have to resolve the conflict of laws. Has this been explained to you? He can bring a lawyer from Italy."

"He works here, so the hearing must take place here."

"Yes, but he has the right to bring in his own lawyer and demand that legal proceedings take place somewhere else."

"So what! I'll make the same demand!"

"And insulting is considered a crime only if you have proof."

"I know. It is in the Criminal Code and in the Constitution."

"That's correct. People's rights are protected by the Constitution."

"You see? I'm defending my rights! What will he get from the law?"

"Article 130 of the Criminal Code. I'll read it aloud. 'An insult, which is an offense against the honor and dignity of another person, expressed in an indecent way, is punished by a fine of up to 100 times the monthly calculation index, by 6 months of forced labor or by 120 hours of community service.'"

"Good! He'll be convicted under that article."

"Do you understand he won't be imprisoned? He may be fined or be forced to do community work."

"I'm not asking to put him in prison, I'm asking for justice."

"If he apologizes and pays you compensation, let's say a million tenge, would you withdraw your complaint? We can sign an agreement right away. I'm telling you as an experienced lawyer that you will not get a million tenge from him through the court. Moreover, you'll have to prove that he's guilty. They'll call witnesses. What if the witnesses refuse to testify?"

"No, I want him to go to court! I've been warned you'd be on his side."

"You're wrong. I defend the interests of our company, yours and Luigi's. Is he still insulting you?"

"No, he's stopped cursing since I filed the complaint. He must be scared. But I won't drop it, otherwise you people will dismiss me from the company. Something like that's already happened. I've been warned about that, too."

"Well, Kulaisha, think it over and let me know, all right? Talk to your husband."

"No, I won't drop my complaint."

"Okay, then, but consider that this will be a very long process."

Kulaisha left the lawyer's office determined to take it to the end. "We sell our oil, we sell our honor. Soon we'll start selling our land!" were the thoughts boiling in her head.

The Italian chef did not bring in a lawyer from Italy. About a year later the court ruled in Kulaisha's favor. The Italian chef had to pay her 226,000 tenge, not a million. It was rumored that all foreigners in Atyrau had stopped cursing. Allahu akbar, there is some justice in the world, after all.

PROCEDURES WITHIN

BY ORAL ARUKENOVA

*Translated from Russian by
Sam Breazeale*

I.

Flights were getting cancelled left and right. Clara spent the day sitting in the departure lounge, watching as hundreds of passengers passed through, many of them unmistakably oil workers. Indeed, right across from her sat a young woman who was clearly in the oil business, eyes glowing and nose upturned. An older woman sitting nearby asked the younger one when the flight to Shymkent would board.

"I don't know, I'm headed to Almaty," the younger woman said pointedly.

"Do you work here?" asked the older woman—and it was off to the races. The young woman began talking about her oil project so theatrically that Clara recognized herself back in her first year of work.

A herd of tough-looking guys with winter coats and heavy backpacks barged in and made a beeline for the bar. Shift workers.

At the cafe counter, two ladies in pantsuits sat down and immediately took out their laptops. Accountants.

A man sat down next to Clara, tossed his duffel bag under the chair, leaned back, and closed his eyes. Middle management.

A man who could have been anywhere from thirty-five to sixty years old walked into the VIP lounge, followed by a full entourage. Exec.

A pompous woman with a purse and several duty-free bags wiped a metal chair with a moist towelette before sitting down. Expat wife.

A tall, skinny guy with glasses stared nervously at his smartphone. Financier.

A woman with a small, shabby rolling suitcase was nervously writing messages on WhatsApp according to instructions someone gave her over the telephone, constantly contradicting himself. Administrator.

Clara had just gotten comfortable, leaned back, and closed her eyes, trying to doze off, when someone called her name.

"Clara, hi! I can't believe it!" said a vibrantly dressed lady in her forties, suddenly standing there.

"Aiman! Long time no see!"

"You look great! Have you had work done?"

"Nope, I just left the oil business. And what about you—Botox?" They both laughed.

"Let's go get some coffee, I haven't had breakfast yet," said Aiman. They ordered coffee and sandwiches and sat at a table.

"I seem to remember you promising you'd never come back to Atyrau—not for any amount of money," Aiman said, grinning.

"And I still haven't—I can't seem to get out of Aktau. Almaty won't take me."

"Were you leading training sessions in Aktau?"

"Yeah, they had me explaining to this one expat who Kazakhs are."

"Like intercultural adaptation, that kind of thing?"

"Right. He asked me why we Kazakhs don't like Uzbeks. Can you imagine?"

"I'd have just told him about Agzam."

"Isn't he a Uyghur?"

"I don't know. What did you tell him?"

"I told him it's an ancient conflict between farmers and herders."

"I'd say you nailed it."

"Yeah, even I was surprised to hear that one. By the way, do you know where Agzam is these days? Still in the head office?"

"I heard he got married to that woman from the tech department. That tall one, the one he was secretly dating."

"Yeah, I remember, a head taller than him."

"And now she's twice as fat, too, because they're expecting. They got sent to some place in Africa for a new project. But listen to this—did you hear about Romka, his deputy?"

"The guy who kicked Dana out of the department?"

"Yeah—basically, he's a Swiss citizen now, he works for some contractors of ours. A fool's dream come true."

"And how'd he get there?"

"Like always—he failed upwards. He divorced his first wife and married a Kyrgyz immigrant with a Swiss passport."

"You're shitting me! His wife was so sweet, she worked in one of the big four auditing firms. Oksana or something, right?"

"Ksenia. She still works for Deloitte. He left her with the kid and sued her for part of the apartment and the car."

"What an asshole! Listen, how does he even get women? He's all crooked and limping."

"Yeah, well, why do you think he limps?" said Aiman, and they both cracked up.

"How did Ksenia take it all?"

"They almost sent her to the psych ward. But she got herself together for the kid, and now she's fine."

"Yeah, you do what you've got to do. So where are you now?"

"Amsterdam, I've been working there for two years now."

"Good for you! Husband, kids?"

"They're there with me. Arsen's getting his doctorate, and the kids are in an international school."

"That's great! Do you like it there?"

"I liked it at first, then I got a little tired of it. I miss home. I'll work two more years while Arsen finishes up his degree, then I'll get out of there, go into consulting, or maybe just relax."

"Good for you. Are Yerzhik and Lera still in Atyrau?"

"Same as ever. I actually just met with Lera today to discuss a charity project for gifted children from low-income families. Every summer, we fly them to Europe for a month, take them to museums, put together master classes, that kind of thing."

"Well, of course—charity's in Lera's blood!"

"That's what I mean! But listen to this—I put together the list, and almost all the last names are ones I know. I can't make eye contact with the shareholders anymore!"

"You should just give them a warning, so they can change their kids' last names ahead of time," said Clara.

Just then, a slim blonde in patent leather shoes walked by them, leaving a trail of perfume in her wake. She looked around for a place to sit and, when she saw Clara, gave a nod and said hello.

"That's Mara, do you know her?" whispered Clara.

"No way, Max's Mara?"

"Yep, they're a cute couple. Well, it sounds like they're starting to board. Damn, I sat here alone all day, and as soon as I run into you, they call me to board."

"Listen, let's talk sometime. You can fill me in," said Aiman, motioning towards Mara.

"Of course. I'll call you."

They kissed goodbye.

"Have a good flight! I'll give you a call later today."

"Yes, tonight. Safe travels!"

II.

As the plane made circles over Almaty, Clara quietly whispered the only surah she knew by heart.

"Ladies and gentlemen, this is your pilot speaking. Due to adverse weather conditions, we're unable to make a landing in Almaty at this time. Instead, we'll be going to Shymkent."

"You've got to be kidding!" thought Clara. "I'll have to catch the train from Shymkent."

Walking into the Shymkent airport, Clara turned on her phone, which rang immediately.

"Clara, it's me! Almaty wouldn't take you?"

"How do you know?" Clara said, then immediately saw Aiman waving at her from the crowded departure lounge.

"We couldn't fly to Astana, either," said Aiman, smiling.

"Listen, I've had enough. Let's get a hotel for the night, and tomorrow we'll take the train," Clara suggested.

"Oh, please," said Aiman. "There's already a driver waiting for us and a double suite reserved, so you're staying with me. We'll go to the sauna and have a bottle of wine."

"I forgot how nice it is to be a higher-up in an oil company!"

After getting massages and going to the sauna, the women stayed up past midnight in their suite, ordering snacks and wine.

"Wow, I had no idea that sweet couple from your project made it to New York. I'd heard so many stories about them," said Aiman.

"Yeah, who would have thought. And how's haughty Miss Fati doing?" Clara asked.

"You're speaking in rhyme—Fati would be pleased."

"Fati and poetry—now that's always an interesting combination," said Clara.

"It's not as ironic as you think. She finally published a collection."

"'Zyuzya worked the soil till one day he struck oil/Then he flipped the bird at Grishka and watched his blood boil.'"

"I don't know about the poetry, but that certainly sounds like her personality," said Aiman, laughing.

"I'll have to read it."

"I'm begging you to read it. You can get it at any bookstore—she published it on her own dime, with a huge print run."

"What does she write about?"

"Usually one of her ancestors. She calls herself the Kazakh Akhmatova."

"Okay, got it. I'm guessing she randomly sticks the word 'maa' in her poems?"

"Just for the rhyme," Aiman giggled.

"Uh-huh. My great-grandmother, maa, that great woman, maa . . ."

"No, wait, you have to put it at the start, not at the end: Maa, that great woman . . ."

"Do you remember when that girl sued her boss, that Italian guy, who supposedly cursed at her constantly and it offended her sensibilities? How did that end?" Clara asked through her laughter.

"You'll never believe it. She won the lawsuit a year later. And she wasn't a girl—she was a married woman."

"Well, that's stupid. Curse words mean nothing to Italians."

"That's what you think, because you worked in Italy and you know their ways. But she's never left Atyrau, not even to go to Almaty."

"I mean, I don't know. I've noticed people in Atyrau love taking things to court."

"Yeah, and in the South, they write to the prosecutor's office. They also complain to the party."

"You're kidding!"

"Not at all—they respond immediately, and they do a thorough investigation."

"Listen, how's Mishka doing? Or now I guess it's Mahmud," asked Aiman, as if it had just occurred to her.

"Don't ask me. It's probably about time for us to go to bed, isn't it? It's already three in the morning," said Clara, frowning.

They went to their separate rooms.

III.

The next morning, Clara woke up to the sound of a phone ringing. She reached for her cell phone but then realized the call was coming from the next room. Clara looked at the clock: half past five in the morning. She heard Aiman answer the call—first sleepily, then with increasing alarm as she asked questions. When the conversation was over, Clara went into Aiman's room.

"Is something wrong?" asked Clara.

"One of my colleagues, the former director of the oil refinery, died. He was killed. Can you even imagine?"

"You're kidding."

"And the primary suspect is his son, an employee of ours. They asked me to come right away."

"Seriously? What, like they don't have lawyers there?"

"This strange old auntie called and told me this is delicate business—they need someone with experience, and the locals aren't good enough. I told her I'm a local, too. But she still insisted."

"What, you don't know her?"

"They just hired her recently. Our boss is on leave, he left her in his place."

"He's covering his bases. Is she a foreigner?"

"Nah, seems like she's one of us, but I couldn't quite catch her name—it's either Gala or Cally. I told her I need to fly to Astana, and then to Amsterdam tomorrow. And then she says not to worry about it, they'll send me on the company jet."

"But the company jet only goes to Almaty."

"She said I can go through Almaty, I'll just exchange the ticket. Anyway, they're coming for me in an hour."

"She reminds me of someone—do you remember Jani Akman, who demanded to see the French ambassador?"

"Oh my god, you're spot on."

"So I'll order us breakfast, you go take a shower."

Clara followed Aiman out of the room. "What do you think, was your director murdered by his son?" she asked.

"He's a weird guy—such cold eyes. I don't know why, but they stuck in my mind."

"Remember in university when they told us about Lombroso's theory, how you can identify a killer from his appearance?"

"This guy's a blue-eyed blond with a cold look and portraits of Nazis. He's not messing around! But hey, why'd you get up so early? Your train isn't until tonight."

"Yeah, well, this is the kind of news that wakes you up. I'll take the opportunity to explore the city a bit."

"You should, everything's much cheaper here in Shymkent than it is in Atyrau or Almaty."

"You can buy anything you want."

"And at a fair price," Aiman reiterated. "By the way, don't buy a train ticket back yet. I'll ask Cally or Gala about the plane to Almaty—maybe there's a spot for you, too."

"Oh, thank you, darling! But, you know, I think I'm good for now," Clara said, smiling.

"Deja vu, I get it. Well, safe travels then!" said Aiman, and they kissed each other on the cheek.

A WOMAN OVER FIFTY

BY LILYA KALAUS

Translated from Russian by
Shelley Fairweather-Vega

Somebody on Facebook sent me a picture: a typewriter with a planter inside it, holding a cactus. It's a pretty planter, and a pretty photo, a conception of the otherworldly everyday that feels understandable and right to me. Typewriters have gone out of print, and so have their spare parts; that's the formula by which things go extinct as a principle: as long as the world has electricity and PCs, mechanical typing machines will lie lifeless in their graves, striking arms destined to never again touch a piece of A4 paper. There were different species. Electric, cylindrical, spherical, double, two-color, wide-carriage. Now they're all buried under a heap of payment orders and mediocre novels, four ancient copies each. But the frail expanse that was once its printmaking heart can also hold a flowerpot. Earth has come to fill the space between the typing arms, like it would the mouth of a corpse. Flowers and cacti see them off on their final journey. The sound with which the metallic letter landed on the surface of the document is disappearing into eternity, an unheard echo. The chirp of cicadas, the tick tock of a mechanical heart, the hoofbeats of centaurs, a pause, the slide of the carriage, a whispered curse word, the typo is whited out, the carbon copy is adjusted, and on, and on, and on.

But I wonder what happens to extinct things in Plato's world of ideas? Double oblivion? A second death? Ideational suicide? If a shadow on the cave wall disappears, what happens to the item which cast that shadow?

Tearing myself away from philosophy, graves, and tombstones, I pondered the thought that this photo could be considered a portrait of a woman over fifty. The blossoms of youth had been reborn into the cactus of maturity, and everything she had worked for over the years—experience, style, ideas, dreams, desires—those were the mechanical levers nobody needed, never to pass over ribbon and carbon paper again.

What can our current reality offer to a woman over fifty? No need to specify her status, family situation, presence or absence of children or career.

Finding a new job is practically impossible. A friend has told me how many times potential employers have rejected her resume precisely due to her age. I suggested there was a professionalism gap or some particular skill she lacked. "No!" my friend told me. "I thought so, too, at first. Then I realized. They just don't want to see an old biddy around the office. That's all." It's not even a matter of sexism. It's a question of aesthetic preferences. Like it or not, she'll have to conjure up her own business, become a freelancer, dive into the swamp of multilevel marketing.

Starting a family is extremely problematic, considering the intense competition from younger women who target the same segment of the bachelor community.

Finding new interests or hobbies is unlikely, unless you mean knitting, crosswords, and good old book-reading. Of course, public lectures on different topics, from art to psychology, are firmly in fashion these days, and that's not too bad an option.

Going back to school, maybe, but only if there's a specific purpose and obtaining new knowledge doesn't get subsumed to the goal of increasing the number of certificates decorating the walls.

What's left? Singing in a choir, webinars, life coaching, cross-stitching, healing and self-healing, healthy lifestyles, cooking, raising the grandkids, social media, watching soaps.

Now let's hear the outrage: How have we come to this? We're full of strength and ideas! We've raised our children and worked our hearts out! We're still capable of so-o-o many things! But there will be no outrage. Because it's all the truth. Yes. We're old and unattractive (mostly, anyway), on the brink of menopause, which does no favors to anyone's personality; we haven't just gotten older, we've gotten obsolete. I often think of my grandmother as an example. My dear old grandma passionately loved the television and watched it with great pleasure. But she was afraid of it. She tried to avoid even turning it on herself. The problem was that the universe had changed too fast. My grandmother couldn't keep up with it. I adore my computer and the internet and my iPhone and social media. I use them all with great pleasure. But—alas!—I'm afraid of them all too, just like my grandmother was afraid of the TV. The tiniest thing goes wrong, and I'm paralyzed in fear and call my children. Obsolescence is the truth we are going to have to accept.

So what do we do? Moan and groan in the clinic waiting room? Meet up with other old toadstools and cry into our beer? Desperately work to make ourselves younger?

No! Again, we don't need the outrage. How you live out the golden years you have left is up to you. Even if you want to spend them in a vegetative state. I think we ought to just relax as much as possible. Talk, dress, walk, drive, communicate, work, sit around, have fun, mourn, and love as we want and not the way it's supposed to be done "at our age."

Banal? Yes. Then I'll say it a different way.

Pick up that typewriter. Put it on the desk. Slide back the carriage, cough a few times, crack your knuckles, visualize all the missing parts of the structure, including A4 paper. And type whatever your little heart desires, directly onto the cactus.

HOW MEN THINK

BY LILYA KALAUS

Translated from Russian by
Shelley Fairweather-Vega

They know an awful lot, these males of the species. It's a marvel. The mechanics of various materials. Putin's geopolitics, Dirac's constant, stock market postal codes, World of Tanks tactics—all kinds of useful things. What you might call information of primary importance. And yet, sometimes male thinking is so inscrutable, so breathtaking, that ordinary insight and the rest of gestalt psychology can only huddle nervously, smoking, in the corner.

A disclaimer: I'm not talking about the men who are hopeless idiots, the dumb little lambs, or the geniuses submerged far into the depths of self-actualization. I'm talking about good, solid specimens, properly nourished, educated, clever, reasonable, and well socialized. Specifically, in other words, my husband.

So. Early one morning I creep into the kitchen with my mind on something to drink. And there I find my husband, who is digging with a spoon, glumly, in an empty sugar bowl, trying unsuccessfully to scrape away the sugar stalactites that have accumulated inside it.

"What the . . . ?" I ask. (I'm a little stupid first thing in the morning.)

"We're out of sugar!" My husband's voice is tragic, and he demonstratively pours his tea right into the sugar bowl.

"What do you mean we're out?" I ask, awake now.

"We're out!" My husband frowns and gulps his tea. "I spent all night looking. All kinds of garbage we don't need, barley or something, seven types of macaroni, garlic powder—what even *is* that?—but sugar . . . There's no sugar! We'll have to go to the store . . ." He trailed off, pondering the burdens men have to carry, staring into the dark wave of tea sloshing against the inner walls of the sugar bowl.

Now I admit that home economics is not my forte. In fact, I'm basically an untamed beast when it comes to raising the children and keeping the house. Still, there's nothing wrong with my fundamental values. I'm not one of those women who spend days on end making their kids memorize poetry, dragging them to clubs and classes, going over homework with a magnifying glass, and chasing the brats around with a big fat book at the ready to instill something educational into them. But I never forget a kid at daycare, I feed them something every day, and I dress them in clean clothes. It's the same thing with housekeeping. Maybe I don't display any particular enthusiasm for it, but my kitchen cupboards contain all the necessities.

I open the doors to one cabinet. Hello! Seven dwarves, fat and happy. Which is to say, seven bright red jars for sprinklable ingredients, standing in a row, bright golden labels across their bellies. The second from the left reads "Sugar." I take it out and open it for my husband to see.

A whole dune of sugary sand sparkles inside.

My husband is abashed.

"No way! I never thought to look in there."

There is a medical fact which is widely known: Women have peripheral vision, and men have tunnel vision. A woman can go into the pantry looking for sugar and find it immediately, and at the same time she'll notice that the salt is running low, and she'll need to buy some flour because her daughter has been asking for blini, and she needs to remember to check to see if there are eggs, and by the way, yesterday she saw a link to a story about how to tell if eggs are fresh, and actually maybe she should make an omelet, because she'll end up scarfing down most of the blini herself, with jam, no less, and she'd been planning to cut down on sweets for a while, but what's the point of putting sugar out, it's just pure temptation, no, she'd better run to the market for cherries, plus—yes, the flour! Must remember the flour. But if a man goes into the pantry for the same purpose, he'll fix his molish tunnel vision on two or three separate objects, taste their contents, spit them out (not sugar!), and go drink his tea out of the sugar bowl, longing wistfully for the golden days when his mama made his breakfast.

British scientists have this to say about the phenomenon. A man, presumably, is a hunter by nature, and he needs to set his eyes on his target, avoid getting distracted by peripheral details, and track it through the primeval forest to victory. In contrast, a woman has to survey everything in her broad field of activity at once. Here there are hides to mend, pots to shape, a mammoth to smoke, babies to bear, and please don't let that fire go out in the hearth, and you need to dig up some roots that are at least barely edible before the bread-winner comes home. Because while tunnel vision is surely a remarkable thing, it's far from perfect. A stranger pops out of the bushes, a vine whips you in the face at the worst possible moment, or you step in something nasty, and that's the end of the tunnel-vision hunt. All you can hope for is some roots to chew on with your beer that night in the cave.

In short, since the dawn of time, there's never been a huge supply of women with empty sugar bowls at the market among their warrior girlfriends.

I'd offer one amicable moral to this story. Ladies, keep working on your peripheral vision! Gentlemen, pay attention to the labels on those jars!

And we'll all be very happy together.

THE STAIRWELL

BY LILYA KALAUS

Translated from Russian by
Shelley Fairweather-Vega

This stairwell remembers everything: white knee socks and darling little yellow shoes, black stockings and serious pumps, jeans and sneakers, trousers and ankle boots, cream-colored high heels, then snow-white, lacy, one-of-a-kind . . . Later, midseason practical brown, patent leather for going out (obnoxious and too tight), soft suede slip-ons like moccasins, and finally orthopedic and safe. The rhythm has changed as well. Percussive rappings, two steps at a time, elegant glides, a flickering cha-cha-cha, now much more even, slower, calmer, now more careful. Weariness, veins, tripping, a step then a stop, two steps and out of breath, three steps and arrhythmia sets in. The echo dies away, dripping sounds down the stairwell like a gigantic icicle. Silence. Suddenly, many, many unfamiliar footfalls, and they are carrying something heavy, angular, something enormous, a box of potatoes, no, no not of potatoes, it lurches inside when they turn the corners . . . Sometimes those bearing the box freeze and breathe, unspeaking, listening to the beat of their own living hearts.

OPERATIC DRAMA

BY LILYA KALAUS

Translated from Russian by
Shelley Fairweather-Vega

ere's a thing that happened. A couple years ago, a dude came to our office on business. He was a Muscovite named Vadya. The management assigned me to him. I was supposed to keep him entertained, arrange a cultural expedition, things along that line. This Vadya turned out to be a really great guy. He proposed that we ditch the historical and cultural aspects of my assignment and focus on a detailed examination and analysis of the local drinking establishments. Which is exactly what we eagerly proceeded to do.

But we also visited a temple of the arts. I talked my new buddy into going to the opera house to see *Carmen*. Naturally, I regretted it later. I'm a provincial guy, so nothing surprises me, but Vadya, poor thing, snorted hard when our plump, aging Carmen crawled up onto a table, grunting loud enough to fill the hall, and danced her dance of youth and beauty. Anyway, we didn't finish watching the show. Without even discussing it we got up and left for the snack bar. We downed fifty grams of cognac apiece.

I was much ashamed.

"Opera is that kind of thing, brother. You have to think meta-phorically. Adjust to the circumstances. Who knows what the hell kind of people might be strutting around on stage. What's important is their voices. And those seem fine."

Vadya shrugged.

"That could be. Listen, since our night out is a bust anyway, maybe you can help me with something? My wife asked me to go check on a distant relative of hers. An old woman. I'm supposed to see if she needs anything, give her some money, and so on. Will we make it before bedtime?"

"No problem," I told him, sneaking a look at my watch. "What's the address?"

His wife's relative lived in a quiet, moss-covered city neighbor-hood. After conquering a few flights of stairs decorated in a light blue mosaic design with almost all its pieces missing, we wound up before an apartment door wallpapered with a brightly flowered plas-tic stick-on tablecloth.

Valentina Vasilyevna, the lady of the house, opened the door. But not right away. First there were tough negotiations and a showing of passports through the peephole (even though Vadya had called her earlier about our visit).

The old lady's apartment was modest but tidy. When you got used to the smell of poverty and loneliness and took a closer look at the 1960s furniture on its worn wooden feet, it even started to look cozy. Valentina Vasilyevna was all wary cordiality. She spread a hand-embroidered cloth over an end table and put atop that a kettle of yellow tea, three Madonna teacups, a worn-out sugar bowl, and a plate holding five tiny cookies. It was a lucky break we had bought her some chocolate bonbons, crackers, and cognac at the kiosk around the corner. To the tune of the same moans and groans she had made digging out the sugar, three dusty shot glasses made of Czech crystal were also extracted from the bowels of her china cabinet.

"My dear Valentina Vasilyevna!" Vadya began heartily. "I'm so delighted to meet you! And to get to the point, let's drink to our friendship and to your very valuable good health!"

We drank. The old lady looked a bit ruddier now, and he handed her an envelope full of charitable relief. In response, she swiftly cleared the candy and cognac from the table. She was preparing to get up and usher us out. But just then, the cognac hit Valentina Vasilyevna's head, clearly induced by the alcoholic pressure on her bladder.

From behind the couch, she extracted approximately half a metric ton of family photo albums, draped in spiderwebs complete with dead spiders.

I sighed and made myself comfortable. Vadya, in contrast, tensed up.

Anyway, we blew the spiders away and started looking. The pictures were yellow with fluted edges, snapshots from the nineteen thirties. Amateur work.

"My father won a prize at work, a Zeiss camera," Valentina Vasilyevna told us as she turned the stiff pages. "There, you see? It was a very rare thing back then. That's me. And that's my half-brother Shurka. He had an unhappy marriage . . . And that's our neighbor, lame Frosya. They called her Rotfoot at school, and in 1950 they found a tumor on top of that . . . And there he is, the man himself, our father, Vasily Ignatyevich, with his colleagues from work. A fine fellow, isn't he? And look at these young men . . . You can't find any like them these days."

I looked, and I shuddered. A fraternal circle of maybe ten people stood arranged in a semicircle, a sepia-brown flag in the background. Fine fellows, indeed. Half of them wore leather jackets. Intelligent enough faces. Ugh.

Vadya swallowed.

"So, errr . . . your father was in the security services? The NKVD?"

"He got a medal!" Valentina Vasilyevna said proudly, and her eyes went moist. "And an order of valor. I'll show you, I've got it here somewhere . . ."

She went to rummage through the cubbyholes in her desk.

Vadya's face was frozen, expressionless. I spoke through the awkwardness.

"Yeah . . . there you go. My great-grandfather was exiled here, to Central Asia. They said he was a kulak. He had a family—like a dozen kids, land, cows, and pigs, you name it. A bird. A kulak, they said. They brought him here and made him dig a dugout. There was nowhere else to live. His kids started to die. Then he built a barn, and he went and hanged himself inside it."

Vadya looked at me.

"A kulak? Big deal. My grandpa and grandma were arrested for being Trotskyites. They were both teachers at the workers' college. They were sent off nobody knows where, not a grave or anything left of them."

I was offended.

"You say that's not a big deal? My grandpa was the only one of those twelve kids to survive. He lost a leg in the war and drank himself to death after that, before I was born. On my mother's side, my grandma served time, too, for stealing scraps of wheat. Her kids were wasting away from hunger, her husband was killed early in the war.

She used to walk through the field at night. She collected the left-overs, and some bastard reported her. What a time that was—"

Vadya ignored me and kept talking.

"My other grandfather was raised in an orphanage, and from there, he went straight to the army, to the front. He got captured, sent to a German concentration camp, escaped, and came back home, the nitwit. And fine fellows just like these gave him ten and a half years for treason. Sent him to the prison camp in Norilsk. He served his time . . . I still remember him. Really nice, kind eyes. He died of tuberculosis—"

I was ready with my answer.

"My other grandma and her whole village were deported here right before the war started. She lived out in a hamlet near Petersburg somewhere. She was Finnish or something, a real chukhonka. We only have one picture of her. You know the type: all this wavy hair. Ten rows of bobby pins in it. They were making a lot of arrests in the areas that got annexed back then—"

Vadya countered.

"All you've got is kulaks and Finnish villagers and internal exiles. My people were all card-carrying intellectuals, *that* social group. The kind who chucked bombs at the tsars in the 19th century, then got twenty years each in Petropavlovka for their populist convictions—"

I was furious.

"Oh, Mr. Intellectual! Your family's all Chernyshevskys, I guess. My aunt was from the merchant class, and her grandfather was Siberian, healthy as a bear. He was arrested when he was just about to turn ninety. They had him chopping trees in the Arctic. He died of tetanus, by the way. From a splinter in his finger."

Vadya fired back.

"Well, my dad, by the way, was an honest-to-God dissident. Five years in the psych ward on Sulfozin. They caught him with a copy of Solzhenitsyn's *Archipelago*."

I sneered.

"Come on, those were hardly even sentences in the GULAG, more like safekeeping for, what, seven years? Bullshit!"

Vadya stubbornly went on.

"He had epilepsy, they sent him to the nuthouse, and we still don't know who had it worse, the ones in the prison camp or the ones they kept stoned with the mental cases."

I was about to tell him about my own dad, who spent his whole young adulthood trafficking paperbacks and neckties on the black market and even got kicked out of the Komsomol for it, but I didn't want to move the bar so low. I took an indifferent shot of cognac.

That's when we both heard a dull thud.

The little cardboard box holding her father's medal had dropped from Valentina Vasilyevna's trembling fingers. The old lady was white as chalk, backed up ass-first against her rickety old desk. She could not take her eyes off the renegades and abominations before her—which is to say, us.

Vadya spoke first.

"Umm . . . Valentina Vasilyevna, thank you very much for your hospitality; I think we'll be on our way."

"She's about to call the cops," I whispered, feeling around in the stinking recesses of her entryway for my boots.

After that we went to a bar. We drank a lot, thinking we ought to honor each and every one of our repressed relatives. I remember us linking arms with a pair of middle-aged women, stomping along the street, shouting the Nautilus Pompilius lyrics about being forged in a chain. I remember Vadya's idiotic laughter when he was explaining to some bartender the difference between a *line* for Zhigulis and a *line* from a Kalashnikov. And later I remember the beefy fist of some Leps lover flying into my face.

By the time Vadya and I said goodbye, we were the best of friends. We're still close. Not long ago, he texted me. *Come see me in golden-domed Moscow in June, and we'll go to the Bolshoi to see* Queen of Spades. *Let's incite some more operatic drama,* he said.

BLACK SNOW
OF DECEMBER

BY ASEL OMAR

Translated from Russian by
Shelley Fairweather-Vega

TRANSLATOR'S NOTE: *Asel Omar's "Black Snow of December" presents a version of events from Kazakhstan's recent history that, alas, are still little discussed today. In December 1986, as the Soviet Union struggled with glasnost and perestroika, the ruling national Communist Party removed Dinmukhamed Kunayev, an ethnic Kazakh, from his post as First Secretary of the Communist Party of Kazakhstan and replaced him with a non-local, Gennady Kolbin. In Alma-Ata (now Almaty), people, at first mostly students, gathered in the streets to protest. The protests spread to other cities and remained peaceful until troops were brought in from Russia to put them down by a bloody show of force and mass arrests three days later. To this day, no reliable count of deaths and arrests is available, the topic is still politically delicate, and no real national reckoning has occurred to come to terms with the underlying ethnic tension behind the unrest.*

"We stayed home. We were frightened. There were rumors that those men on the square were storming nursery schools, killing children."

Mikhail Yuryevich, the newspaper's executive secretary, stood half-turned away from the desk, tapping his fingers on it nervously, the way old men do. His fingers were short and plump, but tapered, and suffused with cigarette smoke. His index and middle finger were marked with iodine-colored stains from always holding a smoldering Sortie. The smell of Mikhail Yuryevich's Sortie filled the whole small editorial office, and his thick black sweater and goatee gave off the scent of aged, pressed tobacco.

Over the years, Mikhail Yuryevich had taken on the physical manifestations of caution and endless patience: a stooping posture and a sad gaze. Shifting his weight from one knock-kneed leg to the other, he even seemed slightly delicate; in the absence of any trace of physical labor, his body had to work constantly to maintain coordination.

"How I understand all that, God knows!" is what his eyes seemed to say, mourning all the injustice of this life, but at the same time, those eyes expressed a mysterious sympathy at the sight of twenty-three-year-old Rustem, a representative of the youthful nation. Between the two of them, at their respective ages, they personified the earthly history of Shem, Ham and Japheth. Mikhail Yuryevich didn't eat pork, he used the informal "you" with everyone except the Editor-in-Chief, and he did his time in his chair from morning to late evening every day. Rustem felt comfortable with him, intimate, as if he were a wise old Asian relative. Nobody had ever given Mikhail Yuryevich any diplomas, and he spoke so vaguely about his college years that nobody could even be sure what country they took place in. His lazy "g" and a stubborn insistence on pronouncing *chto* instead of *shto* betrayed his parochial origins.

As he spoke, he nodded understandingly (understanding Rustem, specifically—not the all-powerful Moscow of 1986, not Kolbin or Kunayev or Gorbachev), but he also steered clear of putting himself in Rustem's position, a position he assessed very carefully, as if balancing on a tightrope stretched between two towers, obliging Rustem to treat him with sympathy and understanding in turn. He spoke quietly, with no strain, cajolingly, counting on Rustem's good will and on the common human values they shared. At this moment, the conversation's direction depended on Rustem. Mikhail Yuryevich would follow his lead.

"But Mikhail Yuryevich, did you personally see a single vandalized nursery school or a single bloodied child?"

"No, of course not, not personally."

Suddenly a very clear image appeared in Rustem's memory: his mother's room and he himself, a twelve-year-old boy everyone called Rustik, with Auntie Galya, Uncle Kostya, Sofia Yakovlevna, and Auntie Galya's sons Dima and Vladik. Little Rustik and his mom were hunkered down at Auntie Galya's house, scared and distraught, and Sofia Yakovlevna, prowling the room, was the only one talking. "Lord knows, Gulya, I'd go straight to Kolbin and tell him, 'Get out of here! Get out—can't you see what's going on because of you?'" That was December 17. The next two days Rustik and his mom stayed home because, on the morning of the seventeenth, his grandparents called and told them not to even stick their heads outside the building. His grandpa had been furious. "What more do they want, those students? They've got food and a roof over their heads! Study, work, what's the problem?" And they stayed home, while events unfolded in the city that they learned about through rumors and sometimes from the view out the window.

Rustik had always thought his mother and Auntie Galya had a strange kind of friendship. They had been close since grade school, and they lived in the same apartment building. Now, in their early thirties, they still got together, rarely but very happily, and their conversations went on long past the time they started saying their good-byes. Usually what prompted those visits was a need to borrow money from Auntie Galya. She never refused, and his mother always repaid her quickly.

One time Auntie Galya asked Rustik to help Vladik learn solfeggio. Vladik obediently went through his lesson, listened carefully to Rustik's explanations, and shyly moved his chubby fingers to shape the right chord. His round eyes, framed with blond lashes, gave Rustik a frightened look, and he asked, almost inaudibly, whether he was doing it right. Rustik felt terrible for him. He was afraid to accidentally hurt his feelings somehow and even tried to speak more quietly. Auntie Galya walked in, took one look at Vladik, and gave him a firm thump on the forehead. "You're Jewish, so you will always have to be better than the rest, because you'll always have it worse! Got that?" Dima, the older brother, helped Rustik with his computer class in his final year. When Rustik finished school, Auntie Galya's family moved away to Israel. They wanted Rustik and his mother to go, too, but what would they do there? His mother wrote them a letter once, but there was never an answer or a call in return.

But in those December days, Galya's family had wanted to stick close to Gulya and Rustik, seeing them as protection. Rustik and his mom might have been searching for protection, too, but they had no chance of finding it. Near evening on the seventeenth, they decided to leave the building. His mother gave in first. "There's something happening to our people out there, and we're just sitting here!"

They walked, holding hands, along the slippery, grimy, trampled snow. There was no traffic at all, as if every car had gone into hiding, and it seemed that civilian life had sequestered itself deep in the warm apartments, their doors shut tight. Meanwhile, a terrible and thundering force marched down the streets and boulevards, yielding to nobody, incubating tension and terror.

Then, at an intersection where, on ordinary days, the cars are bumper to bumper and there is an impenetrable wall of churning tires and wailing horns, they encountered a group of men, dressed in black with red armbands, marching in a straight column as if they owned the place. Their somber, orderly movements made these civilians look like a militia on the move. Yes, that's apparently what they were, because each one of them carried a piece of metal pipe or a heavy wooden club studded with nails. They were Russian men, and they were marching uptown, toward the square. Rustik and his mom turned quickly into an alleyway.

They were between the yellow apartment buildings, sturdy and Stalinist, between the remains of the old courtyard gates, hanging off yellow plastered columns. During Stalin's time, all of this probably got refurbished regularly, painted, every link in the fence polished with oil. In the middle of this stage set of old Almaty, which used to seem so sturdy, a boy was running, slowing around the corners to avoid slipping: seventeen years old, wearing a malakhai, carrying a dombyra—and with two men from that crowd, wielding pipes, in pursuit. Two more in police uniforms came running around a corner and headed straight for him. They were still some distance away, and

Rustik's mom shouted to the boy with the dombyra: "Where are you going? Hide! Why have you stirred up all this trouble?"

"No, apai! It's better to die on your feet than live on your knees!"

"My God, he's just a child!" His mother was aghast.

They rushed past, both pursuers and pursued. Only fear remained, an almost animalistic fear, suffocating and rabid. Not cowardice, but fear. "People need to be afraid of somebody," his grandfather used to say. "Otherwise there will be anarchy." He wasn't happy with anything that had happened. Grandma, on the other hand, said nothing. He remembered that exhaustion had flashed in her eyes, the same exhaustion that Rustem saw several years later in the eyes of Mikhail Yuryevich, the only difference being that in Mikhail Yuryevich it was genetic and centuries old, whereas Grandma's exhaustion came from her own life, from her work in the Communist Party Central Committee, from the war she had survived. His grandfather's exhaustion was of a different kind. Grandpa was pre-revolutionary. The upheaval in thinking he had had to live through was passed down to his descendants. He outlived three alphabets for his native language: Arabic, Latin, and Cyrillic. He learned Russian, German, and several Turkic languages, the latter of which were not very difficult from his philological point of view. But the three alphabets were like three different mentalities, right to left then left to right, or like going from a madrasa to a Soviet school. The Bolsheviks had killed his parents in 1918, as beys of the feudalist class, and he was raised in a miner's family. His adoptive mother, who had the pagan nickname Baqa, meaning "frog," taught her granddaughter—Rustem's mother—to say *bismilla-rahman-rahim*, and they spent most of their time together, so she didn't know any Russian until she was four. They lived in Almaty, and Rustem's mother remembered how the Russian kids in their neighborhood didn't want to let her into their games. "Kalbitka, kalbitka!" they screamed at her. His mother didn't take offense because she didn't understand. Grandma Baqa comforted her when she came home empty-handed. Later, they moved to cold, uncivilized Tselinograd, when Grandfather was transferred there for work. Grandma Baqa had died by then, and in that virgin land, populated by settlers, Rustem's mom nearly forgot her Kazakh grandma. In Tselinograd she started going to a one-story wooden schoolhouse with an out-door toilet. Her classroom included children of various nationalities and also different ages. The whole class repeated after the teacher's Ukrainian lilt: *Oi, za ghaem-ghaem, ghaem-zelenen-kim.* When the mud was too deep, Rustem's mother's mother carried her to music school. After a few years, the family returned to Almaty.

In their apartment there, the old folks kept quite a few things from the heyday of Soviet-Chinese friendship. A tablecloth with silken fringe, embroidered in gold—peonies, clouds, birds of paradise. Thin-walled wooden vases on stands, painted landscapes, a strikingly beautiful porcelain horse on a wooden pedestal in a glass case, bam-boo chopsticks engraved with Chinese men and Chinese women, Chinese books, some covered in velvet and gilded with Chinese char-acters, silk-screen postcards, and many other little knick-knacks.

After his grandfather's funeral, Rustem remembered sitting with one of his grandfather's old friends, Uncle Kazbek, in a waiting room of the ministry where Uncle Kazbek worked. Uncle Kazbek patted dry the sweat beading on his forehead, adjusted his glasses, and said, "Spies, my boy, never say much about themselves."

That made Rustem remember how quiet his grandparents always were. The outward trappings of their life, yes—his work history, the fact that Grandfather changed his last name because his older brothers, twins, had been sent off forever to Siberian camps, and he still didn't know where they were buried; one had been the chairman of the rural council—but Rustem knew nothing at all about the rest. He thought about that Chinese horse with the brown mane and blue saddle covered in tiny designs, about his own enormous country and its global cataclysms, in which one person's fate was just a microscopic gulp of air, and suddenly, with an anxious, careful, tentative pride, he realized that the Soviets naturally couldn't have used ethnic Russians as Stierlitzes in Asia. But no, of course not, none of that could have had anything to do with his grandfather! And yet . . . Uncle Kazbek looked at Rustem warmly, like family, and both of them felt somehow relieved by their mutual discovery after all these fateful years.

"But then why did he . . . ?" Rustem hesitated.

"He signed a lifetime non-disclosure agreement. And if that's not what you meant, then . . ." Uncle Kazbek tried to put a calm expression on his face and succeeded. "Well, you know what happens if you refuse to carry out an assignment the party gives you."

Then Rustem told Uncle Kazbek about the two photographs from his grandfather's archives. One was dated 1939. In it, Grandfather was sitting at a desk, smiling, light-haired, in a wool suit. The second was from 1945, taken in the Far East, in Manchuria, during the war against Japan. In that one, Grandfather wore an officer's uniform, and there was a note in unfamiliar handwriting: "Major Omargaliyev Tulegen." The face almost didn't look like his; it seemed foreign, like the strange writing on the back: dry, pinched, his gaze lackluster, his hair shorter and thinner on his head.

That was the source of the exhaustion entrenched in Grandfather's wrinkles, in his shrapnel scar. Nothing but war, in Belarus, in

Ukraine, in Poland, Czechoslovakia, and Manchuria, Southeast Asia . . . And in the end, how much could a person bear? How much would he agree to tolerate after the murder of his parents, after a revolution, after Stalin?

Rustem's mother's aunt, who was just a baby during Stalin's time, used to tell Rustem about the silver saddles and swords and daggers their family used to own, most of which they had given away or "accidentally" lost to rid themselves of certain memories, from before 1917—in order to save themselves, in order not to be associated with those infamous beys, the feudal overlords. At some point, back when his grandfather was still alive, during a time when scandalous truths were being revealed daily in the press, it suddenly occurred to Rustem to wonder, with surprise, how on earth his grandfather had survived. Why hadn't they taken him away? What made him better or worse than the rest? Grandfather had laughed. "It's just that back then, I wasn't a Communist yet. I joined the party in '41 and went straight to the front lines." One of the first books his grandfather got during perestroika was a poetry collection by Shakarim with a glossy photo of the poet in prison. The same Shakarim who wrote the verses that one time had gotten Grandfather summoned to the NKVD and let go after a scolding—after all, he wasn't a Communist yet.

Rustem's grandmother's life was the complete opposite of her husband's, so dissimilar it was difficult to believe it. She had an authentic, genuine biography that was her pride and consolation in her older years. Her stories about her childhood were much more expansive than his grandfather's, although was it fair to call something more expansive than silence? It seemed to Rustem that what surrounded his family was one big expansive silence, about everything. His grandmother made him tear things to bits, even his student notebooks after he filled them up and was ready to throw them away, even their covers, where he had entered his last name and his school's number; young Rustik learned he needed to tear off the edge from an old newspaper where the mailman had written their apartment number before he used it to wrap up garbage. Letters got shredded, too, along with their envelopes, so that the address could not be read. This was the apotheosis, the logical conclusion, of his grandmother's stories about following around the combine, during her Young Pioneer years, picking up stray grain in the field. That was how his grandmother seemed in those stories, and it seemed quite likely to have been the truth. "You can consider me to have come from a family of farmhands," she used to tell Rustik, her lecture never varying; it always ended with a wish for him to take a good look at how they were all living now, to understand his own helplessness and insignificance before this terrible life, in which they were lucky enough to have everything handed to them. As if there could be any limit to the good you could get out of what you did or didn't receive at birth, thought Rustik; there was no universal scale of happiness and good fortune, and even if there was a zero point— like picking up the grain the combine dropped . . . but probably that wasn't the zero point. The end points were existence and non-existence, life and death, and all the rest swarmed around and between them.

After the events of December, General Zaviryukh stopped saying hello to Grandmother when they ran into each other outside. The General used to live one floor down but was given a much more fashionable apartment for using water cannons to break up the demonstrators. "He's probably ashamed," Grandmother said. But when the war in Chechnya began, she told Rustik, "Our men have entered Chechnya." How did all those parts fit together inside her—"our men" in Chechnya and her disrespect for Zaviryukh—in a party-member grandmother, brave and strong, never bending under any blows fate dealt her, not knowing how to cry, brooking no dissent, able to cure a person of any sickness, except probably AIDS (even that was an open question—it might be possible if fate forced her hand), and she could rescue you from any tangled-up political situation as well, when heads were just about to roll. How did all of that fit inside this hook-nosed old woman, proud and confident as a camel trotting across a borderless expanse, knowing she would get where she was going and would never lose her way?

They went home, and Rustik sat down to write in his school notebook about what he had seen during those December days. He also wrote the rumors circulating about trucks spraying icy water to disperse the students. It was the blockade diary of a boy in December's Almaty, written to the sound of the classical music that usually gets played before another national leader is buried, to the now-inaudible shouts of the people on the square, to the sound of the old people calling to check on things, to the music of superstition and pagan prayers for this dear country, loved in such torment, in which the gods were gradually dropping dead.

Of course, that's not precisely what he was thinking at the time. He and his mom were thinking about whether he should go to school the next day, given the riots. Conferring with the old folks resulted in a firm answer: Go, probably everything will be fine. And so he did.

The first lesson of the day was replaced by a conversation between two teachers at the blackboard—"So what's their complaint? The gall of those young people!"—and so on and by the compiling of a list of

AMANAT

students absent from school. "Where are they if not out on the square!" they said, and on that list was about a third of the student body. "Good thing I came," thought Rustik.

The next day, when everyone was there, Stalina Georgiyevna got mad at Kulakhmetov, the class dunce, and tossed the grade book down on his desk. "Don't look at me like that, you bey brats! So, you're all dressed up and don't feel like studying!" The class was stunned silent. Rustik didn't blame the teacher, and everyone always tiptoed around her, like fire, anyway; that day she gave him a five, the best grade, but Rustik always learned his history lessons because he loved the subject. Still, he told his mother about the incident, and all his classmates told their parents, too, and the principal personally delivered some kind of warning to Stalina Georgiyevna, as his mother told him later.

The Soviet myth about the unforgettable, kind, beloved first teacher always remained just that, a myth, for Rustik, a static symbol on a lovely picture in his reading book: a woman surrounded by children, like some wise good fairy. Even as a little boy, Rustik knew that, in his reading book, everything was always perfect and not like it was in real life. You get used to that. There, in big fonts and stupid dialogues, a girl named Sima is always helping her mother wash a windowframe, Vasya is forever reading a book, and even that naughty, lazy Petya always admits his mistakes in the end and becomes a better person, more like, let's say, Vasya. Later, somewhere beyond the reading book, Sima and Vasya graduate and get married, and they have well-behaved children who read books and wash windowframes, and Sima and Vasya will go to the theatre and afterwards sit and watch TV with their grandmother. This story of mythical, faceless people continued later in the English class textbooks. And it was

180

annoying that kids who already knew how to read before they started school still had to repeat the phrases about the windowframe, and if you got distracted, then Vera Fyodorovna, the first reading teacher, would jog right over to you in a thundering of platform heels and throw a fit, tossing all your rulers and pens and books on the floor. But what happened to Rustik with the Little Octobrists star was the worst. He didn't like to eat in the school cafeteria. In punishment for that, one time Vera Fyodorovna whacked him in the head, and to protest, he turned around, back to the table, and stared, tense and gloomy, at the tiled cafeteria wall, green at the cracks, rightfully expecting even more unpleasantness to come. Vera Fyodorovna's shouts and scoldings were as ordinary as bread and tea for breakfast. What annoyed him the most was her saying, "You're wearing a star with the portrait of the young Lenin, and you behave so shamelessly!" The blood rushed to his head, and his helplessness in the face of his teacher's injustice collided, strangely enough, with his own stubbornness and desire to stand up for himself, because all of this was so unbelievable, deceitful, unfair: what did Lenin have to do with it? Many other horrors and kindergarten fears of teachers flashed before his eyes, until he felt like he was falling and couldn't stop—this had all gone too far, and why were they doing this to him over some stinky bowl of soup, like the one that starts the revolution in Eisenstein's *Battleship Potemkin*, but fine, go ahead along your foolish path, maybe it's foolish, maybe it's useless, but at this point, there's no other way, even if half of Vera Fyodorovna's class still hadn't learned to read and write three years later, even if the sky fell down with all its heavy weight, he was already bearing too much of a burden.

"I don't have to wear it, Vera Fyodorova."

"So you can just put it down on my desk for me?" She provoked him, and the star got unpinned as if by somebody else's disobedient hands, and it was put on the sheet of plexiglass that covered the sketches of kittens and puppies on the desk.

That very evening they went to a concert—Maryla Rodowicz was singing about the colors of the fair, and her guitarist was on stage in a suit, with his head bandaged, dyed a bloody red ("That's because we sent troops into Poland!" his mother explained, under the rumble of the speakers). Rustik's head bobs in time with the music, he loves all of it, they're sitting in the second row, they bought the expensive tickets, and in the next seat over is Vera Fyodorovna with a date. The same Vera Fyodorovna who called his mom into school that day and told her she would probably have a heart attack any second now and Rustik would never make it into the Young Pioneers. Whatever irony of fate brought them all to that concert, this was one of those everyday twists, without which perfect story plots probably could not exist. Someone *could* have thought up this plot, certainly, but it would be extremely difficult to imagine the real-life Vera Fyodorovna; she could only crop up in the most commonplace, everyday settings.

In the school principal's office, Rustik's grandma, shifting her dour gaze from Vera Fyodorovna to Rustik's mom, who had made the criminal decision to cheer him up with the Maryla Rodowicz concert, smiled coldly at the principal. The woman responded with the same Soviet party-line smile: this was an error by the teacher; of course the boy will be accepted as a member of the Young Pioneers; there's no question about it, come now.

Throughout his years at school, he remembered Vera Fyodorovna, thin and blond, in her black turtleneck and chamois suit. He remembered the touch of her dry hand and her downtrodden son who was in the other class, just as blond, who wore the shirt with the girly collar.

Rustik's mom met him after school, and the occasional pedestrians seemed not to just be walking down the street, but rather hurrying, looking somehow harassed. Now his mom didn't know whether to send him to his music lesson. Fortunately, Lyubov Borisovna, the teacher, called them herself and said the accompaniment lesson would take place not far away, in Oleg's apartment. Oleg was Rustik's friend and another pupil of Lyubov Borisovna's. Rustik headed over to Oleg's place, and they tried to practice, but the conversation kept turning to the bothersome topic of what was happening on the square. Oleg's parents came in: Everyone is afraid of the Kazakhs, and Lyubov Borisovna's husband has started wearing a malakhai so that he looks like a Kazakh, and what's happening in the nursery schools, and what are we supposed to do now? Rustik tried to be objective, take everyone at face value, even himself, and he tried to bring some peace to that room full of grownups, all while an invisible line, a gap, a crack, was being laid down between them, one that nothing could patch.

"If that Kolbin would just leave, everything would be easier," he said.

And, sitting sideways to the piano, from where the only one he couldn't see was Oleg's dad, who was behind him, he sensed that the gap was expanding, fast and relentless, and that nothing could ever reconcile them again in that room full of Oleg's toys and books, which at that moment became foreign and uninteresting to Rustik; the warmth and pleasure of being in this home had disappeared, and Rustik no longer had any right to enjoy it.

That evening, when it got dark, somebody who was completely hammered held a loud conversation on the pay phone outside Rustik's window. "Kolya! We won on the square today, we dispersed those students. We won, Kolya!" A lamp burned on his desk. He didn't feel like writing in his journal. The demonstrators had been dispersed. It just made him think: this was actually his native land, and these daily events, whether in December, January, August, year-round—it wasn't some huge Soviet Union, it wasn't Kazakhstan, it was this city, suffocating tonight from fear and hatred—this was his home; it was looking out through his eyes, flowing in his veins, venturing out on the now-terrifying streets. This native land of his had been battling for three days on the square where he wasn't allowed to go.

His mother burned his diary. First she hid it under the linoleum in the corner of his room, but then she couldn't put up with it being there and burned it, with Rustik's permission. He couldn't blame her. Too much had already happened in this lifetime, up till then, and God only knew what was yet to come.

Once, his grandfather had advised his mother not to join the Party: in the district where she worked, the Communists were reporting a recruitment shortfall among ethnic Kazakhs, and she received an application to join. But during that memorable period called the Stagnation, his grandfather had unexpectedly made a seditious statement. He said the Party was a temporary phenomenon. Then he entered another long period of saying nothing about politics, until perestroika, when it was revealed that he had always known Mandelstam, Shakarim, and Gumilyov by heart. He recited amazingly long scraps of verse to Rustik. Rustik thought that for someone pre-revolutionary, that's the only way it could have been, actually.

Now, of course, it was a good thing his mom wasn't a Communist. She hadn't wanted to do it, but they thought it might come in handy. It didn't come in handy. What's more, that sweet stagnation handed Rustik's mother an unforgettable encounter with a provocateur in the artistic realm. He offered to give her some samizdat Bulgakov and Solzhenitsyn. That's why his mom kept hiding Rustik's school journal. Nothing that was burned ever let the family go. It got passed down from generation to generation. His grandfather burned all his poems from the war.

They had to buy some cognac for Uncle Sasha Kukushkin, who worked with Rustik's mom. He and Uncle Mukhtar, the son of the former prosecutor general, tried to find them in the stirred-up city, and finally they did, and they came over to say they should all drink to the friendship of the peoples . . . That evening, Auntie Lyuba Konovalova called, too, and told Rustik's mom, "Let's stick together, Gulya."

Mom called the library where she worked and talked to the director, Alexander Filippovich. "I haven't disappeared," she told him. "I'm doing my work, everything is fine."

Mom worked at the library of the Society for the Blind. Alexander Filippovich had lost his sight long ago, when he was young. He learned Kazakh perfectly after going blind. Now he answered her in Kazakh, too. "No problem, Gulya. I'm with you. Don't worry. I understand what you mean . . . You know, Kazakhs have a very strong tradition of obeying their elders without question, and that's why they followed the elders today."

That day they were more thankful to the blind man than to many who could see. A blind man doesn't see faces, so for him, the race problem doesn't exist.

The crack that had appeared in Oleg's apartment quietly continued to grow. The New Year's holiday everybody had forgotten about was approaching. There was nobody around to make the students stop, many of their families lived far away in uncivilized places, and these students, who didn't belong in Almaty, couldn't fathom why a boy like Rustik couldn't talk to them in their native language, even though the same blood flowed in his veins. How could he explain any of that, anyway? About his grandfather, his mother, Almaty, about the eternal cycle of survival? How to explain that his grandfather had told him, during a time when that infamous national consciousness was awakening, that he ought to at least learn Russian well?

Rustik understood that in those days, the police officers who had helped to suppress the student uprising thought differently. One of them, a Kazakh man they knew, ran into them outside one day, satisfied and mean all at once: "Today the students got their heads bashed in, and I got a medal for dispersing them!"

And how hard was it for his mother to bite her tongue when they made an announcement at work that nobody should speak in Kazakh, even in a private conversation, if other people around wouldn't understand. What do those other people have to do with it? What do they understand, ever? And why should anyone in Almaty have to constantly think about what other people will think? Rustik knew that their Korean neighbor, a police officer who had refused to accept a prize for dispersing the demonstrators, wasn't thinking about other people. What did he care? What was it to him? After all, if Rustik had been older that year, instead of just twelve, he probably wouldn't have been there on the square. The old folks would have already called him. They would have had time. And it would have been a vital, simple truth.

"They made us stand in a cordon," said Mikhail Yuryevich.

Snow was falling outside the window. A woman was out in the courtyard, a chef in a white peaked cap, between the restaurant's storage sheds. She threw out the garbage, then navigated back through piles of snow and disappeared behind a steel door. A truck drove up, noisily, leaving black clumps on the fresh snow.

Twilight, long and tedious, penetrated through the window into the room. *But a man's country comes first. Ireland first, Stevie,* Rustem thought, remembering *A Portrait of the Artist as a Young Man. You can be a poet or a mystic after,* the book said. But what came next? *Ireland is the old sow that eats her farrow.* Enough. Stand up. Close the door. Hand the key to the caretaker on duty and go home.

"We've stayed too long, Rustik. Time to go." Mikhail Yuryevich seemed to crumple even as he rose to his feet. "Tomorrow, it's a new issue, we'll be up late again."

"Goodbye, Mikhail Yuryevich."

"See you tomorrow." He hunched over some more and walked out.

———————

Tonight, the walk was joyful, easy. The frost crunched pleasantly underfoot, and even his new dress shoes, with their soft soles, had a nice spring to them. Rustem pulled his scarf more tightly around him. Mikhail Yuryevich had been made second in command at the paper. Rustem had been fired. His investigation into who was to blame for the deaths of those students on the square, back in December 1986, had seemed premature to somebody up at the top.

That's what the editor had said, rolling his eyes to the ceiling: "It's just too soon, you understand?" But even that couldn't spoil this lovely, sparkling evening. Before him was a new life, and even if he didn't know what kind of life it would be, it would be new, and Rustem had plenty of mental energy to spend on it. New Year's lights played over the street he knew so well, Communist Prospect, and orange squares of light from each window were arranged on the snow.

"Stop. Let's see some ID." In the dark, Rustem hadn't noticed the two police officers and the cop car hiding around the corner. Rustem reached into his inner pocket for his passport.

"You been drinking?"

"No."

"Then where's that smell coming from?"

Rustem dug out everything in his jacket pockets, and winced at the flashlight beam in his face. The sergeant's face was lit up, too. A billy club rested threateningly on his shoulder, and the breath coming from his mouth, twisted into a smirk, reeked of alcohol. That face was stingingly familiar, and the surprise of recognition made Rustem drop the money he had taken out.

"Listen, brother—"

"Get lost!" the sergeant muttered, handing the money to his partner. The cop car wailed over the slippery snow, its doors banging shut once it was in motion.

Yes, it was that same guy, in the malakhai, with the dombyra, whom he had seen running between apartment buildings. Rustem froze.

"Listen, brother! That was you. It was you . . ."

He no longer knew who he was talking to.

The shadows gradually turned violet from all the neon light on the avenue. The snow piled up, solemnly, in no hurry; the pines shed the light from street lamps and shop windows, and it all created the impression of a New Year's fairy tale, fast approaching, the kind in which you feel calm and blissful, right down to the pleasant numbness in your joints.

THE FRENCH BERET

BY ASEL OMAR

Translated from Russian by
Shelley Fairweather-Vega

To the memory of my grandmother
Toidyq Bulatova

lack and slick as if it were paved with mica, lined with a frosty foam of ice and gray-haired burdock, the road led toward town. Crested tits chirped occasionally in the pink, chilled sky, wary of the intimidating cold. Clusters of small red berries hung in a tangle of branches against a background of cottony clouds. In the distance, a steam engine blew its whistle.

Togzhan glided along on her long, skinny legs. Her ankle boots were too big for her. Her red nose she kept tucked into her mother's downy shawl. She carried a bundle containing sheep's cheese, a hunk of boiled beef, and one cube of sugar. Her mother had gotten up at three o'clock in the morning to pack that bundle.

The girl passed the water tower and turned onto Karl Liebknecht Street. There in the outskirts of the old city, she ventured down a quiet, nameless alleyway, on her way to a building with a metal door painted in dark blue oil paint. This was the investigative headquarters of the Joint State Political Directorate, and Togzhan was hurrying there to see her older brother. They had arrested him three months ago on charges of subversive activities.

Inside it was warm from the crowd of women who had brought things to hand over to their loved ones, just like Togzhan. She took her place in line and squatted down against the wall, her fingers pulled inside her coat sleeves to warm them. Finally, a voice from the door to the next room shouted out "Kenjegaliyev!" and Togzhan hurried to her feet. They led her to the visitation room.

She walked in, and as usual, they pointed her to a seat at a heavy wooden table. The door opposite opened, and in came her brother, accompanied by a guard. Togzhan's big brother was strong and powerfully built, two heads taller than the man guarding him, but his face looked exhausted, he was skinnier than before, and there were dark circles under his eyes. The dreary scent of the prison's inner chambers wafted into the room along with him. That scent appeared every time the barred door cracked open. It was the smell of a large number of men living in close quarters, destitute.

Togzhan's brother sat down heavily on the chair facing her. She put her bundle on the table. The guard, a Kazakh man with a severe crew cut, getting on in years, untied the bundle of cloth and sifted through its contents. Then he re-tied it and walked off to the side of the room.

"Togzhan, I wrote a letter. Send it to Moscow for me," her brother said.

He pushed across the table toward her a sheet of lined paper folded in quarters, tightly packed with handwriting, and cast a wary look at the guard. Togzhan stared, worried, not sure if she should take it. The guard had turned and was looking out the window, in a way that seemed somehow purposeful. Togzhan took the sheet of paper.

"How can I send it? I don't know the address."

"They'll tell you at the post office."

"Your visit is over," the guard announced loudly.

As her brother was being led away, he called over his shoulder to her. "Togzhan. You have to send it!"

Togzhan nodded, swallowing back tears.

"I will! I will send it," she said to him, even though she had already been escorted out of the visitation room.

She hurried to the collective farm's central market, wiping her eyes, holding the paper tightly in her hand. The crowd she pushed her way through at the bazaar left on her the smell of mothballed fox fur from someone else's coat. Box-calf boots hanging over a soldier's back poked her in the shoulder. The aroma of lemony soap came from the hardware shop, and the wind carried the cries of the shop workers: "Candy on a stick! Lollipops!"

Tired, panting for breath, she went down the stone flight of stairs by the Triumph movie theater and slumped against a column. The stiff cuff of her wool coat wouldn't let her wipe the tears away properly. She took the French beret off her head. She had knitted it herself, and it had turned out just the way she wanted, stylish as Greta Garbo's, whose giant portrait she just happened to be sitting under now, on these stone steps. She had spun the yarn on her mother's old wooden wheel, and pricked her fingers on all the sharp parts before she learned to spin safely.

Togzhan had just turned twelve. She was a Young Pioneer, in seventh grade in the Russian-language high school. Her shoes and coat had been bought in sizes she could grow into, because lately her arms and legs had been growing so quickly that her clothes got too small before she could wear them out. So there she sat on the steps of her favorite movie theater, skinny and awkward, one leg stretched out before her and the other tucked beneath her, one sharp knee angling off inside her striped woolen jacket. A passionflower, covered in frost, bowed over her foot. Togzhan wiped her face with the beret, straightened her hair, which had been cut with tailor's scissors in an abrupt, square bob, and opened the folded sheet of paper.

Dear Comrade Kalinin, her brother had written. *I was arrested on September 2, 1937.* Togzhan started to cry again. September 2 was her birthday.

> *I was obliged to resign from the mechanical engineering and mathematics department in the Saratov Technical Institute and return to the city of Aktyubinsk, where I went to work for the Leninsky District Executive Committee, because my family, consisting of my elderly parents, Temirbulat and Jamal Kenjegaliyev, and my two school-age sisters, Togzhan and Maylash, were in dire need.*

Togzhan did not recognize her brother's changed handwriting. The letters, made with indelible pencil, were extremely close together, probably to save paper, and looked somehow gnarled and too long. His fingers were hurting, Togzhan thought to herself.

> *The district newspaper, which I supervised, made a technical error. The incorrect version of the Kazakh vowel U was printed, resulting in the word Улы, "Venomous," instead of Ұлы, "Great," in reference to Comrade Stalin. There was no malicious intent*

in the error. Our typesetter, a partially blind, elderly man, simply mixed up the letters. Our newspaper has no proofreader, because we are temporarily understaffed . . . As for my own peasant upbringing, any one of my friends or neighbors could attest to it, as we have lived in Aktyubinsk Province since time immemorial. Our property consists of pots and pans and a single piece of felt we keep in our one-room state apartment at 3 Vodoprovodnaya Street. In light of the information laid out above, I humbly request your assistance, dear Comrade Kalinin, in reconsidering my case. I am not guilty. Komsomolets Islam Kenjegaliyev.

The post office door banged shut on its tight springs. "How many times do I have to tell you people? Don't slam the door!" shouted the woman behind the counter. Togzhan bought an envelope from her, walked over to an old table stained with ink blots and scribblings, and dipped a rusty fountain pen in some ink. She thought for a moment, then wrote out very carefully: "Moscow. Comrade Mikhail Ivanovich Kalinin" and her own detailed return address. She blew on the envelope to dry the ink, slipped the letter into a mailbox, and hurried away to school.

One month passed. Togzhan was in school when her sister Maylash knocked on the door to her classroom and asked the teacher if she could see her for a minute. It was an emergency.

They stood together in the hallway. "Toshka, why are you just standing there so stiff? Dance with me! They let out Islam!" Maylash shouted. "He's not guilty!" She started spinning around in a crouch and kicking her legs like a Russian dancer, throwing her hands in the air, laughing with her mouth wide open. Togzhan got over her initial shock and joined in, her face twisted awkwardly but passionately with joy, hands high over her head.

The cold December sun hit the gray walls of the school in long stripes. The wooden floor creaked and groaned, echoing the girls' stomping feet, and jackdaws cawed past the streaks of frost on the window. They ran home in a craze, hats knocked back off their heads, singing and laughing.

"Why did they let him go?" Togzhan asked on the way.

"Mama said a letter came from Moscow. But Toshka, don't get close to him if he hasn't had his bath yet."

"Why not?" Togzhan stopped.

"He's lousy!" Maylash shouted in glee. "We ran to hug him, and he said, Stay away from me, I'm lousy! And Mama cut a photo of Comrade Kalinin out of the paper and put it on the windowsill, and she's already prayed over it three times."

"Oh, Musya, stop it, you silly thing!" Togzhan exclaimed and hugged her sister to her. Arms around each other's shoulders, they ran the rest of the way home.

Islam was sitting at the kitchen table, against the wall. He wore a neatly ironed white shirt, and he looked freshly washed, but also even thinner and more haggard than the last time Togzhan had seen him. Her father sat across from him, an open bottle of vodka between them on the table. Mama was fussing around a boiling pot on the kerosene stove, and onions and peeled potatoes gleamed on the wooden counter.

Togzhan froze at the kitchen door, not quite willing to approach her brother.

"Come on over here, Togzhan!" he said, forcing himself to smile through his weakness.

Togzhan gave her mother a questioning look. "What's wrong, aren't you glad to see him?" Mama asked.

Togzhan ran then, fast as she could, and threw her long, skinny arms around Islam. Tiny coals still burned, with a pale pink fire, in the heavy iron on the windowsill. "Thank you, my darling. Thank you!" Islam whispered.

———————

A black car, polished to a shine, drove slowly down Karl Liebknecht Street to an unnamed alley and stopped at the gates of the pretrial detention center. The guard, a young police conscript, stuck his head out the window of the checkpoint booth. The driver opened a door, and a tall young woman in a long coat, an Astrakhan muff on her arm, stepped out. She looked around, lifting her black veil with her delicate fingers, as if examining someone closely.

The guard stared hard. He had never seen this woman before. A man getting on in years, a major with a severe gray crew cut, was standing at his office window on the second floor, looking down at the courtyard. Some time ago, he had worked there as a prison guard. Something made him turn from the window, walk downstairs, and stand just before the front door. In this lithe young woman, ringlets streaming out from under her black hat and then tucked neatly into a mesh hairnet, he recognized the gangly girl who used to come here with packages, who often used to stand outside the gates, looking through the barred windows. That hat of hers, angled a little to one side atop her magnificent hairdo, reminded him just for a second of a black beret on a child's round head. One time he had felt sorry for that girl, and so he had pretended not to notice when the prisoner she had come to visit slipped her a letter while they met. Yes, he recognized her. It was the same girl. Only he couldn't remember her name.

Her eyes met his, her lashes flashed as if she were glad to see him, and she walked closer. "Do you remember my brother, Islam Kenjegaliyev?"

"No," he said.

"Do you remember me?" she asked, anticipation in her voice.

"No."

"Here. This is for you," she said, and without another word, she held out a small box, perched on the palm of her hand.

"No, I couldn't."

"What's your name?"

"Sadvakas Absattarov."

"Thank you," she said, and she put the box down on a railing.

"How is your brother?" asked the old man.

"He's fine, praise God. He has six children." And she hurried away, waving goodbye.

The old man opened the box. Inside, there was a gold wristwatch with a malachite face.

The black car disappeared around the corner. The major watched it go and went back upstairs to his office.

18+

BY AYA ÖMIRTAI

Translated from Kazakh by
Zaure Batayeva

You've probably had moments like this, when you just wanted to sit down and talk, like adults. You certainly have. A natural thing for human beings. Without discriminating and without defining who is a man and who is a woman. You have two arms, two legs, just like anyone else, and there can be no doubt that you are a human being. How many times have you found yourself in such a situation? No need to hide, it must have happened at least once.

Hot tea has just been served and you are about to share your thoughts about today's society, the future of the nation, and other important issues that have long preoccupied you. Then, suddenly, something interesting: The man sitting in front of you starts awkwardly moving his fat body. With no prelude and with the agility that he inherited from our nomadic forefathers, he unbuckles his belt and frees his belly. The fat on his neck is preventing him from looking down, so his fingers run blindly around until he manages to unbuckle his belt from the hole, pierced next to the third, no, the fourth hole. The dirty, greasy waistband of his underpants shows: he hasn't changed them for many days, he's on a business trip. Nothing to be ashamed of, an important statesman can be forgiven for anything! Slovenliness makes him cuter.

Here we are. See it. Enjoy it. Didn't you want this? Didn't you come to this meeting because you needed this? Don't pretend, we know all about you. Your behavior and so on. Who needs your pretenses?

What's your name? What did you say it was, dear? No need to tell me, I won't remember it anyway. Lately I've had some issues with my memory, they say that eating big amounts of salmon helps. It's better that I name you myself. My beloved birthplace is Bozqaragan. Do you know it? Uuui, such juicy grass and so much honey water! Fertile land, wade in it until evening! How about we call you Bozqaragan, to honor my birthplace, eh?! Don't be so pale, stop hiding your arms in your sleeves, take them out. Look at your peers! They promptly found a common tongue with the right people and they untied the flies of the right people, without getting themselves into knots, and by now, they're holding fatty bones to chew on and will never let them go. Do you know Aqbastau? She must be your age. Recently we had a good time together at the sauna. She's working under my personal supervision now. She has sent her younger brother to university. What else does she need? A smooth little tongue, she's fantastic! And look at yourself, you've accomplished nothing!

He stops just in time, his nostrils flaring, about to explode. Bravo! Bug-eyed bull! Long live your short legs, curved like the two sides of a qobuz!

No patch of land is left on which you have not stepped in search of work. Show me, what's on that shiny paper, your CV? Give it to me, he says, and throws it on the table without looking. Your perfume, what a delight! I bet your own smell is even more miraculous, he continues, and suddenly darts, stretching his neck like a goose chick—eyes shut, mustache quivering. You see right away what he's targeting: your neck. You cannot slap bald men like him, their self-esteem will be injured, their revenge will be hard. Then, forget about asking for a job, you won't even be allowed to open his door.

Wow! When you run like that, you look like an ancient batyr who hooks everyone he comes across on his white-pointed spear, you say, dodging to the right just in time. Like a predator whose prey was taken from his mouth, his eyes sparkle with anger. His wrinkled face says, what's this bullshit? When I run how? he says, quickly regaining his composure. Like this, you run like this: digidik, digidik, you mumble some nonsense. You already know that you shouldn't stay any longer. You've triumphed over his defeated organ, but now you've been plunged into a pool of guilt.

In short, he says, pausing for a few seconds, if you want a job, this is the situation. You have my phone number, call me anytime, he says.

You're so lucky you're looking for a job in the springtime! It is not so hot that it will boil your brain, not so cold that it will freeze your intestines. This must be God's beneficent eye, otherwise in which corner of the city would you be shivering?

You sit down on a bench at the very end of a long boulevard and take out a lemon. You rub it against your sleeve and you begin to eat it, spitting out the skin and the seeds. It burns your tongue. You bite into it again.

Little sister! You look up: a complete stranger with a neck of long hair is standing in front of you, pulling up his trousers.

In a flowery spring,
In the city of dreams,
The beauty of beauties,
Let me offer you a drink!

This he declares happily. He's so drunk, he can hardly stand on his feet. You recognize the type immediately: another would-be poet, penniless, poor as dirt. Yet he has that extra piece of meat between his legs, and that is his main quality. It is enough to make him the master of the universe.

You couldn't handle the others, but this type you can certainly handle. You look around: no one seems to be in the vicinity, except for some children playing nearby. You grab him by the back of his neck. The poet lets his tongue loose: Bitch! You don't respect men, witches like you should be tortured, flies should nest in their eyes!

Here, take that! Here, take that, you bastard bard! You kick his ass hard, you kick and kick.

POET

BY MADINA OMAROVA

Translated from Kazakh by
Zaure Batayeva

Autumn had come quickly to Almaty. The summer heat had disappeared in one day, and a cool wind from the mountains had enwrapped the city. The city became unhappy.

I noticed the man first. We were walking towards each other. Suddenly his eyes fell on me. He stared and then smiled. He started walking faster. I also smiled and took his hand when he approached. He hugged me, squeezed me, and kissed me. He had aged. I'm not saying that he had become an old man, but he looked older. He said we should go to a nearby café and have a meal. I had nothing else to do, so I followed him. He took tea for himself. I asked for laghman noodles and fifty grams of cognac. And for bread. "And some bread, of course," I shouted to the waiter.

"I'm exhausted," he said. "Lonely."

"Where's your wife?"

"The wife's there, but I've got nobody to talk to."

"Hmm . . ."

"When we were working together, did I ever hit on you?"

"No, never."

"That's strange."

"You hit on every girl around, but not me, not a single time."

"Interesting."

"Perhaps I'm not your type."

"No, you are, you are."

I wanted to smoke. "If I remember right, you don't smoke, do you?"

"I don't. I go to the Union every day. Just wander around and go back home. Nobody's there."

"Why not?"

"All my friends are dead. They're in another world."

"I see."

"How about we make love?"

"I don't know, nothing interesting will come of that."

"You've never slept with me. If you do, you'll never leave me."

"Maybe."

"More cognac?"

"No, I need to go back to work."

"I'm exhausted," he said again. "This world has become meaningless. I'm tired. Everything is in vain." He squeezed my hand. Autumn falls quickly in Almaty.

ONCE UPON AN AUTUMN EVENING

BY MADINA OMAROVA

Translated from Kazakh by
Zaure Batayeva

t was going to rain. An old injury, where my arm had broken once, started aching. An unpleasant feeling. So unpleasant that it nauseated me. I needed some fresh air. Outside, my neighbors Nazira and Mariash were sitting on the bench with their babies. I sat down next to them.

"You don't mind if I smoke?"

"Go ahead," said Mariash. "We live in car exhaust anyway."

I lit up a cigarette and blew it out in the other direction. There were many children in the yard. If you stayed long enough, you could witness funny, hilarious, sometimes even shocking things.

"Has Zhanna come today?"

"I haven't seen her yet," replied Mariash. "Lately she has really scared me. When I see her coming, I shiver and my hands get cold."

"Don't be silly. She's a five-year-old child," I said.

"All right girls, we're going home," said Nazira, getting up.

"Bye," I murmured. Nazira did not like me. She was jealous of her husband. Tall and handsome, a sultan among men, how did he fall into the trap of this anorexic?

"She's tiny, that's true. Yesterday she took Askhat into the bushes. I got worried and followed them. Guess what I saw! They were lying down, hugging. I didn't know what to do."

"Lying down?"

"Yes, on the ground. Hugging. Askhat's a baby. It was Zhanna who was on top. Sniffing him."

"What did you do?"

"I said they'd catch cold, and I made them get up."

"What are we going to do now?"

"I need to talk to her grandparents, I suppose."

"Hasn't she got any parents?"

"She's got a mother, but it's her grandparents who are looking after her."

"Shouldn't we walk a little?" I asked Mariash.

"No, I'm looking after Askhat."

Askhat was sitting in the sandbox and building a house. Plump, pouting his lips, talking to himself. Carefree. I got up. It was going to rain. I walked around the playground and went out to the street. Everywhere there are summer cafés. Full of people. And I live in a studio all by myself. How scary to be lonely in a city with more than a million people. No, a city is not a cozy place.

When I came back, the yard was empty. I hurried home. In the entrance hall, the smell of cat pee choked me. Heading towards the stairs, I noticed a dark silhouette. I flinched.

"Is that you, Zhanna?" I don't know why I said so.

"Yes, it's me."

"Why are you here? Your grandmother must be looking for you." I was frightened. I had seen Zhanna from a distance a few times but had never spoken to her. What would you talk about with a five-year-old?

"No, she isn't. She's visiting someone."

"Why don't you go home?"

"I lost my keys. Can I wait at your place?"

"If you want. Come on!" These words slipped out of my mouth. I was like a puppet tied to ropes.

Zhanna followed me like a ghost, making no sound.

"Did you get wet? It's raining."

"No."

"I did. We'll have tea."

I started boiling water while drying my hair. Zhanna sat down in the armchair in the corner.

I knelt in front of her. Her eyes quickly turned away. I caressed her hair and touched her thick braid. Compared to the braid, her body was too slim. So slim, that I wondered how she could not be dead. "Tell me the truth. What are you doing?" Blood ran to her pale face. She would start crying soon. Let her cry.

"I'm in love with Askhat."

"But my dear, he is a five-year-old baby. And you? How old are you?"

"Seven." Her voice hardly made a sound.

"You two are too small." I heard water boiling and stood up. "Let's have tea. I will change my clothes first." I took dry clothes from the wardrobe and felt that she was following my every movement.

"Your grandparents must be looking for you."

"They're visiting friends."

Under the kitchen light, her face was even paler. I was about to offer her wine but stopped myself. "Why aren't you eating any candy?"

"I'm not allowed."

"Then take some bread and jam."

She shook her head. "I wrote a letter to Askhat."

"I know. His mother told me."

"Are you friends?"

"Not really, we just chat sometimes."

"What does she say about me?"

"I don't know. She says that you two are too small, and it would be better if you wait until you grow up."

She sighed.

"Is there a phone at home? It is almost ten. Your grandparents must be looking for you."

"Yes, I've got to go," she said.

"Let me take you home."

"I'll go myself."

I did not give up. We went outside. She said that she lived on the other side of the road. Her thin, long fingers held my hand firmly. Tiny being. I squeezed her hand. She did not react.

"Which entrance?"

She pointed to the door in the middle of the building. "I'll go alone."

"Let me take you to the door."

"Please don't, auntie."

There was so much pleading in her voice that I let go of her hand. She snuck into the dark block of flats. I never saw her again. Later I found out that no girl by the name of Zhanna had ever lived in that building. Where does she live now? Does she still love Askhat? Why did she come, why did she leave? Little ghost girl, befriending loneliness.

EXCERPT FROM
SCHOOL

BY ZAURE BATAYEVA

Translated from Kazakh by
Zaure Batayeva

I.

It was one of those cold years, when winter comes in October. The school's heating had been cut. I heard a rumor that the building had been acquired from the State in payment for some old debt that our institution had not been willing to settle, and the former superintendent of the building was unhappy about its privatization and had sued the new owner, our boss, the school's President. So, that winter, staff and students had to keep their winter coats on everywhere they went, even inside the classrooms. One afternoon, I was called to the President's office again. I found the President sitting in his private suite behind the main office. He had called me to say that a TV channel was going to film a report about the school.

"I'm giving this task to you."

"Me? Why not Akhmet?"

"Akhmet is a demagogue of the old Soviet school. That means you are the one who should be interviewed. Prepare carefully." The President looked at me. I was wrapped in my old coat, my nose red from the cold and my hair unwashed and uncombed. Working at the school that winter had made me slovenly.

"I'll instruct Nadya to give you some money so that you can take care of your hair."

I jumped at the opportunity. "I don't need money for a beauty salon, sir. I need money for food."

The President did not like my comment, but he replied without anger. "Salaries will be paid late this afternoon."

Did he say late afternoon? At 5 p.m., I stood at the accountant's office. The window was open, but nobody was waiting in line. People must have left, tired of waiting. Or did nobody know about it? Nadya appeared and put a pay stub in front of me. I saw the amount: less than 700 tenge.

"Nadya, this isn't right! My salary should be more than this."

"More objections from you? Everything is correct. Only 30% of the salary is to be paid."

"Why?"

"Ask the boss."

II.

A few days later, Alya, a mathematics teacher, walked into my office, crying. Through her sobs I could gather that a sixth-grade student, the son of an athlete, had called her an idiot in class. "If he doesn't apologize, I won't go back to that classroom. How am I to face the children?" The next day, the child's mother came, wearing a short leather coat and expensive leather shoes with high heels that made her look even taller. "What kind of teacher doesn't know a child's last name? He was absolutely right to call her an idiot!"

"I'm sorry, but our teachers have to teach several grades in one day. It's possible that they sometimes forget a surname."

"My child's last name is not the kind of name you should forget! My husband is the athlete who made Kazakhstan known to the world."

"You know, sports fans may know their favorite athletes, but people with no interest in sports may not know your husband's name. And the teacher apologized for mispronouncing his name. She's your child's teacher. You should not be defending your son against her."

The athlete's wife stood up and left, banging the door. The next morning, the athlete himself, big and tall, came into my office. "Dearest Shynar, if you don't know my name, you should look it up in the encyclopedia. It's not just my name, you know—it's the pride of the nation! My son has won many competitions, too. Why wouldn't his teacher pronounce his name correctly?"

"It's wonderful that the child has won so many competitions, but the rules of the school are the same for all students. He insulted someone older than him, and he must apologize."

"You're an ill-mannered peasant. Who are you to tell me what to do? You don't know your place."

"I may not know my place, but I know my job. It is my duty to defend hard-working teachers from people like you."

The athlete raced out of the office. Half an hour later, the university rector's secretary called me to her office. When I entered, the athlete was there, drinking coffee. Balzhan pointed to the chair on the other side of the table.

"Take a seat. Mr. Baimurat told me everything. Why do you treat a person defending our nation's honor with such disrespect, Shynar? Apologize, my dear."

"Why should I apologize, but not the child who cursed a professional with a red diploma for no reason?"

The athlete looked at the rector and shook his head. So Balzhan took the apology on herself. "Mr. Baimurat, I'm sorry. You know as well as I do that ignorant people exist."

The champion echoed her. "Oh, yes, it's hard to express in words how ignorant these third-rate people can be."

I could not restrain myself. "Mr. Champion, if you need publicity so badly, I can send out a press release about your behavior to all the newspapers of the country."

The champion stretched out his hand towards me. I quickly grabbed a little sculpture standing on the rector's table. The champion jumped out of this seat. I jumped up as well, shouting that I could defend myself. Only then did I notice that I was half his height.

The next day I would be told that the athlete had transferred his son to another exclusive school. The parents were too proud to pick up their son's documents and sent the rector to do it for them.

III.

I urgently needed some literature on how to administer a school, so I went to the school's library, where I ended up staring at a newly arrived collection of Everyman's Library Classics instead.

"Asylgul, didn't the British Embassy donate this same collection last year? What are you going to do with this one?"

"Nothing's too much. I'll display these books as well."

"Can you donate the Virginia Woolf to me? Who else will read it here?"

"How dare you? These books were a present for our students."

"You see, some readers like owning books. They're called possessive readers." My justification did not impress Asylgul.

"By the way, congratulations on your new position," Asylgul said, smiling.

"Have you already heard about it?"

"Of course, everyone's talking about it. Now you have to change your image. You can no longer dress like a hippie. You need to present yourself as a businesswoman." Asylgul and I were the same age, but she always spoke to me as if I were much younger. On the way out, I snuck a Jane Austen novel from the pile.

IV.

A new issue had arisen. The President had ordered us to nominate one student for the national Golden Sign award, but none of our students met the requirements. The teachers suggested that we nominate Ainur, who had participated in several Olympiad competitions in different subjects. She was the niece of a prominent politician. Ainur's mother came to a teacher meeting. From what the mother said, I understood that for Ainur's family, the Golden Sign award was as important as finding a wealthy husband. I told her we could nominate her. "All right. Our best teachers will prepare Ainur. You also need to hire tutors, so she will have double the preparation."

Shortly before the national examinations, we conducted a test. Ainur had excellent results in mathematics and English, but her essay in Russian was weak. Ainur's teachers said that it would be impossible to improve Ainur's Russian in two weeks' time. Some of the experienced teachers confided to me that Ainur's teachers would have to write the essay for her in advance. During the examination, we put Ainur in a separate room. Two teachers of Russian were there to help her. Afterwards, the teachers locked themselves in a room, as if they were a crack team from a top-secret agency. Later in the evening, Talgat, a new colleague who was still in his trial month, took Ainur's examination papers to the City Department of Education, where a special committee would evaluate the tests submitted for the Golden Sign award.

I arrived home very late that day. I was exhausted. That night my cell phone woke me up from my deep sleep. It was after midnight. A female voice spoke hastily.

"Shynar, you need to come to the City Department of Education right now. If you're not here in half an hour, you'll be jeopardizing the school's reputation."

"What is this regarding?"

But she had already hung up. Having no choice, I called a taxi. When I arrived, several women were standing on the huge steps at the entrance. "Are you Shynar?" I nodded, and we went silently inside. The lights in the corridors were turned off. We entered a room where three or four women were sitting. I recognized a former university professor of mine.

"Gulzada Ahmediyarovna! How are you?"

I could tell my former teacher felt uneasy. She was known as one of the strictest professors, someone who made her students shiver. She was considered a Dostoyevsky expert. Now it became clear that she was also the head of the Golden Sign committee.

"Shynarochka, I didn't even know it was you. Why didn't you handle this better?"

"What is it that I didn't handle?"

She looked at me and sighed. None of the women said anything. The woman who had brought me in gestured that I should follow her. Our silent march down the dark corridor continued. We went up one more floor, and she opened the door of a room that was an entrance to yet another room. On the door, upholstered with black leather, I saw a plaque: Sabira Nurgaliyeva, Head of the City Department of Education. A person so unapproachable that I was astounded that I would get to see her, here, in the middle of the night. My guide opened the door.

I entered and offered a greeting. "Good evening."

The woman was writing and did not lift her head. I remained at the entrance. I felt like a child who had misbehaved. A few minutes later, she spoke with a firm voice.

"Take a seat."

I did.

At first, I felt intimidated. I had heard rumors that she was an old spinster with bad manners. But to me, that night, her serious face looked more like that of a petty Soviet bureaucrat who took herself much too seriously, someone out of Bulgakov, maybe. It almost made me laugh. Why do Kazakh bosses always frown?

"Do you realize you've jeopardized Ainur's future? You're so irresponsible."

"Me? Ainur's future? What did I do?"

"This is not the place for sarcasm."

"I'm not being sarcastic. I just don't understand."

The head of the City Department of Education returned to her writing. I returned to the previous room.

"Gulzada Ahmediyarovna, was Ainur's essay so bad? I had it checked by three excellent teachers."

"And why didn't you take care of the rest?"

"What else was I supposed to do?"

"Are you pretending to be a fool? They say you did not provide financing."

Damn! They needed bribes! Why had nobody told me?

"Is it too late?"

"No idea. Go and find out!"

I went outside and called my boss. He did not answer. I called his home number, and his wife answered. I explained why I was calling. "I'll find him. Just wait there." Some time passed, while I stood alone in the dark yard of the building. Finally, he called. "Go home. I will take care of it myself." In the end, Ainur did not receive a Golden Sign. Only a silver one.

V.

It was Friday, and a staff meeting with the President was scheduled for 6 p.m. that evening, but an hour later the President had still not shown up. I left the building and ran to the bus stop. The bus was crowded. My feet hardly touched the floor. I had ten more stops. Then I heard my phone ring. On the screen of the new phone I had received, I saw I had six missed calls from the President's secretary. I returned her call. The secretary demanded that I come back to the school immediately. I told her I had an appointment and could not return. The phone rang again. It was the President himself. I switched off the phone.

VI.

On Monday morning I did not go to my office. Instead, I went directly to the President's office. The secretary made a face as if to say "it's your own fault" and announced my arrival. The President was sitting at the big desk by himself. He did not ask me to take a seat.

"Have you declared war?"

"No. I waited for an hour."

"If necessary, you wait three or four hours! A career requires some sacrifice. Why did you turn off your phone?"

"I've got a life outside this job."

"Return your phone. That will be your punishment."

I put the phone on the table and slid it towards him. "I would like to resign. I don't need this career. I need money. I have to eat and take care of my parents."

My reply made him furious. "A sacred place will not be empty. Go."

So I went to the accountant's office. "Nadya, I've just resigned. I still haven't received the other half of this year's salary. When do you think I can receive my money?"

"Shynarochka, I was told not to give you any money."

"Why? I wasn't fired—I resigned myself!"

"All questions must be directed to the boss. I've got nothing to do with this."

I could see that Nadya was shocked. She knew better than anyone what it meant. I had worked for free for more than half a year. The accountant's office was next to the boss's office. All I had to do was turn and go back inside. I tried not to think about my salary anymore. I went outside. The day was warm and bright. I felt free. It was a great feeling.

EXCERPT FROM *THE* *ANTHROPOLOGISTS*

BY ZAURE BATAYEVA

Translated from Kazakh by
Zaure Batayeva

I.

Two Americans sitting in a corner of the café were speaking too loudly. Renée looked at them for a while, blinking her big eyes. "Americans are so egotistical. How embarrassing!" She went on. "I'm researching Kazakh folk songs and also the Kazakh language. I need a translator who can assist me with materials and interviews. I need someone who can go to concerts with me. From my grant money, I can pay you three hundred dollars."

Three hundred dollars, free concerts, a chance to practice my English—what else did I need? I agreed immediately. The next day we met at the Academy of Science at 9 o'clock sharp. As a graduate student, I used to go to the library there all the time, but only now did I really notice the grand marble steps leading up to the building. "Do you see how great this building is? This is how the Soviet Union built the foundation of our sciences today," I said enthusiastically. Renée stopped for a moment, smiled at me, and squinted, her head tilted to one side. What was that about? I quickly walked up the steps.

We stayed silent until we reached the end of a long corridor. The girl at the desk was our age, but she frowned, indicating she had a problem with our visit.

"Does she have a permit?"

"Yes, she does."

"Give me your identity cards. Do you think she cares about our folk songs? She must be a spy. She stands there like an ostrich."

I checked Renée's reaction. She did not seem to understand. She really looked like an ostrich, turning her long neck to look away from us.

"Why do you say such things? She knows Russian very well."

"So what?"

"Why would a spy look at Kazakh folk songs in an archive? What's wrong with you? You should be happy that Americans want to learn our language."

"Why should I be happy about it? And what does it have to do with you?"

At last she returned our identity cards. We took out several volumes of folk songs published between the 1940s and 1970s. We started copying down the themes and places of performance. I liked working like this. So many songs I knew were passing before my eyes. Exciting. At some point, I noticed that Renée, eyes wet and blinking, was trying to catch my attention.

"I'm very tired. And hungry. Can we go?"

"But we just arrived! Shouldn't we finish this?"

Renée started to cry.

"What's wrong?"

"That woman at the desk was so mean to me."

"Don't cry. She didn't mean to hurt you. She seems to be an unhappy person."

Oibai, who would have thought that my new friend was so sensitive? I quickly gathered the papers into folders.

By the time we were outside, Renée had cheered up.

"Let's go the Uzbek restaurant. We can have laghman."

"It's expensive. I don't want to go there."

"It will be my treat."

I followed her. We never went back to the archive together.

II.

The next day Renée invited me to a party.

"Who are they? Anthropologists like you?"

"Some are journalists. Will you go with me? Let's go!"

"If you're inviting me, why not? Are there any single men?"

"Plenty!"

When we arrived at the party, the two-room apartment was full of people, all speaking English. A group of people were standing on the balcony. How did they all fit in here? People were moving around. The music was loud, everyone was shouting. Renée met some acquaintances and disappeared. I went to the living room, where I saw my other American friend, Peggy. Peggy waved me towards her.

"When did you come back to Almaty?"

"Um, just yesterday . . . What are you doing here?"

"I came with Renée."

"Oh, pretty Renée? She has already enchanted everybody."

"You girls compete like two sister wives."

"We like to gossip. I'm just kidding. Don't tell her!"

"I won't. Why didn't you tell me that you were coming back so soon?"

Peggy pretended that she hadn't heard me and introduced me to the man sitting next to her.

"This is Michael. He's just arrived. Michael is a historian."

Michael waved to me and said "Hi!" in English. Peggy stood up and walked away.

"Are you going to study Kazakh history? Even Kazakhs don't know their own history."

"I'm studying the methodology of historical research."

"That sounds intriguing. Do you need a translator?"

"I have a Kazakh friend who helps me with Kazakh."

"You have just arrived and already found a friend?"

"I have known him for a long time. He studied in America. I'm also staying with him. He works at a bank."

"If he studied in America, lets you stay in his apartment, and works at a bank, then he must be a real shala Kazakh."

Michael shook his head. "You should be careful talking like that. The girls here are calling you a bossy nationalist."

"The anthropologist girls? Yes, they are like second-year medical students. They diagnose everybody with nationalism."

"Yeah, well, they've probably read too much Benedict Anderson."

"Who is Benedict Anderson?"

Michael laughed. "You're better off not knowing."

At midnight the music was still playing. I sat in the corner with a bottle of beer that Michael had handed me a long time ago. I started regretting that I hadn't eaten dinner at home. Peggy and Renée occasionally waved at me from a distance. The Russians and Kazakhs at this party dressed and behaved just like the Americans. I could see that all the people here were leading lives that were different from mine. Images of a shabby village flashed through my mind. For a moment, it seemed to me that rural Kazakhs were awaiting the same fate as American Indians. My heart ached at this sudden thought, and tears filled my eyes. A slim man with very blue eyes sat down next to me.

"Why are you so sad?"

He had a slightly different Russian accent, and I understood that he was from Europe.

"No reason. Just tired. What are you doing in Kazakhstan?"

"I'm an anthropologist. My name's Eyvind. I've been doing archaeological digs in Kazakhstan for seven years."

"So you are a real anthropologist, the old-fashioned kind!"

The man did not seem to understand my excitement.

"Seven years is a long time. Are you going home soon?"

"I don't want to go back."

"Why?"

"I don't know. The country where I come from is strange. The people there think only about material things."

"Isn't that an indication of a good life? We Kazakhs only think about our daily bread. There is no room to think about anything else."

"That is exactly what I mean."

I saw Peggy and Renée standing on the balcony in the middle of a group of Americans. They were all speaking loudly, shouting even. After a while I noticed that people were leaving. Then I saw the archaeologist pick up the empty bottles and put them into a bucket.

"Eyvind, why are you cleaning up? Do you live in this apartment?"

"No. Who else is going to do it? We need to gather the bottles separately. Otherwise someone will put them in the trash."

"But we don't allow our guests to clean the house."

Eyvind continued his work. "Separating garbage is important." He stopped for a moment, took out a card from his back pocket, and handed it to me. It was his contact information.

Michael approached us.

"Michael, do you have any idea why Eyvind is cleaning the house?"

"That is exactly what I asked too. Isn't it weird?"

"You are all weird. What kind of party is this? Nothing but beer! No food, nothing!"

III.

Renée had been invited to an academic conference and asked me to come along.

"What is it about?"

"History."

"You're not a historian. They just need foreigners to dress up their fake conference."

"There you go again! The person who invited me is a well-connected academic. I need to interview lots of people for my dissertation, so I need to have a good relationship with her. Her father is a famous professor."

After the conference, the organizers set a big table, full of food. They sat us in the middle of the table, just opposite two young men, Russian-speaking Kazakhs working in the university's administration.

"Devushka, are you an American?"

"Yes."

"Wow! *An American Tragedy*! Have you read Dreiser?"

"No, who's Dreiser?"

"An American writer."

"What are you doing in Almaty? Spying?"

Both men laughed. Renée started blinking and replied firmly in Kazakh.

"I'm not a spy. I'm learning Kazakh here. What about you guys? Do you speak any Kazakh?"

The men froze. Now it was our turn to laugh.

IV.

We were told that the dean of the music college had agreed to be interviewed by Renée. The next day, we stood outside his door at the appointed time. A lady in her sixties opened the door. The professor was not home. The professor's wife, Baqytjan-apa, was a retired theater actress. Her apartment was clean, and the furniture was dark, expensive, and overwhelming. A big table in the living room was already set for us. Wrapped in her long silk robe, she lifted a porcelain teapot with hands covered in gem stones and poured tea with such elegance that no sound of liquid escaped. Soon we learned that her son had a good position in a foreign company and that her son-in-law was a big fish in the local government. She continued boasting about her children and her in-laws, using a language that mixed Russian and Kazakh and that Renée sometimes failed to understand.

"My daughter is so diplomatic."

"Really? In which country?"

I was too lazy to correct Renée's lack of understanding. Why on earth should I have to translate other people's bragging? I had made a rule for myself, that this wouldn't be part of my job. Suddenly Baqytjan-apa yelled at me.

"Hey, why are you acting so important? Translate!"

"She understands Russian very well. You can continue in Russian."

"A real Kazakh . . . she is sitting there as if she is invited."

"I apologize, Baqytjan-apa! Interpreting wears me out quickly, and I was saving my energy for the interview."

Renée, blinking again, turned to me.

"What's going on?"

"Nothing. She is upset with me."

Baqytjan-apa continued, recounting the story of her daughter's lost diamond earring. Meanwhile, I was enjoying the tasty bread and horse sausage on the table. Renée nodded her head occasionally, but I saw that she was mostly occupied with the horse sausage as well. Poor Renée, she probably did not understand Kazakhs' admiration for expensive jewelry. I had never seen any of the Americans wear gold. Suddenly, Baqytjan-apa turned the focus of the conversation to me.

"Why are you still not married?"

"I don't know. Earlier there was nobody I could marry, and now I'm too busy."

228

"No time? You must be imitating *them*. Do you think that it suits you? Not a bit. If nobody marries you, just have a baby for yourself. A Kazakh woman's duty is to be a mother and stay at home."

Was she hinting that I was hopelessly old? I was barely thirty. I was offended, but I reminded myself that I was her guest.

"I will get married at the right time. Do you think I'm just out having fun? I'm working. This is my work. Who makes a child for herself? That would be cruel."

The professor called. He told us to come to his office. Confused as to why we had not gone there at once, we thanked the professor's wife for the tea and went to the office. We were received by a man in his sixties, his white hair carefully combed back. Renée spoke Russian as much as she could. The professor called his secretary and instructed her to bring tea. The secretary brought a big tray with all kinds of delicacies and set the table. The professor walked slowly towards the armchair next to the tea table, sat down, and turned to me.

"So, girls! What is this lady's profession?"

"Anthropologist."

"An anthropologist who studies skulls?"

"In America, anthropology is understood differently. American anthropologists study the interaction between human beings and their environment."

"My grandson studied in America. He wants to go back. Their propaganda is powerful!"

"He may have liked it there."

"Why should he? Kazakhstan is paradise on earth. Everyone is coming here. Tell this girl that Kazakhstan is five times the size of France."

"She has heard that before."

"Hmm. Ask her if she has read Dreiser's *American Tragedy*."

"No, she hasn't."

"How do you know? Ask her!"

"Have you read Dreiser's *An American Tragedy*?"

Renée's eyes had started blinking as soon as she heard Dreiser's name.

"Why do they keep asking me about this Dreiser? Is he someone I should know?"

The old man had already reached his conclusion.

"So it's true that Americans don't read books. I have a personal library at home. All four walls are full of books. I've read them all."

"You love books!"

"Oibai, this thing speaks Kazakh!"

Renée adjusted her glasses with her index finger. "A little!"

"Good girl! Will you have a glass of cognac with me?"

"No, thanks, I don't drink cognac."

"I have prepared a concert for you."

The professor led us to a conference hall with a small stage, where a group of sad-faced musicians was sitting, hugging their folk instruments. They all spoke at once.

"Working hours are over. We have children, families! Let us go home!"

"Hey, stop talking! Play *Kosh Keruen*."

After the orchestra had played the piece, the professor introduced each instrument. "This is a sazsyrnay. No other people in the world have an instrument like this." Thus the lecture went on. The professor took a dombyra and showed off his musical talent. Renée looked disappointed. She surely had not expected her request for an interview to be turned into a concert in her honor. When the professor had left, she invited all the musicians to dinner. The women declined, saying that they had to rush home. The men liked the idea very much.

A group of men carrying their instruments led us to a small restaurant nearby. The restaurant was still empty, and the waiters put together two tables that took up almost one quarter of the room. I could see that the American among us had put them under a spell. Was it the Soviet habit of showing off in front of foreigners, or was there a secret hope for money to be gained? As soon as the refreshments were served, the singers started performing. Some of them were rising stars who had already appeared in big national concerts and on TV shows. Now it was the turn of a young man sitting quietly at the end of the table. His strong fingers slid along the long neck of the dombyra, and his deep voice began a famous song. Shiny black hair, high forehead, almond eyes, straight nose, and dark skin, his big body motionless, he reminded me of the Indian chieftain Chingachgook, as played by the East German actor Gojko Mitić. I could not help but whisper: "He looks just like an Indian chief!" The handsome man smiled. Afterwards, Renée and the men started competing in aytis, inventing witty rhymes one after another. Renée kept up with them. She improvised with the same speed as the men.

We were enjoying ourselves so much that we did not notice the people coming in. Three Kazakh men sat down at the next table. At some point, one of them shouted in Russian: "Hey, enough with this mambet bazaar!" The singers slowed down and asked each other what had been said. The offence was too big to let go. One of the singers stood up and said, "Who are you to forbid us to sing sacred Kazakh songs here?"

That was it. Within seconds, the restaurant turned into a battle-field. It was too late to run to the exit, so I followed Renée to the wall. The sky seemed to have fallen. Chairs were flying in the air. Someone must have been injured: blood was splattered all over the room. A man behind the bar was now showing his head, now disappearing, just like in a Western movie. He was shouting but not able to stop anyone. The men were going insane—someone could have been killed. The handsome singer stopped for a second and yelled at us: "Why are you still here? Get out! You will be hurt!" I pulled Renée by the sleeve, lowered my head, and ran for the door. Only outside did we notice that Renée's white shirt was covered in blood. "Are you hurt?" Under the street lights, she looked pale but uninjured. I hailed a taxi.

V.

The TV channels were reporting about the American invasion of Iraq. Peggy called to invite me to an antiwar roundtable. Renée had been at the US embassy all day, and she decided to join us as well. In the evening we met at the gates of the Italian cultural center, a fancy white building in the heart of a poor residential district of Almaty. In the shiny conference hall, people were sitting on expensive chairs and discussing the war. The moderator, a big man in glasses, spoke Russian with a foreign accent. Most of the participants were foreign-ers. There were no seats left, so we stood at the entrance. Renée and Peggy had guilty faces as if they were the ones who had started the war. When I was accidentally given the microphone, I said that it was not good to ignore the opinion of international organizations. That is what my sister had told me earlier that day on the phone. When the event was over and people were offered refreshments, the big Italian approached us. He stretched out his huge hand and introduced himself as Tony. After a short conversation with the Americans, he turned to me and said that he was looking for a Kazakh translator. "Can you come back tomorrow?"

I returned the next day. The gates were closed. I pressed the doorbell. A young Kazakh man met me at the entrance. He was wearing a white shirt unbuttoned at the top. My eyes fell on his silver necklace: a Christian cross. "Hello! I'm Maqsat." His brown eyes were smiling. Tony was already in the office, together with the director, a woman named Andrea. Maqsat was Andrea's assistant. As we spoke, it became clear that this cultural center was in fact the headquarters of the Italian Catholic missionaries in Central Asia. Andrea and Tony were the leaders of the mission. They had called me because they were looking for someone who could translate *Ystoria Mongalorum* into Kazakh. Having been raised in a family of communists, I blurted out, "So, in fact, your mission is to convert Kazakhs into Catholics. Is that it?" Andrea and Tony exchanged looks.

"Yes. And to take care of orphans. We help several orphanages in Almaty. Isn't that good work?"

"What do you gain by converting people into Catholics?"

"Christianity is not new in Central Asia. What about the Nestorians?"

"That was a long time ago! Why don't Buddhists impose their religion on anyone?"

"They do propagate their own religion. And as for us Christians, it was Saint Paul who told us to build churches."

"My grandfather was a mullah. I have never seen him impose Islam on anyone, not even on us, his grandchildren. Okay, I will think about it. How much would you pay for the translation?"

"It is not an easy text, so we would consider paying 60,000 tenge."

A pretty good sum of money. I could buy a washing machine for my mom. But something was holding me back. The next day, I sent an email to Andrea telling her I needed some time to decide, but asking her to sign me up for their Sunday film club.

———————

I joined the Sunday film club, run by Andrea and Tony's friend Valentina, and returned every week to see another Italian film. One Sunday, I arrived too early. The door of the conference hall was open, and I could see a priest conducting Sunday mass. Tony gestured to me to come in. I sat down in the last row. A long line of people was slowly moving down the narrow aisle between the chairs. When they reached the priest, they knelt in front of him, touched a bowl with their lips, and kissed his hand. Kazakhs and Russians, all of them young. I had seen this ritual in films, but seeing it with my own eyes was a different experience: now I felt with all the fibers of my body how strange and alien this culture was to us. It was such a strong sensation that I felt dizzy. It seemed just yesterday that atheism was a big part of our life. How did these young people succumb to religion so quickly? Valentina, sitting in the same row, turned to me and tried to smile. "I cannot explain it to you. You are an atheist."

———————

We went in several cars to a newly built orphanage on the outskirts of Almaty, taking birthday presents to a few of the little ones who had been placed here. Going in, I caught a familiar smell. Once experienced, this smell haunts you all your life. It is not the sweet smell of babies; it is the bitter smell of the tears of babies missing their mothers. We went right to the cafeteria. Around thirty young children were sitting at low tables. A silent room full of toddlers is an odd thing. The sharp sounds of metal spoons touching metal bowls broke the silence. Several adults were sitting awkwardly at the low tables along with the children. Some children looked at us with surprised faces, and some did not pay us any attention. I sat down on a bench along the wall. As a student, I once volunteered to work in an orphanage, and afterwards, I told myself never to go back. I did not want to see this scene again. Back then, most of the orphans were Russians, and we were told that their parents were either alcoholics or criminals. A sculpture of the Virgin Mary was hanging on the wall. So this was Tony and Andrea's answer to all my prickly questions.

A little girl walked up to me and stood in front of me, holding her little fingers crossed somewhere around her face, as toddlers do when they observe something unfamiliar or interesting. Then she leaned on my knees. I lifted her and put her on my lap. Her several layers of clothing gave off the strong smell of an unwashed body. I took off the ribbon attached to her short hair and smelled her head. The toddler, breathing heavily through her congested nose, put her head on my shoulder. When Tony offered her candy, she quickly filled both her pockets and grabbed more with both hands. Holding her candy tight in her pudgy little hands, she put her head on my shoulder again. I did not dare to move. We both sat there until I had to leave.

On our way back, nobody spoke. I was looking through the windows at the shabby streets of Almaty, full of people with striped

Chinese bags. Around the bazaar, I could see elderly women engaged in illegal activities: selling sunflower seeds, fortunetelling. Who was going to tell fairy tales to our children if the grandmothers were out in the streets all day? We had almost lost our language and culture to the Soviet regime, and now this alien Christian culture would confuse us even more. I was frightened by my own thoughts.

"Tony, you are an educated man. Tell me, is it fair to confuse the young people of this country with religion? They are too young."

"Religion will guide these kids. I cannot even imagine what would have happened to Maqsat if he had not met us."

"Maqsat will be a good Italian. He speaks Italian and Russian, but he does not know Kazakh. He already despises the language of his own country."

"So, for a nationalist like you, it would be better if Maqsat ended up in the streets? Look at you! You're making money assisting American spies!"

"Why not leave the children of this country alone? If people want to run away from themselves, they have the right. But I have no desire to participate in it."

My friendship with the missionaries ended there. But the Americans would keep asking, occasionally, what had happened with Tony.

THE LIGHTER

BY OLGA MARK

Translated from Russian by
Shelley Fairweather-Vega

K ind people, have compassion for a poor orphan!" The girlish voice rang out through the bus and beat against the windows, as if to flee the stuffy air and escape outside.

When this voice suddenly intruded into their pre-holiday routine, demanding enough as it was, the passengers gave a start. Some glared at her with annoyance, this petite figure wrapped in a warm coat that wasn't terrible looking, but most had a favorable enough reaction to both the voice and its owner, and wrinkled bills dropped generously into the thin palm of her hand.

Verka was happy. She smiled at everyone who gave her money, knowing her pretty little face would move people to kindness and increase the size of their donations.

"Where are your parents?" asked a middle-aged woman, concerned.

"We're refugees," Verka answered cheerfully. "From Chechnya." Then she added, just in case, "There's a war there."

The woman shook her head regretfully while Verka headed for the exit. The tribute had been collected, and it was time to move on.

Humming something and skipping as she went, filled with joy, Verka walked between the new, tall apartment buildings in the fanciest part of the city. It was dangerous to work for a living here, too many cops and alert citizens, but Verka liked to take risks. She stopped near one doorway, examined it closely, rejected it, and moved to the next. She walked inside that door and waited. To make things more fun, Verka took a half-eaten hot dog from her pocket. She chewed off tiny bites, not in a hurry—her belly was full—and like an actress before her entrance, she went over her lines. After about ten minutes, a man walked through the door. Clutching the rest of the hot dog in one hand, Verka hurried over to meet him.

"Want a Lolita, a nymphette, a juvenilette?" Verka sang the words, opened her coat, and quick as a bat blocked the way to the stairs. She wore nothing other than that coat. Her pointed little breasts poked out threateningly, the dark nipples contracted maybe with cold, maybe with arousal. A flat stomach and blond puffy triangle below, the strong thighs and angular knees of a creature half girl, half woman . . . Frightened, the man took a step back, away from the glow of the bare young body. Verka advanced. Her whisper rang out loud, now beseeching, now commanding, fast, rapid-fire, over and over.

"Have compassion for a poor orphan, Uncle! I'm a pretty girl, a good girl, you've never seen anyone like me, you've never had anyone like me . . ."

The man was retreating to the exit, but then he stepped forward abruptly, grabbed Verka by the shoulder, and shoved her out the door.

"Little wretch!"

Verka flew outside and fell, almost knocking a woman who was walking in off her feet. The woman stopped, distraught, staring at the naked Verka spread-eagle on her coat.

"He raped me!" Verka said, speaking very clearly and staring right at the woman. "He took my clothes! Me, an orphan!" The picture of despair, she covered her face in her hands.

The man ran outside, and Verka, catching a glimpse of the look on the distraught woman's face, shouted, "Help!" Then she jumped up and dashed off between the buildings.

She stopped to catch her breath a couple blocks away. Shaking with laughter, she spent a long time resting near one of the young trees they had planted two years ago. Verka took the souvenir bottle of vodka from her pocket, the one she had fallen in love with for its beauty and miniature size and bought that morning at the bus stop kiosk. She opened it and took a gulp. Then she walked off to another building, dancing along the way, in no hurry at all, pretending to be Laime Vaikule on the TV. The doors here had locks controlled by keypads. She waited until a kid was going inside, hopped in after him, and stood there waiting again.

A man appeared almost at once. Opening her coat, Verka went to meet him.

"Want a Lolita, a nymphette, a juvenilette?" The man stopped and looked her slowly up and down.

"How old are you?"

"Eleven!" Verka said cheerfully.

"You're lying," the man said.

"Fourteen," Verka corrected herself. "I don't remember, Uncle. We're refugees from Tajikistan. There's a war there."

"Where'd you learn to talk like that then, Lolita from Tajikistan?"

"I'm really smart," said Verka, coming closer to the man. "I read books, watch movies, play the guitar. You've never even dreamed of someone like me."

The man examined her closely again, reminding her of a doctor at a checkup.

"All right, let's go to my place," said the man.

"No, Uncle, I'm not stupid. Here, please. I won't go to your place."

The man hesitated for a second, then grabbed Verka and dragged her up the stairs to the first landing, where there was a small niche in the wall.

"Uncle!" Verka whimpered, "I'm just an orphan. What about a little money?"

"How much do you need?" asked the man. "Enough for ice cream?"

"A thousand."

The man pulled out some money—Verka got a glimpse of the contents of his wallet—and thrust it at her. He fumbled around in his winter clothing and spent five minutes trying to find a comfortable position.

Verka waited patiently, and she earned the money she had gotten just as patiently and dispassionately, staring, aloof, out the foggy stairwell window. She felt in her pockets for the rest of the hot dog and started chewing.

"You could at least not eat," said the man.

"I don't waste food," Verka snapped back.

"Now where will you go?" the man asked, when Verka was fastening her coat, in no hurry. She took two steps down and stopped to fix her hair.

"I'm not going anywhere until you pay me, Uncle."

"What do you mean, until I pay you?" The man was angry. "I gave you a thousand!"

"A thousand of our stuff," Verka said. "I meant a thousand dollars."

The man swore. Verka froze for a second, then rolled her eyes theatrically, threw up her arms, and shouted so the whole building could hear her.

"Help, help! I'm a child being raped!"

The man rushed at her, but Verka was ready for that, and she dodged, then dashed upstairs, banging on every apartment door as she went.

"Stop! Quiet down!" the man shouted at her from behind.

Verka turned and hissed at him.

"You give me my pay, you child rapist, or I'm going to the cops, and that's it!"

Somewhere a door slammed, and they could hear voices. The man, his face pale, pulled out his wallet, took three hundred dollars from it, and threw the cash at Verka. One keen glance at the wallet told her there was nothing left inside it, so Verka picked up the money, pulled her coat closed, and ran downstairs, past all the worried "What happened?" and "Who screamed?"

Once she was far enough away, in the empty lot near the place they were building another tall building, Verka leaped high in the air, doing the victory dance of some unknown tribe. She finished her vodka and headed to the Ramstore to turn the useless green paper into good things she needed.

The city was muffled up in the early winter evening. The afternoon smog had settled in a poisonous cloud to fill the streets. Bent under the weight of several stuffed shopping bags, a green alien beast printed on each, Verka slowly made her way past the long concrete barricade walling off a construction site abandoned ten years back. Once they were planning to build a new department store here, the biggest one in the city, and they had even managed to put in a good solid foundation and build the first four floors.

Then times changed, there wasn't enough money, the lot got overgrown first with weeds, then little trees. By now, there were supermarkets all over the city housed in imported prefab structures. They grew before your eyes like houses made of cards. Nobody cared about an old Soviet behemoth of a project anymore. Verka walked, and to distract herself from her aching arms, which could barely lug the heavy load, she repeated the new words she had read for the first time today in the store, in ads and on products, on book covers and cassette cases. *I-beam. Consulting services. Mortgages.* She loved the mysterious combinations of sounds, which you could repeat and savor until, pretty soon, what you had heard or seen or read suddenly became clear and made sense . . . People laughed at her weird fixations, and the almost forbidden pleasure grew even more acute.

When she reached a break in the concrete wall, Verka slipped the bags through first, then crawled through herself. She followed the well-beaten path to the unfinished building and knocked at the basement window. None of the upper stories had walls, just framework and barely a roof, but the basement and the storage cellars underground were finished. All they needed was to put some plywood in the holes for the windows and vents, and the place was ready.

A cardboard shutter slid down fast, and the shaggy head of a fifteen-year-old boy appeared in the window.

"Verka! Come on in. You cold?"

"Here!" Verka, proud, handed him the shopping bags one at a

time. The guy oohed and aahed happily as he took each bag, trying to figure out what was inside, and Verka laughed.

When she had passed them all in, Verka slipped through the window herself. The guy caught her and helped her down, then hurried to cover the window. They brought the bags into the next room, where it was hot from a burning cast-iron stove and noisy. Five young teenagers had evidently been living there for a while. Blankets were spread in the corners, dishes sat on homemade tables cobbled together from boxes, and a dark boarded-up window was decorated with a curtain.

Verka was met with joyful shouts, and when she started laying out triumphantly the things she had bought, the joy turned to jubilation. They applauded the slightly bent sticks of sausage, rounds of Dutch cheese and pinwheels of smoked cheese, baklava and pastries, food in cans, bottles of vodka and Pepsi, candy, chocolate, mints, and other treasures.

"How did you carry all that?" asked the strong, bony girl who was always sniffling. But Verka had caught her breath by then and waved her off. "No big deal."

When everyone had eaten their fill and had plenty to drink, when they were waiting out the brief stupor of satiety, smoking with relish, and everyone was having a good time, Verka spun in circles in the middle of the room and told them about the events of her day. She acted out all the roles, mimicked the men's voices and the women's frightened faces, and told them how skillfully and smoothly she, Verka, had done it all.

Everyone was laughing, copying her words and gestures, and as she basked in their love and admiration, Verka felt happy.

"It was getting cold this afternoon," the strong girl said suddenly. "Should we go spend the night at the orphanage?"

"Nah," said the shaggy-haired boy, looking over the meager remains of their feast. "Let's go tomorrow."

"Tomorrow, tomorrow!" Verka cheered. They only showed up at the orphanage when things got really bad on the streets, or they needed to hide out and wait for some kind of trouble to pass. And the caretakers had long ago stopped paying attention to the older kids' frequent disappearances. They were often gone for days on end in the summer, and sometimes in the winter too.

"I bought this, too," said Verka, and she took a lighter from her pocket.

"So?" somebody asked her, giving her purchase an uninterested look. "It's just a lighter."

"It's everlasting. It lasts forever." Verka held the little red rectangle with rounded corners proudly above her head.

"Nothing lasts forever," laughed the dark-skinned boy who looked like a gypsy.

"This one does, this one does!" Verka chanted, and she traced a finger lovingly over its smooth surface. "They told me it does!"

"You're so lucky," whispered the girl who always sat quietly in the corner, the youngest of them all. "You always have money, and you know so many big fancy words."

"That's the way I am!" Verka crowed.

She spun across the room, one hand flicking the lighter, the other holding an open vodka bottle, and she was happy, the warm room felt good, the little flame flickered and went out, the kids around her were getting ready for bed but she wanted to go somewhere, do something, it didn't matter where or what, as long as this drunken happiness could go on.

"Let's go upstairs!" she called to them. "Let's look at the city! It's night, it'll be great!"

"You're wasted!" the shaggy-haired guy told her, getting under a blanket with one of the girls. "It's cold out there. We'll freeze."

But Verka was already going up the rickety flight of stairs. She opened the door at the top and then up, up, up, to the last finished floor. The sharp, cold air seized her, she gasped in delight, and she pulled her coat closer around her.

Verka walked to the very edge. The city winked at her with dozens of bright windows, the holiday lights in the streets, the colored flashes of the ads. It was cold. At night, nature forgot that this was a southern city. Verka took a hurried gulp of vodka. She flicked her lighter mechanically, as if adding one more small flame to the sparkling night, and she looked off into the distance. For her, the view from up above was always spellbinding. She looked for a long time over the city, sprawling in all directions, and then, frozen, she started to dance. Soon, laughing and yelping, spinning in circles, she had her head tossed back and her arms thrown out wide. When she stopped and went back to looking at the city, it seemed to her that the lights in the windows were being carried away, whirling unrestrained, into the measureless blackness of space. Everything was swimming, the headlights, the houses, the streets . . . The wayward planet was flying into the unknown, drawing after it the slim lobe of the moon, and the sun wherever it was hiding, and the fragile winter stars. Barely holding back, full speed ahead, Verka shouted at the lights smeared into thin, bright streaks.

"Kind people, have compassion for a poor orphan!"

MY ELEUSINIAN MYSTERIES

BY ZIRA NAURZBAYEVA

Translated from Russian by
Shelley Fairweather-Vega

The trail of light formed by the headlamps of cars racing across the steppe highway dwindled to nothing in the darkness. That light was powerless to illuminate the darkness around us, but nevertheless, there it was. I felt it was not just lighting our journey. The very road in front of the car seemed to appear out of nothing under the rays of light, and then dissolve, disappear into the darkness behind us. My little girl was sleeping on my lap, my traveling companions were sleeping, too, and the driver wasn't talking, so I was alone in the night. I felt as if I were the only one experiencing, with every cell of my body, our miraculous flight through the darkness. I alone could recognize this darkness as a wordless, eternal threat to the life flickering warm inside the car. My daughter felt heavy by now, her little body warming my stomach, and somewhere deep inside me—much lower than my heart—I was melting, softening, being somehow carried back to the time that this little nubbin, just tiny then, breathed and moved there inside me . . . And just as a woman's womb encloses and protects her unborn child, I felt now that my whole body and the circle of my arms were protecting my small daughter from the darkness, behind us and all around us, and only the weak rays of light ahead of us remained open for her. Suddenly, I thought about my own mother, now dead, and my mother's mother and her mother and the thousands of generations of my great-grandmothers on my mother's side, about their lives, giving birth to their children and feeding them, in a yurt blanketed with snow among the frozen and threatening steppe, or on the road during a migration, and often, too often during war times, while waiting for their husbands to return, never knowing whether they were still alive, whether they'd be used as living shields to repel the enemy, whether raiders would appear that night in the defenseless aul. They gave birth, and regardless of what forward-thinking modern people might say, it wasn't any animal instinct to reproduce, because there are situations in which even animals do not multiply, saving their strength instead for self-preservation. And if even one of those thousands of links in the chain of my great-grandmothers had lost the love of life, the faith in life, which women need to bring defenseless human beings into this world, then I would never have existed, and neither would my little daughter . . .

Our lives are like the light from headlights, so bright at the source, dwindling so quickly in the unyielding darkness. One brightly lit slice is our present. A slice of weakening light is our future, for which we make plans that make Someone laugh. And we are never allowed to know what lies beyond the boundary between light and dark. We can only assume, hope, that past that point, our path will continue. And we have only our love and faith to guard our children from the darkness that gobbles up the past and threatens the future.

My daughter lost her maternal grandmother when she was nine months old and lost her paternal grandmother twenty years before she was born. But even before she turned two, she would sometimes laugh heartily in her sleep, then wake up, look around, and ask, "Where's grandma? Where did she go?" Out on our walks, she peered intently into the faces of old Kazakh women, and she toddled around the ones that sat on benches outside, bringing them presents, putting little leaves and pebbles into their wrinkled hands. And one time, she looked at a group photo in an album I had left open and recognized her immediately: "Look! My grandma!" And in the next photo, she saw her again. It wasn't her memories from babyhood at work, because it was her father's mother she had recognized, not mine. And I thought that perhaps that meant that her paternal grandmother's spirit had come to my child in her sleep, to play with her twentieth or twenty-fifth granddaughter . . . But my mother's spirit hadn't shown up to visit her first, immensely beloved granddaughter, and I struggled to understand why.

Later, when my daughter was a little bigger, she started to wonder why other children had two grandmothers, often even great-grandmothers, and she didn't even have one. She asked me: "If I don't have a grandma, that means my kids won't have a grandma. Right?" And I vowed to my four-year-old daughter that her children would have a grandmother, certainly they would, and a lively one at that. Any time I remember about living a healthy lifestyle, or getting some exercise, that vow I made is the reason.

An old bit of folk wisdom says that as long as a person has a mother, she remains a child. But I don't think this is about infantilism. When my mother died, I was out on a walk with my baby daughter. I carried her into the house and someone told me the bad news, but from my chronic lack of sleep or for some other reason, the information did not really get through to me. "All right, I'll bring the stroller in and start clearing out the spare bedroom for guests. And I'll need to clear a room for the body," I said. By then I knew all too well what death and funeral rituals meant. Several hours later, when I had begun feeling terrible, my closest friend called from Paris and asked what was wrong. Even then I answered her calmly. "Oh, I'm fine. My mother died." With the men, I drove to the cemetery and went through all the formalities. With the women, I cooked and baked everything we needed for the meal at the wake. All night I sat next to the cold body, I did something like grieving and crying, but . . . But I only genuinely understood what had happened when I was standing at the edge of her open grave, holding a clump of clay soil dug from the pit, when my mother's body, wrapped in a white shroud, was lowered into the grave, and people began dropping that soil onto her.

I finally comprehended my loss, and I wept with grief, but even then I did not understand that from then on my fate, as the oldest woman in the family line, would be to stand there, on the edge of that grave. I was now first in line to follow her, to walk away into the darkness. I can only pray to God that that order be preserved, so that nobody takes away my sacred right to go next. A woman does not only bring a child into the world. A mother must stand between that child and the darkness, as long as she can, sheltering her from the sight of the gaping jaws of oblivion. Perhaps women are forbidden, in Islam, from participating in funerals because life and death are not supposed to go together in their minds, so that death does not desecrate or sap that feminine power we need for birth. But us, we've been raised differently by our mothers and grandmothers. When she buried her 43-year-old son, my paternal grandmother climbed down into the grave herself to arrange his head more comfortably where he lay. I think there was no desecration on earth, physical or moral, that could have sullied my Azhe, her overworked brown hands, her brave motherly heart.

In ancient Greece, the Eleusinian Mysteries were endowed with the highest honors and accompanied by the most secret rites. Every poet and philosopher in the Iliad sings their praises: death cannot touch anyone blessed by the Eleusinians, and no man can be happy who has not undergone those ceremonies or glimpsed their secret wisdom. "Happy is he who has been received! The uninitiated will know not fortune, and be destined to remain in the sorrowful gloom," they say.

Experts believe that at the heart of the Eleusinian Mysteries were dramatic performances telling the story of two goddesses, a mother and daughter, Demeter and Persephone. Persephone was abducted by the god of the underworld, and her goddess mother grieved, causing all of nature to stop flowering and bearing fruit. Then her daughter returned for a time, and Demeter and the gods reconciled. That myth explains the natural cycle of death and rebirth: when Persephone returns to Demeter from the underworld kingdom, the mother rejoices, and spring comes; when Persephone returns to her husband in the world of the dead, Demeter puts on her mourning clothes again, and nature dies. As they watched these performances, the people who participated in the rites, including men, made their own journey into the darkness, came face to face with the god of the dead underworld, and contemplated the new shoot that grows thanks to the death of the grain buried in the earth. They were supposed to experience the cyclical nature of life and death, the eternity and persistence of life, handed down from mother to daughter, from woman to woman. This truth, expressed in words, seems banal, probably because the Eleusinian Mysteries really were shrouded in mystery. But recognizing this banality during the multi-day ceremonies of cleansing and trials was a source of peace and wisdom for perishable human beings.

My own Eleusinian Mysteries lasted for nine years. I set off on my path into the darkness when my Azhe left us. My grief was ferocious. I could not understand why this woman in particular, who had marveled in life, whose Light had softened even the most hardened souls, had gone away, and why so many contemptible people went on living. I wanted to scream loud enough to tear the moon from the sky, to make this whole indifferent world shatter and sink into hell. I kept my head lowered when I walked, so I wouldn't see the hateful, thoughtless faces of passersby, so I wouldn't frighten them with my own gaze, and also because I couldn't tear my eyes away from the earth that had taken in my Azhe. A year or two years passed. It must have been my one hundredth solitary bus ride to the cemetery in Kensay. At one bus stop, a little removed from the crowd, there stood two members of that most unpleasant class of old women, the ones with the sharpest elbows and shrillest voices, the kind who would shove someone else's child out of line when waiting for the cheapest scraps of meat. And suddenly, through the dirty window, I could see them clearly, in bold relief. I realized that these old women were dying, as were we all, and that they knew all about their imminent deaths and were afraid of them, the way my Azhe had never been afraid. I felt sorry for them. They were my sisters in death . . .

In the car racing across the nighttime steppe, I thought about how my daughter would take the cup of life from me, the one our grandmothers had carried through the darkness of millennia, through war and hunger, through victory and defeat. And I also felt that we were not alone in the night, that our foremothers were there, invisible, protecting us. "Keep this daughter of mine safe from the evil eye, from illness and pain, from trouble and strife," I remember my Azhe praying in Kazakh as she combed my hair. And I whispered those words now, as I embraced my sleeping daughter.

ABOUT THE TRANSLATORS

ZAURE BATAYEVA (1969) is the driving force behind this anthology, the one who first dreamed of bringing a collection of Kazakh women's writing into English. Besides being the author and translator of two pieces included here and a noted cultural commentator and critic, she is a prolific translator into Kazakh, recently of Sarah Cameron's groundbreaking historical work, *The Hungry Steppe.*

Photo credit: Marlis Jeenbaev

SAM BREAZEALE (1996) is currently working on an MA in Russian at Middlebury College and an MA in International and Regional Studies at the University of Michigan, where he focuses on Central Asia and Russia. He served as a Fulbright English Teaching Assistant in Kyrgyzstan during the 2021-2022 academic year. He also works as a translator for *Meduza in English*.

SHELLEY FAIRWEATHER-VEGA (1978), a graduate of Johns Hopkins University and the University of Washington, translates fiction, poetry, and screenplays from Russian and Uzbek to English. Aside from extensive work with the authors included in this volume, she has translated short stories and novels by the Uzbek writer Hamid Ismailov and the Kazakh musicologist Talasbek Asemkulov, and her translations have been published in *Words Without Borders*, *World Literature Today*, *Brooklyn Rail*, and *Translation Review*. She has been translating Kazakhstani authors since 2017 and recently completed an intensive course in the Kazakh language.

ABOUT THE
AUTHORS

ORAL ARUKENOVA (1967) is a proud graduate of the Open Literary School of Almaty, founded by the students of Olga Mark (see below). She also holds a degree in German and English language teaching. Arukenova has used her experiences as a working professional (interpreter, purchasing officer, market researcher) to nourish her fiction writing. Her first collection of stories, *Neftyanka Rules*, was published in 2018. Arukenova writes in Russian and in Kazakh.

RAUSHAN BAIGUZHAYEVA (1954), an engineering graduate of Polytechnic University in Almaty, worked as a scriptwriter at the Kazakhfilm movie studios for several decades. Baiguzhayeva's short stories and novellas were gathered and published in a book titled *Voyage* in 2014. Baiguzhayeva writes in Russian.

NADEZHDA CHERNOVA (1947) is a graduate of Kazakh State University and a member of the Writers' Union of Kazakhstan. She worked as a TV journalist and as the editor of two literary magazines (*Zhalyn* and *Prostor*). She is the author of numerous books of poetry and fiction. Chernova writes in Russian.

LILYA KALAUS (1969), a graduate of Kazakh State University, is a fiction writer, painter, and former publisher. Kalaus has published poetry and fantasy books, but her preferred genre has always been the comical short story. Currently she offers private literary courses and is working on a new collection of short stories. Kalaus writes exclusively in Russian.

AIGUL KEMELBAYEVA (1965), a graduate of Kazakh State University (Almaty) and the Maxim Gorky Literature Institute (Moscow), is the author of three film scripts, one novel, and numerous short stories. A member of the Writers' Union of Kazakhstan, Kemelbayeva is also considered a prominent literary critic. Although she is equally adept at writing in Russian, Kemelbayeva prefers to write in Kazakh.

AYAGUL MANTAY (1983–2021), a graduate of RUDN University in Moscow, was a blogger and fiction writer. She published two collections of short stories in Kazakhstan and was a frequent contributor to literary magazines. During her too-short career, Mantay wrote in Kazakh.

OLGA MARK (1963–2008), a professor at Almaty State University, authored two novels, one collection of stories, and a monograph on poetry. Mark is also remembered for her role as a literary mentor and organizer, and especially her ability to galvanize young people, while being bound to a wheelchair at home. In 1993, with the help of a group of volunteers, Mark founded the first independent journal of arts and literature in Kazakhstan: *Appolinarii*. She ran the journal, and the many events associated with it, from her three-room apartment in Almaty. A few years later she managed to obtain funding for the journal and its related activities from private donors, paving the way for the establishment of an independent writers' workshop in the early 2000s. Mark wrote in Russian.

ZIRA NAURZBAYEVA (1967), a philosophy graduate of Kazakh State University, is a fiction writer, journalist, and researcher, with special interests in Turkic mythology, Kazakh folk music, and Kazakh identity. She is the author of a monograph on Tengrism and hundreds of articles, published in a wide range of newspapers and magazines. A one-time host of a weekly radio program about Kazakh music, Naurzbayeva frequently incorporates musical themes into her writing. Though she is bilingual, Naurzbayeva mostly writes in Russian.

ASEL OMAR (1973), a graduate of the Maxim Gorky Literature Institute in Moscow and a member of the Writers' Union of Kazakhstan, has taught literature at various universities. She is the author of four books of fiction, a collection of poetry, and numerous articles. Omar's fictional portrayal of the December 1986 uprising in Almaty, excerpted in this anthology, caused great controversy at the time of its publication. Omar writes in Russian.

MADINA OMAROVA (1975), a graduate of Almaty State University, is a playwright and fiction writer. Omarova's writings focus on the lives of ethnic Kazakhs. Though best known in the country for her plays, Omarova also writes short stories informed by a gritty feminist awareness not found in any other Kazakh author. Omarova writes in Kazakh.

AYA ÖMIRTAI (1992) was born in the Bayan-Ölgii province of Mongolia. That same year, Aya's family moved to Kazakhstan as part of a re-immigration program that had been launched in the wake of Kazakhstan's independence. The difficulties that her relatives encountered as first-generation immigrants (including linguistic and cultural discrimination) inspired Aya to become a journalist and a writer. Aya holds a bachelor's degree in journalism from the Kazakh State University and has been working for various Kazakh-language media outlets since she graduated. Ömirtai writes in Kazakh.

ZHUMAGUL SOLTY (1948), a graduate of Kazakh State University, started her writing career as a journalist for the Kazakh edition of the Soviet propagandist newspaper *Leninskaya Smena* in the 1970s. After the collapse of the USSR, Solty took up playwriting and short story–writing as a way of reflecting on her generation's struggle to adapt to the new post-Soviet reality. Solty has published articles and stories in a wide range of magazines and newspapers in Kazakhstan. Solty writes in Kazakh.

PERMISSIONS

ABOUT GAUDY BOY

From the Latin *gaudium*, meaning "joy," Gaudy Boy publishes books that delight readers with the various powers of art. The name is taken from the poem "Gaudy Turnout" by Singaporean poet Arthur Yap, about his time abroad in Leeds, the United Kingdom. Similarly inspired by such diasporic wanderings and migrations, Gaudy Boy brings literary works by authors of Asian heritage to the attention of an American audience and beyond. Established in 2018 as the imprint of the New York City–based literary nonprofit Singapore Unbound, we publish poetry, fiction, and literary nonfiction. Visit our website at www.singaporeunbound.org/gaudyboy.

Winners of the Gaudy Boy Poetry Book Prize
Time Regime by Jhani Randhawa
Object Permanence by Nica Bengzon
Play for Time by Paula Mendoza
Autobiography of Horse by Jenifer Sang Eun Park
The Experiment of the Tropics by Lawrence Lacambra Ypil

Fiction and Nonfiction
The Infinite Library and Other Stories
    by Victor Fernando R. Ocampo
The Sweetest Fruits by Monique Truong
And the Walls Come Crumbling Down by Tania De Rozario
The Foley Artist by Ricco Villanueva Siasoco
Malay Sketches by Alfian Sa'at

From Gaudy Boy Translates

Ulirát, edited by Tilde Acuña, John Bengan, Daryll Delgado,
   Amado Anthony G. Mendoza III, and Kristine Ong Muslim

Picking off new shoots will not stop the spring, edited by Ko Ko Thett
   and Brian Haman

CPSIA information can be obtained
at www.ICGtesting.com
Printed in the USA
BVHW072041200522
637573BV00005B/6